I0690887

BLOOD BOUND

COURTNEY MAGUIRE

CITY OWL
PRESS

This book is a work of fiction. Names, characters, places, and incidents either are products of the author's imagination or are used fictitiously. Any resemblance to actual events or locales or persons, living or dead, is entirely coincidental and not intended by the author.

BLOOD BOUND
Youkai Bloodlines, Book 3

CITY OWL PRESS
www.cityowlpress.com

Cover Design by MiblArt. All stock photos licensed appropriately.

Edited by Heather McCorkle.

For information on subsidiary rights, please contact the publisher at info@cityowlpress.com.

Print Edition ISBN: 978-1-64898-134-0,

Digital Edition ISBN: 978-1-64898-133-3

Printed in the United States of America

In memory of Anne Rice.
"May flights of devils wing you to your rest."

ONE

Train Wreck

HIRO

SPRING 2004

YOU CAN LIVE A HUNDRED LIFETIMES AND THE WORLD WILL STILL surprise you, hit you like a high-speed train and drag you along the rails before dumping you off a thousand miles from where you started. Sometimes the ride isn't as violent as all that. Sometimes it feels like a vacation, an escape, like falling in love. But the end of the line is always the same—a broken, bloody mess far from home.

Sitting on a hard cobblestone path in my two-day-old funeral suit, I stared at a pillar of granite with his name on it, a fifth of Jack in my gut and my soul shattered into a million pieces. Aikawa Takanori—the name of the train that hit me.

A broad shadow fell over me, and I closed my eyes against it. I knew who it was, knew the sound of his steps, the way the air trembled in his presence. Sakurai Hideyoshi. He sat down beside me on the stone path without a word, so close our shoulders touched. Over two hundred years had passed since the day we met, and his nearness still made my skin prickle. His fingers brushed against mine as he slipped the nearly empty bottle of whiskey out of my hands and raised it to his lips.

"You knew it would end this way," he said, his voice low and cold. Not a judgment or an accusation, just a statement of fact.

"If you're here to lecture me, you can save it," I said, snatching the bottle back out of his hand.

There was something shocking about seeing him again, sitting there like an inkblot on my vision. The same solid frame, the same dark features, sharp as cut granite and just as immovable. How much time had I spent pounding myself against that hardness, like the ocean against a rocky cliff, trying to break it away? Now I observed him as if from a distance. Something bitter pushed up against my grief, but there was no room for it, so it settled back into my gut. He had been my home before Takanori, but now he was almost unrecognizable. He hadn't changed, of course. I was the one who was different.

"How long since you've drank something besides whiskey?"

"Not since—" I broke off, my eyes darting to the gravestone. My hands trembled as I took a long pull off the whiskey bottle. It could have been hours or years, every second since that day stretched into an eternity.

"Come with me," he said, pulling himself gracefully to his feet. I didn't move. "Hiro."

"I can't," I choked. I struggled to breathe around the ball of grief wedged in my throat. He was here for a reason. He wanted something, and I couldn't give it to him. "I'm not...ready..."

"He's dead. It doesn't matter if you're ready," he barked. The words were sharp, the edge of a blade iced over, and they cut deep.

He grabbed the collar of my jacket and yanked me to my feet. Without even waiting for me to catch my balance, he turned and stomped off down the path. It had been this way since the day we met, Hideyoshi plodding ahead without looking back, so confident I would follow. I found it comforting somehow, like nothing had ever broken between us. We would always be Hideyoshi and Hiro. The shape of his back would never change. He would never get sick and die.

I ran my hand over Taka's name on the granite and felt my heart tugged in two different directions. Another train had come, this one promising to take me back to somewhere familiar, but part of me was afraid. What if I got there and found it wasn't my home at all anymore, but just another strange place that would leave me even more broken?

But Hideyoshi was right. Taka was dead, the home I could have had here reduced to ashes. I had nowhere else to go.

My chest constricted, and I cursed under my breath as I ran to catch up to Hideyoshi, falling in step just a few paces behind. The sun was setting as we exited the cemetery, and darkness fell quickly over the narrow streets of Tokyo. Neon signs lit up one by one with an electric pop as we passed, the early evening crowds already taking their places in the izakayas that lined the street and disappearing into basement bars. Hideyoshi led me all the way to Ikebukuro and the busy streets surrounding Sunshine City. Wires hung like spiderwebs overhead, feeding power to the garish artificial light. Loud music and cigarette smoke filled the streets, and the smell of sweaty bodies started a scratching under my skin that had me gritting my teeth.

He stopped in the most crowded part of the busy street and looked over his shoulder at me for the first time. My gut clenched. I knew what he wanted. I scowled and shook my head, but he simply pinned me with those needle-sharp eyes that didn't take no for an answer until I relented.

His silent command: *Sing.*

I closed my eyes and took a deep breath. The scratching under my skin intensified and the sounds of the city died away as something else rose to the surface, something dark and dangerous. When my eyes opened again, the electric lights paled behind the glare of human life, every movement leaving a streaky afterimage in blue and white. My pulse sped and my mouth watered. I pulled in a deep breath, and my voice rose from the depths with an old song, something traditional that took me back to a different Tokyo. Despite its terrible purpose, it warmed me. My heart swam in it, cleansed its wounds in it.

My voice flowed soft and deep through the crowd, its magic slithering along the air like a serpent. A few turned their heads, hearts twinkling like fireflies. Some even stopped briefly to listen before moving on, but none of them were right so I kept singing.

Finally, a woman who had been rushing through the crowd with her eyes on the street stopped and looked up. The light inside her glowed soft and warm as the spring sun, heating my stagnant blood. She was the one. Her eyes glazed over as my song took hold of her, wrapping around her mind and leaving her helpless. I gave her a sad smile, a small apology for what was about to happen to her.

Hideyoshi had magic too, and when he touched her, she fell immediately under his spell. He took her hand and silently led her away from the crowd into a dark alley behind a string of clubs. I followed, head down, hands in my pockets. Once we were safely away from prying eyes, Hideyoshi slipped an arm around her waist and pulled her to him.

They could have been lovers standing there. My skin vibrated with the pounding of her heart as he moved in and whispered something in her ear, something that made her sigh and lean into him. Her head fell back, and he cupped it in one hand as he brushed her hair away from her neck with the other.

My pulse quickened at the sight of her pale skin, the veins pumping blue beneath. The whisper of a thousand voices rose in my ears. A pang of grief cut across my heart.

Are you in there, Takanori?

A slow smile spread across Hideyoshi's face. "Would you like the first taste, or shall I?"

I swallowed hard and turned my face away. His smile faltered and his obsidian eyes started to change, just a little at first, white leaking into his irises from the outside in. His lips peeled back, revealing a pair of deadly, sharp fangs.

She gasped but didn't struggle when his teeth pierced her skin. Her eyelids fluttered, the magic of Hideyoshi's touch keeping her in a dreamlike semiconsciousness, dulling the pain and leaving only pleasure, the only gift he could give her in return for her sacrifice.

I tried to look away, but the smell of blood made my breath quicken and hunger burned in my veins. The light inside her pulsed and swelled until it was all she was. Without breaking his hold on her, Hideyoshi's hand slid down her arm and lifted her wrist. A thin sound escaped me. It was more than just her blood he was offering. I heard the words as if he spoke them in my ear.

Come home, Hiro.

I dropped to my knees beside them. The itch beneath my skin became an all-over burn and I took her wrist in my hands, plunging my teeth into its tender flesh. The skin popped, and she shuddered as her blood released in a hot, coppery stream. A primal, almost sexual heat radiated through me with every swallow.

My body throbbed. Grief dropped away, and I gave in with a groan of relief as the blood washed away my pain. I felt light, the effects of the whiskey doubling and sending me spinning. I reached for Hideyoshi and found his arm, my hand bunching in his shirtsleeve. Heat poured off him, throaty moans vibrating through us both as we played tug-of-war with her veins. My skin flushed and the hairs on my arms stood on end, every drunken cell of my body jumping to life as hers wound down.

Like a candle flame, she burned out, sagging in Hideyoshi's arms. He let her drop. Our eyes locked, burning with the high of what we'd just taken. Once again, he pulled me to my feet by my collar. He took my face in his hands and pressed his lips to mine. Panting and high on blood, I gave in fully. I gripped his waist and leaned into him as he pushed his tongue against mine, fighting over the last drops of blood that clung to our lips.

The train had left the station. There was no stopping it now. My heart swelled with remembered love for him, crowding out my lungs as it competed with Takanori's. For a dark, guilty moment that will haunt me forever, I wanted it to win, to drown out the pain of loss and leave only this. Tears poured down my face, mixed with the blood on our tongues.

The thing was, I *had* lived a hundred lifetimes. And not one had prepared me for this.

TWO

Homecoming

SPRING 2004

I FOLLOWED HIDEYOSHI HOME IN SILENCE. HIS HOME. OUR HOME. THE high of the blood we'd taken faded with every step, and grief overwhelmed me again as I stared at his back. I'd loved him once, desperately, passionately. A ball of confused emotions hardened in my chest, and I rubbed at my sternum. It would be so easy to slip back into this life, comfortable even, if it wasn't for Taka. Before him, I thought I could be happy, content at least, with my life with Hideyoshi, despite how time had dulled us. But then Taka appeared and shone a bright light on all the things we were missing, and now I wasn't sure how to return to the dark.

The large traditional manor tucked behind high stone walls looked out of place among the modern houses and tight-packed apartment complexes that surrounded it. The city encroached closer and closer every year, but somehow we'd managed to protect it. Hideyoshi's house remained largely unchanged in the more than two hundred years we lived there. Our oasis in time. We'd added a few modern conveniences, of course—electric lighting, running water, and a completely redone kitchen—but its soul was the same.

Hideyoshi pushed through the front gate and stomped up the steps ahead of me. I lingered behind, dizzy with nostalgia as my fingers brushed the front pillars. I remembered dousing the entire engawa with buckets of water to protect it as fire bombs dropped from the bellies of great metal beasts onto the buildings below. The power of them was immense and unlike anything I'd ever seen. Families burned in their homes. Even more starved in the aftermath after losing everything. We lost a section of wall and more roofing tiles than I could count, but somehow we made it through the Pacific War with our home mostly intact, despite the near total destruction of the city around us. Only a few scars remained, hidden under a layer of paint.

With a growl of impatience, Hideyoshi grabbed me by my shirt and pulled me inside. I hovered in the genkan, my eyes sweeping over the expanse of tatami. "It's exactly the same," I said, more to myself than to him.

"Like it never happened." He had already disappeared into the kitchen, and his voice cut through the paper walls. He returned with a bottle of nihonshu and a pair of ceramic glasses. He thrust one into my hand and filled it before filling his own.

"What are we drinking to?" I asked.

"To your return, of course," he said, draining his glass. He immediately refilled it before dropping onto a cushion in front of a low table.

I swirled the clear liquid around in my glass. My return. To him, my return was just the end of a ten-year fight. Maybe a chance to start again, or more accurately, to go back to how we were. But for me, it was the end of something, something meaningful, the loss of which left me adrift in a featureless sea, and I couldn't, *wouldn't*, go back to where we had been.

Hideyoshi's brows sunk low over his eyes as I set the glass down on the table untouched. "I need some sleep," I said in a broken voice. "Goodnight, Hideyoshi."

He called my name once, hoarsely as if through gritted teeth, but didn't follow as I walked away down a long corridor, past the room we once shared, and into the one that was only mine. I slid the door open and found, once again, that nothing had changed. A bare, eight-mat room with a long closet on the back wall, a tonsu topped with an oil lamp and a few meaningless trinkets, a futon neatly rolled up in the corner. Everything just as I left it, albeit under a thin layer of dust. My fingertips snagged on a crack in the doorframe, repaired but still visible under a patch of new stain.

A dark panic sliced through me and I couldn't breathe. Hands shaking, I ripped open the top drawer of the tonsu, throwing the contents out the side until I found what I wanted. A fat, black marker. Heart pounding, tears pressing hot behind my eyes, I bit off the cap and scrawled a vertical line in fat strokes across the shoji:

起こったよ！

It happened!

THREE

Temporary Things

SPRING 2004

My favorite thing about this old house was the bath. Despite all the modernization we'd done, we refused to get rid of the ofuro off the back of the house. I leaned back against the bamboo planks that made up the round tub, submerged up to my shoulders in well water heated by a fire below, and allowed myself to relax for the first time in weeks. Tension melted from muscles sore from being wound too tight for too long. I pulled the citrus smell of hinoki deep into my lungs. As weird as I felt about being here, I had to admit I missed this. With all the doors closed up, the room filled with steam and I could pretend I was floating in a cloud. I touched the ring hanging from a chain around my neck.

He would love this.

The door whipped open, and I jumped so hard I nearly drowned. "Hideyoshi! What are you—"

"Get dressed," he barked.

"What?"

"And wear something presentable. We have an errand to run."

"Well, everything I have here is at least ten years old, so unless we're going to a rave—"

"I got you some new things," he said. "They're in the closet."

The door snapped shut. Argument over.

"Great," I mumbled, sinking back into the bath with a groan. "Welcome home, Hiro."

After a couple more rebellious minutes in the tub, I went back to the house, dripping and wrapped in a yukata. My graffiti from the night before cut a harsh line down the wall, and I ran my fingers over it. Despite the embarrassment of my emotional breakdown, it was comforting in a way that my time away had left a physical mark on my unchanging life.

I opened the closet and poked through the things Hideyoshi had bought for me—button-up shirts and slacks next to a few garish graphic tees and loads of denim. Hideyoshi's feeble attempt to be stylish. Western-influenced fashion left him perpetually baffled. I remember him shaking his head as men began pairing porkpie hats with their kimono and wrinkling his nose at ladies' dresses that showed too much of women's figures. With a soft laugh, I pulled out a pair of relaxed-fit jeans and one of the less offensive T-shirts, topping it with an open button-up. I found my old moto-style leather jacket shoved in the back, the one with cracked elbows and zippers like teeth, and threw that on too.

A pair of heavy leather boots hanging off my fingers, I made my way back to the front of the house. The shoji had been pulled back, and the house was open to the air. Hideyoshi paced in the engawa wearing a black suit with an open collar, his jacket draped over his arm. My heart fluttered as time wound back on itself. He looked quite the modern man, but I still saw the samurai. I saw it in his posture, in his graceful stride, the ghost of his long hair drifting about his shoulders.

I cried the day he cut it. The emperor Meiji had deemed the carrying of swords illegal, effectively destroying the samurai class, and I came home to find Hideyoshi with a knife in one hand and his severed ponytail in the other. He took the loss of identity as stoically as everything else, but some subtle shift happened inside him as if a little of the air had been let out.

"I said presentable, not like you're going to Woodstock," he growled when he caught sight of me.

"Leather is never out of fashion," I countered with a cheeky smile.

"Button your shirt at least." He advanced on me, grabbing my collar and pulling at the buttons.

"Hey! Would you stop?" I said, swatting his hands away. "What's wrong with you?"

"When are you going to grow up and realize you reflect on me?"

I opened my mouth, ready to fire off a rebuttal, but guilt stamped it down. I deserved his resentment. Questions and rumors must have buzzed around him like flies after I left without explanation or warning. The immortal pair, the ideal, the youkai all others were meant to look up to had proven themselves as fragile as anything else. My leaving may not have hurt his heart, but it certainly hurt his pride. And now that I'd returned, I threatened to embarrass him further.

He closed his eyes for the length of a breath and reached for my buttons again. This time I didn't resist him. I used to love it when he dressed me. It made me feel important, special, his careful touch the closest thing to real affection he ever showed. My skin warmed as his fingers lingered on each button, that magnet inside drawing us closer together. My breath caught with a need for him so fierce, I had to grip his arms to steady myself.

"You never asked me, you know," I said, surprised by the roughness of my voice.

"Asked you what?"

"If I was okay."

His brow creased, but he never took his eyes off the buttons. "I didn't ask, because I know the answer."

"Yeah, but…" My fingers curled in the fabric of his shirt, eyes burning. "It would be nice to know you—"

Last button done, he turned and stepped off the porch before I could finish, pulling his jacket on as he went. My stomach lurched as if I'd been dropped from a height, my hands still clinging to the empty space.

It would be nice to know you cared.

THE BUSINESS OF BEING IMMORTAL COULD BE A BIT COMPLICATED IN THIS modern age, especially when one owned property, and the name on our deed was well past its expiration date. Judging by Hideyoshi's foul mood, that meant a visit to our old friend, Asagi. A good family name may not get them as far as it once did in this new democratic society, but Asagi was nothing if not resourceful. Asagi had lived their whole life with one foot in and one foot out of human society. A few well-placed contacts meant they could easily obtain the basic identifying documents—birth certificates, immigration papers, passports, even death and marriage certificates—that served as the backbone to everything that made the modern world run.

I followed Hideyoshi to a basement-level bar tucked in the heart of Roppongi. A paper lamp hung over the entrance of a dark stairwell, BAR SAKURA written in katakana down its cylindrical body. A sandwich board listing drink specials leaned against the wall. A strange young man dressed in deliberately sloppy layers met us at the top of the stairs, only his long nose and one black eye visible from beneath a nest of wild black hair. He was oddly beautiful, and his fearlessness impressed me as he placed himself between us and the door.

"Sakurai-san," he said in a soft voice, greeting Hideyoshi with a shallow bow that made Hideyoshi's lips curl. "We thought you would be alone."

"I'm not," he said, brushing past him into the stairwell.

"Sakurai-san, please—" The boy cut back into Hideyoshi's path and placed a hand on his chest. Without a flicker of expression, Hideyoshi grabbed the boy and pinned him to the wall in a show of strength that made him go pale.

"RYO!" A sharp, deep voice rang from inside the restaurant. The boy froze. Hideyoshi released him, and he scurried down the stairs ahead of us. We followed him into a dark, deserted dining room where he disappeared in a forest of overturned chairs on tabletops. Contrary to the name, the place had a grimness to it, all dark woods and polished brass, the sharp smell of smoke hanging in the air, the only homage to its namesake the pink blossoms decorating the corners of a chalkboard drink menu.

"Yoshi-chan, irrashai." The same deep voice snaked its way through the dimness. I squinted my eyes, tracing it back to the faint, firefly glow of a lit cigarette. "You'll have to forgive Ryo. He gets a bit nervous when things don't go to plan."

Hideyoshi and I weaved our way through the tables toward the source of that deep voice. We found Asagi lounging in a booth in the back corner. While modern fashion confused Hideyoshi, Asagi embraced it. Their short, body-hugging red dress almost certainly carried a label from a European designer I couldn't pronounce. Long, stockinged legs tipped with dangerously high heels with red soles crossed and uncrossed beneath the table. Fair skin glowed despite the dimness from behind a curtain of pin-straight hair.

"Mmm, Hideyoshi and Hiro back together again," Asagi said, running a tongue over painted lips and raking blood-red eyes over the two of us. "I can feel the heart of Tokyo pounding."

Hideyoshi pulled an envelope fat with cash out of his inner jacket pocket and dropped it on the table in front of Asagi. Asagi ignored it, taking a pull off a clove cigarette on a long stem, eyes fixed on me, the corners of their lips curling upward.

"Do you have my documents or not, Asagi?" Hideyoshi said, stepping between us.

"I do."

"Well, let's have it."

"I hear you left your maker for the love of a human," Asagi said, looking at Hideyoshi but speaking to me.

"I left for myself," I answered in a monotone.

"And what brings you back? Human life bore you? Or did he put you out on the street when he found out you were a blood-hungry killer?"

"He's dead." I flinched, surprised by my own tone, flat but somehow still full of bitterness.

Asagi's lips parted in a gasp, and they sank back into their seat. All their snarkiness melted away, replaced by genuine sympathy, and I was reminded of a time when we were almost friends. "My condolences," Asagi said in a low voice. "The love of a human has a way of changing us, of reminding us how precious time can be. There is nothing more painful than losing it."

"What would you know about love?" Hideyoshi sneered. "You keep humans as slaves."

"They are *not* slaves." Asagi pushed the words through their teeth, their pretty face twisting with disgust.

"You're like a leech, sucking the lives out of them little by little—"

"You'd rather I was a murderer, like you?" Asagi's baritone voice reverberated through the small space as they leaped to their feet. Asagi was tall, taller than Hideyoshi by over a head, but Hideyoshi didn't back down. Ryo appeared from out of the dark and whispered Asagi's name, laying a hand on their arm.

Almost instantly, Asagi calmed at the man's touch, brushing their fingers over the back of his hand and taking a deep breath. I studied him for the signs, the glazed eyes, the vacant expression, but saw only genuine affection. Asagi didn't take from him. Ryo, at least, was free.

"Give him what he came for," Asagi said, gesturing toward Hideyoshi as they fell back into their seat. Ryo pulled an envelope out of his clothes and handed it to Hideyoshi before sliding into the booth with Asagi.

Asagi ran their finger over the bit of jawline not hidden behind Ryo's wild mop. Ryo's cheeks pinked slightly, and he lowered his head before pulling Asagi's hand away and wrapping it in his. An intimate gesture, one they'd likely performed a hundred times, and it made my skin ache for all the little touches I could no longer have.

Hideyoshi stuffed the envelope in his jacket pocket and marched toward the door without a word.

"He'll never understand," Asagi said as I turned to follow him. I stopped but didn't look back. "He found something he wanted and immediately made it unbreakable. He doesn't know what it's like to love something you know is temporary."

"The loving is the easy part," I said, my voice sandpaper rough.

"Yes. It is."

I turned just enough to see Asagi's face. Even in the dimness, their eyes shimmered. It struck me then how much loss Asagi must have suffered in their life, surrounded by temporary things. Their hands were now tightly wrapped around Ryo's, but one day he would be gone too.

"It could break you. But you can't let it." Asagi's expression solidified, their voice sharp and edged with fervor.

"Why not?"

Asagi sat back, lips curling into a smile, a bit of their usual smugness flashing in their eyes. "Because you are a king among demons."

FOUR

Relief

WINTER 1993

WE'D HAD THIS ARGUMENT SO MANY TIMES, WE DID IT IN SHORTHAND. A shadow fell over me where I sat on the floor, a disassembled shamisen spread out before me. Strings lay coiled around me like snakes as I ran a rag over the worn neck of the instrument. The shamisen was nearly as old as I was and in desperate need of reskinning, yet still beautiful in its own way. I hardly played anymore, but something about the practice of maintaining the instrument soothed me. Maybe it was the simplicity of it. Replace a broken string or tighten a loose tuning peg, and what was once an awkward hunk of wood and catskin turned into something beautiful. If only everything were so easy to fix.

I glanced up far enough to see the tote bag hanging from Hide's fingers, heavy with a pair of metal thermoses. A dark weight settled in my stomach, and I dropped my gaze back to the rag in my hands.

"We have to go, Hiro." His tone was even, firm but patient.

"No, *I* don't."

"It's our responsibility—"

"This was your plan. Your responsibility." The words were made sharp as they ground past the stone in my throat.

"My plan." Hide huffed, the thermoses clinking together as his weight shifted. "You wanted to protect everyone. This is part of it. You can't keep shoving the ugly parts onto me, Hiro."

"It's inhumane."

"Maybe," he said. "But in two hundred years, I've yet to hear an alternative."

My fingers stopped working the rag and my shoulders slumped. The tempo of the argument may have changed—long, screaming fights trimmed down to a few quiet words between clenched teeth—but it always ended the same. I always gave into his logic. But I kept having it and I would keep having it, because being silent felt like yet another betrayal of the people I pledged to protect.

I swallowed hard. "I'm in the middle of—"

"It can wait."

He wasn't unsympathetic. Despite the hardness of his words, his eyes were soft, and I told myself he was as conflicted as I was. He had to be. It was the only way I could bear it.

I nodded and he turned toward the door, satisfied I would follow. I did, of course, and we walked in silence all the way to Okubo, him in front and me a step or two behind. He walked with one hand, the one he used to keep draped over his swords, tucked into the pocket of his trousers, his wool peacoat bunched up around it. I couldn't stop looking at that bag swinging casually at his side. If any of the people we passed knew what was in there…

We weaved through streets lined with Korean restaurants and groceries until we arrived at what looked from the outside like a construction site, one of those places that was perpetually half-finished. It was tucked tight into the crevice between two office buildings. Wire fences hung with a vinyl banner that read MATSUDAIRA-GUMI CONSTRUCTION surrounding a steel and concrete skeleton draped in tattered plastic. Raw materials and power tools lay strewn about but never really moved—set dressing for what was hidden underneath. Hide pulled a small brass key out of his pocket and unlocked the gate around the side, hidden from the street by thick shadows. It swung open with a shriek.

Hideyoshi's hard-soled shoes crunched on the loose ground around the building. He held back a section of plastic sheeting and stepped aside for me to pass. The light inside was murky and cut with motes of dust. I rubbed my nose and suppressed a sneeze. Dirt clung to my skin, making air heavy with cold feel even more oppressive. My gaze pulled like a magnet through the bones of metal and crumbling sheetrock toward what was hidden in its bowels.

The plastic sheeting rustled as it dropped back into place behind Hideyoshi. He stepped past me, dodging hanging wires and stepping over fallen beams. I followed him to the thing that drew my gaze, the only thing that felt finished in this shell of a place: a heavy, metal door set into the concrete foundation, the kind of door you'd see in a bank, not guarding the basement of an unfinished office building. Hide went down on one knee and punched a code into a keypad. It beeped softly, and the lock released with a heavy, metallic *clonk*.

Hide glanced up at me and I refused to meet his eyes. He released a heavy sigh before yanking the door open, revealing a narrow staircase leading down into a dimly lit space just out of sight. He descended, his shoulders filling the entire breadth of the stairwell. My stomach twisted in a knot as I followed.

When we reached the bottom, the space opened up into a room about the size of a one-room Tokyo apartment with stark, concrete walls and a low ceiling. The fluorescent lights were on a timer and buzzed overhead, giving everything a sickly yellow tint. A long wall of bars bisected the room, the space behind it further divided into three small cells, each with a door just big enough to shove a man through.

As soon as our feet touched the floor, the cell nearest us burst with violent energy. A man launched himself down the length of it and threw his body against the bars. My heart jumped into my throat and I stepped back, nearly falling backward against the stairs. Hideyoshi didn't flinch, instead raising the bag he carried and shaking it in front of him.

"You want this, you need to calm down."

The man in the cell threw his emaciated form against the bars again, sending down a shower of dust. Black hair hung over white eyes that burned into us as he reached a wiry arm through the bars and swept at us with a clawed hand. A gurgling sound somewhere between a growl and a cry pushed up through his throat as he snapped his bared fangs. A youkai gone mad.

Cold leaked into my bones just as it did every other time we came down here. It was for their own good, Hide always told me, as well as ours. They weren't men anymore, but monsters who'd lost themselves to blood and time. They knew nothing now but hunger. Leaving them free in the world would be like releasing a rabid dog. They would kill violently and indiscriminately, potentially exposing us to the world and negating everything we'd worked to build. Caging them was the only way to keep us safe, both human and youkai alike.

But it made me sick. When I looked at that man writhing and screaming with tears in his eyes, I thought of every time I'd let the monster inside me have a little too much control, every time I'd given in a little too much to the pleasures of the blood. We were all just a hair's breadth away from where he was. We were all perched on the edge of a sharp cliff, waiting for a strong wind to push us over.

When I looked at him, I saw myself.

Whether from obedience or exhaustion, the man's cries gradually died down, and he slumped against the bars of his cage. Hideyoshi reached into his bag and pulled out one of the thermoses. When he cracked the lid, a smell like rancid meat filled the room, making us both cringe—blood procured from a local blood bank friendly to youkai. Something happened to blood when it wasn't taken directly from the vein, as if it lost some of its magic. We could live off of it, and some did almost exclusively in these modern times. But it smelled awful, tasted worse, and left us feeling slow, like we'd chugged a bottle of cold medicine.

Hide went down on his knees next to the slumped creature and set the thermos just inside the bars. The man wrapped tired fingers around it and licked his lips. A tear slipped down his cheek, cutting a track in the layer of dust on his skin, and he brought the thermos up. He moaned softly as the blood slid down his throat, Adam's apple bobbing with each thick swallow. Little by little, his muscles relaxed and the lethargy took hold. He would be quiet now, at least for a while, quiet enough to let us believe we'd done something to ease his suffering. Deep down, I knew it wasn't true, that he never stopped screaming even if we couldn't hear it.

"Hiro."

My eyes snapped back to Hideyoshi. He held the second thermos out to me.

"Why don't you go take care of our friend on the end."

I swallowed hard and nodded, taking the thermos from him. Steps heavy, I moved down the row of cells. I tried hard not to look into them, empty and silent as an invitation, and focused instead on my destination. A lump lay in the back corner of the last cell, a tattered pile of clothes in the vague shape of a man. He lay in the fetal position, face tucked into the crook of his arm. As I drew closer, I recognized the familiar shape of his brow just visible through the bend in his arm.

"Hashiguchi-han?" My voice cracked as I called his name. Our old friend, or perhaps our oldest enemy, Hashiguchi Toshiro, had been in the cage for the better part of a year. His girl, Yui, had come to us for help. He'd been missing for days. We'd found him in a dry creek bed, hunched under a bridge like a troll and chewing on a dismembered leg, his hands and face black with blood, his white eyes the only thing visible in the dark. Seeing him like that made all the old stories of my youth make sense—the Kappa crouched at the water's edge, waiting for someone to venture too close.

"Hashiguchi-han," I called again, tapping lightly on the bars. He didn't move. The exposed skin of his forehead was dry and very white. My stomach turned over. A ring of keys hung on a hook on the wall. I grabbed them.

"Hiro, what are you doing?" Hide asked as the door swung open with a groan. I didn't answer. I took one slow step inside, then another, my eyes plastered to that patch of skin. Hashiguchi didn't move, didn't twitch, didn't show any sign of awareness of my presence.

My eyes burned as I squatted next to him. I laid my hand on his shoulder. Something shifted inside him, and like a house of cards, he collapsed in a cough of white dust.

I gasped and fell back against the bars. The clothing that had once been filled by a man settled over a pile of dust. A few ash-colored bones that had not yet degraded poked out of the pile. A rib, the edge of his pelvis, a jawbone. They would be gone soon too.

A creeping panic coated my skin like a layer of ice. I looked up and found Hide standing in the doorway, an uncharacteristically gentle look in his eyes. I covered my eyes with my hand and took a shuddering breath.

"He's dead."

"Mn."

"Someone should tell Yui."

"I'm sure she knows." I looked up at him, and he tapped his chest. Of course. She would have felt it. A fire inside of her snuffed out.

I released a long breath and ran my hand over my face, trying not to wonder how much of the grit on my skin was Hashiguchi. Hide squatted beside me, close enough our shoulders touched, and I leaned into that small bit of contact until he shifted forward to reach into the ashes. Something metal reflected dully in the yellow light of the fluorescents. He plucked it out and dusted it off. A ring.

"I'll take care of this." He handed the ring to me. "Go see Yui."

"No." I squeezed the word between chattering teeth.

"Hiro—"

"I can't keep shoving the ugly parts onto you, remember?"

He flinched, hurt flashing in his eyes. He sighed, his gaze dropping away from mine for a moment. "You're not. This part…" He held up the ring again. "It's better if it's you."

A cold ache spread through my chest as he dropped the ring into my hand. He wasn't wrong. While it was proper to acknowledge her loss, his emotional distance was not what she needed. But what could I give her? What could I say that would possibly fill the hole left by what she'd lost?

I closed my hand around the ring and stood. Hideyoshi didn't move as I walked past him, and I didn't look back. I escaped the artificial light of the basement and burst back into the open air. Claustrophobia pressed down on me even after I picked my way through the skeletal building and back onto the street. Skyscrapers clawed at a patch of pale blue sky. I turned my face toward it, sucking in deep, ragged breaths. I pulled my leather jacket tighter around me, shivering from more than just the cold, Hashiguchi's ring heavy in my pocket.

He shouldn't have died like that, locked in a hole all alone. He didn't deserve it. No one did, and yet it happened over and over. How many piles of ash had we found in those cells? How many people locked in their own suffering until they'd given up, laid down, and died? Hashiguchi may have lasted the longest, but it was always the same in the end.

How long would I last?

I tore my gaze away from the sky and forced myself to move, one foot in front of the other until I reached Yui's apartment in Nakano. The small, four-unit building sat tucked in the far corner of a residential block surrounded by high hedges. I stared at the door a long time before knocking. It swung open and there stood Yui, her youthful face rumpled, her eyes red and puffy. She gasped at the sight of me, hands over her mouth.

"I'm sorry, Yui-chan," I said gently. Her eyes welled, and I caught her by the shoulders as she tried to bow. I reached into my pocket, retrieved the ring, and pressed it into her hand.

"Thank you, Hiro-sama." She clutched the ring to her chest and tried to smile.

"Are you...okay?"

She nodded and scrubbed the tears from her face. "He'd been unhappy for a long time even before this. It is, in a way, a relief." She sniffed, her eyes going far away. "Maybe we're all destined to end this way."

The panic that had just begun to thaw solidified around me once again. I shoved my hands in my pockets and suppressed a shiver. "I certainly hope not."

FIVE

Mystery Man

WINTER 1993

I DIDN'T WANT TO GO BACK TO THE CAGES TO HELP HIDEYOSHI SWEEP UP a pile of ash that used to be a man, but I didn't want to go home either, so I found myself wandering the bustling streets around Nakano station. In the years I'd lived here, Tokyo had become a living thing, swallowing up the towns around it like a great, ever-expanding beast, the same in so many ways and yet completely different. Many of the same streets remained, only now they were paved in concrete and filled with bodies. Harried salarimen shoved past pockets of foreign tourists with their eyes on everything but where they were walking. Paper lanterns still hung on storefronts, only instead of the soft flicker of candles, they burned with harsh, artificial light. It was both beautiful and jarring, this juxtaposition of old and new, of a city racing toward a metropolitan future while stubbornly clinging to its former identity.

I ducked out of the cold and into the steamy humidity of possibly the worst ramen-ya in Tokyo. Tucked into a far corner of the Broadway between a T-shirt shop and an arcade, the place looked abandoned from the outside. Practically invisible in a sea of neon, a faded cloth sign over the door was the only indication of the business within. A wood counter with half a dozen stools shoved under it stretched the length of the long, narrow room opposite an open kitchen. Tall pots of broth boiled over high flames, tossing their sharp, spicy scents into the air. It was the kind of place tourists didn't notice and locals avoided, the perfect place to disappear. I claimed the stool on the farthest end, and my order had just arrived when *he* appeared.

A blast of cold air shoved him through the door, and the surly cook shouted a weak "Irasshai!" from behind the counter. He was small, more coat than man, his cheeks and the end of his nose bright with cold. He rattled off his order without even looking at the menu, shrugging his way out of his big, puffy jacket and pulling his gloves off with his teeth. I jerked my attention away as his gaze stopped on me, hunched over my bowl, swirling overcooked noodles around the murky broth and trying hard not to be noticed.

"Mind if I sit here?"

I looked up and he was right there beside me, jacket already draped over the back of the neighboring stool. He smiled, wide and genuine, exposing a fine fan of crow's feet around his eyes. I swallowed hard around the wad of tasteless noodles lodged in my throat.

He took my lack of refusal as assent and plopped down beside me before thrusting his hand out. "I'm Takanori."

I flinched, blinking as if he meant to punch me in the nose.

He withdrew his hand and settled back into his seat. "Do you live around here?"

I didn't answer, jabbing at a piece of overdone pork instead. My skin sizzled where he leaned in close to me, and a sharp, panicky feeling cut through my chest. The cook arrived with his order and plonked it down on the bar in front of him.

"Oh, I see," he said with a cheeky smile. "Mystery Man, I get it. That's okay, you don't have to talk to me. I'm pretty good at carrying on a conversation all by myself. My sister tells me I talk more than enough for two people anyway. Enough for a whole company of people." He shoved a wad of noodles into his mouth and chased it with a big gulp of water. "I think it's a side effect of working alone most of the time. When I get around other people, I just—hey! Where are you going?"

With a grumbled "Gochisousama," I pushed away from the bar, rose, and went out the door.

Hideyoshi was home by the time I returned and had been for some time by the looks of it. He sat with his legs tucked under a kotatsu, balancing a book in one hand and leaning on his elbow. A fire crackled in the brazier in the center of the room, as if in defiance of the modern electric heaters we'd installed years before. He looked up only briefly at my entrance. The pieces of my shamisen still lay strewn across the floor from its interrupted maintenance, and I drifted over to them.

"Did you see Yui?" Hide asked.

"Yes."

"Good."

"She's taking it well, considering."

"Mn."

Silence fell down around us. Wood shifted in the fire, sending up a cough of sparks. The tuning pegs of my shamisen creaked as I wound the strings around them and twisted them taut.

"She asked me," I started haltingly, "if we were all destined to end like this."

Hideyoshi snapped his book shut and pinched the bridge of his nose.

"Do you think—"

"No."

"Why not?" Heat flared in my cheeks and my sinuses burned. "We all have the same darkness inside us, and we all cope with it in different ways. Some live a thousand years, some are insane from the moment they're made."

"What's your point, Hiro?"

"I don't know." I sighed and scrubbed at the space between my eyebrows. "Maybe people aren't meant to live so long. Maybe I don't want to die alone in a cage."

"Then don't," he said, each word sharpened to a point. "You have a choice."

"Right." I picked at one of the strings, sending a hard, rattling note through the air.

He studied me for a long time, his sharp gaze scraping over me. "Is there something you're not telling me?"

A knot tightened in my stomach. The cold I'd been fighting all day welled up again, and I fought it down. "No." My job with the shamisen done, I gathered up my things and rose. Hide's eyes, dark under his straight, thin brows, followed my every movement. He turned on his hip as I walked past him toward the hallway.

"Hiro—"

"It's fine. Forget I said anything." I forced a smile and turned back far enough to drop a kiss on the top of his head. "I think I'll call it an early night. It's been a long day."

He grunted an agreement and turned back to his book. I knew he wouldn't press—he never did—but something twinged deep in my heart at his quick dismissal.

I slipped into my room and closed the door behind me. Why didn't I just tell him? Why couldn't I confide in him that the hairline fissure in my mind, the split that had been there since the day he made me, sometimes felt like a chasm? How every time we went down to those cages, I saw my own future laid out for me under harsh fluorescents. I wondered when Hashiguchi had first shown signs of madness, if Yui had noticed, maybe even tried to bring him back from the edge before it all fell apart. What would Hideyoshi do if he were in Yui's position? If I were the one going mad?

My chest tightened. I knew what he would do. It was the real reason I didn't confide in him and had allowed this awful distance to grow between us. I loved him. Even after two hundred years, I loved him with my whole heart. But I didn't trust him anymore.

The small room suddenly felt claustrophobic, and I crossed it in two long strides to slide open the door to the outside. The sharp evening air tingled through my lungs as I sucked in deep breaths one after another. Little by little, my knotted insides relaxed and I sank to the floor. Leaning against the doorframe, I pulled the shamisen across my lap and started to play. Not a song, just something to fill the silence. My mind wandered with the notes back to the ramen-ya I had visited that afternoon.

The image of that strange little man flashed clear as a picture behind my eyes, his bright, open smile making my heart race. Just that one momentary interaction had left me unbalanced and craving—not for blood, but for connection. A needle of guilt prodded my heart. All he wanted was conversation, and I'd been unspeakably rude to him. Guilt turned into longing as I tried to remember the last time I'd had a real conversation, one that wasn't loaded with strategy and youkai politics—a *human* conversation.

The notes of the shamisen died out, replaced by the beating of my own heart.

"Takanori." I whispered his name and even that felt forbidden.

I DON'T KNOW WHY I WENT BACK THERE. MAYBE BECAUSE IT WAS WARM, convenient. Certainly wasn't for the food. I knew he was there almost before I reached the door, as if his manic energy charged the air. I should have turned around and gone somewhere else, but it wrapped its electric tendrils around me and pulled me in.

"Mystery Man!" He perked up in his chair as soon as the door swung open and waved wildly. The same puffy coat lay draped over the back of his stool and an oversized wool sweater devoured his small frame, its high neck bunched up under his chin and the sleeves hanging long over his fingers. His feet barely reached the floor, and his black-denim-clad legs swung in the air beneath him. My stomach fluttered as I took a seat at the opposite end of the bar and made a big show of reading the menu. After all, I wasn't there for him.

Was I?

"I have had the *worst* day," he said, popping out of his chair and sliding his bowl down the bar toward me. "The people I work for...it's amazing they're still in business. The way they spend money, honestly. And they wouldn't know a receipt if it spat on their shoes." The flutter turned into an electrical storm as he dropped into the seat next to me. "I'm an accountant. It's not sexy, I know, but—"

"Do you ever stop talking?" I grumbled.

"Nope," he answered with a laugh. "You'll get used to it. Maybe even join in. Then I'll only talk half as much. You could start with your name—"

"Look, I'm not interested, okay?" I barked, slapping my menu down on the bar. What was I doing?

"Well, that's presumptuous," he said with mock indignation. "And what makes you think I'm interested in you? How do you know I don't have a girlfriend waiting at home? Or a wife?"

I arched an eyebrow at him and he laughed.

"Geez, do I have *lonely old queen* stamped on my forehead? Okay, fine. I get it. Wrong tree and all that. If it makes you feel better, I'm not interested either," he said. "Just looking for conversation."

I sank down in my chair. I was doing it again. But conversation was dangerous. Conversation led to friendships, expectations, things I didn't have room for. I came to this under-patronized hole in the wall precisely to avoid this sort of thing. I hadn't counted on meeting someone so willing to throw himself against the fragile shell I'd built around myself and force his way inside. I picked up my chopsticks, set them back down, and pushed around the place setting until everything sat at right angles.

"Hiro."

His face stretched into a wide grin, and something dormant inside me stirred. "Good to meet you, Hiro."

SIX

Not a Date

WINTER 1993

WE CARRIED ON LIKE THAT FOR WEEKS. I KEPT FINDING MYSELF DRIFTING toward the ramen-ya at the same time of day despite my better judgment, determined it would be the last time. He was always there too, yammering away as I stubbornly tried to ignore him, as if he were determined to find the chink in my armor and make me come spilling out. No matter how many personal questions I dodged, there were five more right behind them and something inevitably slipped. He managed to glean that I was born in Kyoto, though my accent had faded away to almost nothing. He'd guessed my age at "not older than twenty-five," to which I didn't comment. He even figured out I lived in an old house in Ushigome.

It was truly annoying, and yet I returned day after day, our verbal sparring matches sometimes the only thing that kept me going. I didn't have to think about cages, or secrets, or a long, daunting future, and I found myself falling into his bright eyes, his easy smile. He gave himself fully to every conversation, held nothing back. It was disorienting, like being shaken from a long sleep.

I didn't tell Hideyoshi.

"You gonna get that?" I asked around a mouthful of ramen, gesturing to the flip phone vibrating across the counter. Takanori crossed his arms over his chest and pursed his lips, turning his face away as if the thing would disappear if he couldn't see it.

"It's my sister," he said.

"You don't get along?" I took a long swig of green tea. He'd mentioned his sister in passing, but we'd never really talked about her. All our talks had been mostly meaningless, things like complaining about the weather while I tried not to notice his long eyelashes or the way his cheek dimpled when he laughed. This felt like taking a step toward something. My mouth went dry. Maybe he'd been holding something back after all.

"It's not that," he said, ruffling his choppy hair. "She's been bugging me about the Spring Festival. Wants to get all dressed up and everything."

"So?"

"So...I haven't worn a kimono since I was ten." He sighed with relief when the phone stopped ringing, only to groan when it picked back up a few seconds later. "How do I get out of this?"

"Just tell her you don't want to go."

"You don't understand," he said, his cheeks pink. "I can't say no to my sister. It's physically impossible. I'd climb Tokyo Tower in a Godzilla costume if she asked me to."

Damn. He's funny too.

"You talk to her," he said, shoving the phone at me.

"What?! I'm not gonna talk to your sister, you weirdo!"

"Please! I'll buy your lunch for a year. Ten years."

"No way. I don't think we're at the talk-to-my-sister point in our relationship."

He tossed the phone back onto the counter with a pout and deflated back into his chair.

"Just go. How bad can it be?"

He picked at a loose thread in the hem of his sweater, his small nose scrunched up. "She just rides me kind of hard sometimes, ya know?" he said, his head hanging. "I love her and all, we're very close, but she can be like an overbearing mom. Always nagging about my job or money or my love life. Sometimes I make up imaginary boyfriends just to get her off my case."

"Sounds like she worries about you."

"I'm the older brother. I'm the one that's supposed to worry." Takanori sat up straight and clapped his hands together. "I just got a great idea."

I shoved a wad of noodles in my mouth.

"You can be my date."

And I choked.

"Oh God." Takanori jumped out of his chair and slapped me on the back. "Shit, I'm sorry. I didn't mean—" Still coughing, I shook my head, and he shoved a glass of water in front of me. "You're not gonna punch me in the face or something, are you?"

"What? No," I said, still coughing up broth. "I just—"

"I know, I know. You're right. It's crazy," he said in a rush, waving his hands. "I mean, you're not even...you don't even know me. I'm just some guy that you sit next to in a restaurant and forces conversation on you."

"It's not that."

"It's okay. Really. You don't have to feel guilty. It's not like we're friends."

"I *like* talking to you, Taka."

We both froze. My hand had landed on his arm at some point, and I pulled it back, blushing as if I'd admitted something scandalous. *Taka.* His name shortened felt like an endearment. I made a list of all the reasons I should get up and walk away. It was a long one, blood-drinking immortal being the least of it, but I couldn't make myself move. As much as I tried to resist it, he fascinated me, slumped shoulders, lower lip tucked in his teeth, and blushing all the way to his ears. All his emotions were written in neon across his body. Talking to him was...easy. Not like...

"Okay, I'll go." His eyes brightened, and I held up my hands. "As a friend. Not a date."

"Yeah, okay," he said, nodding furiously. He smiled so wide, it lit up the whole room and that list of reasons evaporated. He snatched a napkin from the holder next to him and scribbled something down on it.

"This is my address. You can meet me there and we'll walk to the festival to meet up with Maia. It's just a few blocks away."

His address. His home address.

I'm in so much trouble.

"AAAAAAAAGGHH! I DON'T KNOW HOW TO DO THIS!"

Takanori gave a frustrated yank to the fastenings of his hakama and threw his hands in the air. He really was a mess, the collar of his pale grey kimono gaping and his hakama sagging around his slender hips. He looked like a boy playing dress-up in his father's clothes, everything off-kilter and just a bit too big. I laughed and his face flushed.

"Here, let me help you," I said, grabbing the horribly tangled mess over his stomach. He crossed his arms over his chest, puffing out his cheeks like a cranky three-year-old as I loosened the knot and straightened the belts. Warmth teased at my insides, followed by a wash of guilt as I thought of Hideyoshi and all the times he'd helped me dress.

"Why do we have to dress like this anyway?"

"It's a festival," I said, clearing my throat of the knot that had formed there. "It's supposed to be fun."

I smoothed the collar of his kimono and lifted the hakama into the proper position, my arms circling his small waist as I retied the bindings. He watched me with a childish fascination, a little wrinkle forming on the bridge of his nose.

"How are you so good at this?" he asked.

I laughed. "I guess you could say I had a traditional upbringing. There," I said, squaring off the knot and taking a step back. "Now you look like a proper Japanese gentleman."

I slipped a white haori over his shoulders and turned him toward a mirror. His eyes widened a bit, but the stubborn frown remained. His gaze bounced between his image and mine, as if comparing the two. I looked his negative, all black-on-black, my long hair tied up in a wild ponytail high on my crown. Curly hair had become fashionable in recent years, so I no longer made the effort to tame it, letting it explode off the back of my head and tickle at the nape of my neck.

"You look beautiful," he said. My face heated and I turned away.

"Ready to go?" I asked, shuffling into the genkan and slipping my feet into a pair of wooden geta.

"Oh, wait! I almost forgot!" He ran to a shelf in the back of the apartment, tripping on his hakama on the way, and fetched a small wooden box. "I got this for you…for today."

My heart sputtered. "I thought this wasn't—"

"It's just a small thing," he said quickly. "I wanted to do something to say thank you. A totally non-date gift." His eyes sparkled, and he pulled his lip between his teeth as he handed it to me.

I pulled the top off the box. Inside was a long leather strap tipped with a small cluster of white-glass plum blossoms. I gasped, running a finger over the petals.

"For your hair. I thought it would look…" He shifted his weight from one foot to the other, hands wound in the sleeves of his haori. "Do you like it?"

"Yeah, it's…" I paused and cleared my throat. "Thank you."

"Can I…?" he asked, gesturing to the box. I nodded, handing it over and bending at the waist. He reached his hands up over my head and wrapped the strap around the base of my ponytail. His breath smelled like citrus. My heart fluttered and my palms began to sweat as his hands dropped from my hair to rest on my shoulders.

I straightened sharply and took a step back, pretending to admire myself in a nearby mirror while I forced back an encroaching panic. The ends of the strap hung long beside my ponytail, the flowers swinging gently. A burst of white in a nest of black.

"How does it look?" I asked, cocking my head to the side to give him a better view.

He didn't say anything. Didn't need to. It was etched all over his face.

"We should go. Maia's probably waiting for us," he said after a sharp intake of breath. I didn't breathe again until he hurried into his geta and shuffled out the door.

"TAKANORI!" A GIRL IN A PALE PINK YUKATA RUSHED TOWARD US FROM across the street, jumping up and down and waving her arms as she went. Taka's sister, Maia, judging from their striking resemblance. Same round face, same plump lips, same striking features only softer. She was younger than I expected, glowing with teenage exuberance. She wore her light brown hair neatly lifted off her neck in a delicate twist and peppered with cloth flowers.

She skidded to a stop when she saw me. "Who's this?" she asked, a suggestive twinkle in her eye.

"This is Hiro," Taka said, "He's—"

"Cute!"

"—a *friend*." Taka flinched.

"I see." Maia crossed her arms over her chest and gave me a long look-over. "Like, my kinda friend, or your kinda friend?"

"Maia!" Taka gasped and turned about eight shades of red.

I hid a snorting laugh behind my hand, cutting it short as Maia pinned me with a questioning look, her eyebrows lifting. "Oh. Umm…" I glanced toward Taka.

"Damn," she said, hands on her hips. "The cute ones are always gay."

Taka's jaw dropped, his eyes swinging in my direction. I couldn't stop the laugh this time. "What—ow!"

He nailed me in the bicep with a hard punch. "You—I thought—"

"I never said." Another punch. "Ow! Stop!"

Maia had one hand over her mouth, the other around her middle, as she doubled over laughing. It was infectious, and soon I was laughing along with her as I fended off another set of playful blows. I couldn't remember the last time I laughed so hard and so easily.

"You guys are great," she said between gasps. "I wish my dates were like this."

"It's not a date," Taka and I said in unison.

"Why the hell not?" she asked, throwing up her hands. "I mean, look at you two."

We froze where we stood, Taka in mid-swing, me rubbing the bruised spot on my arm. My heart twitched like an electric shock.

"We hardly know each other," Taka said, a tremor of disappointment in his eyes. "He's just doing me a favor, really."

"Yeah, whatever," she said, rolling her eyes in disbelief. "I'm going to find a Takoyaki stall. You boys have fun on your non-date."

She wiggled her fingers at us as she disappeared into the crowd, leaving us in a bubble of awkwardness. Drums pounded in the distance as the elaborate floats bobbed down the street toward us, surrounded by costumed dancers. Taka fidgeted with his hakama. I avoided his eyes.

"It's not...personal," I started when the silence became too much to bear. "I mean, you're…"

"It's fine," he said, waving me off and ducking into the flow of the crowd toward the parade. "I'm sure you have somebody…"

That shock again. I rubbed my sternum. "Yes."

"Been together a long time?" he asked as I fell into step beside him.

"Practically my whole life."

He shot me a cheeky grin. "So it's serious then?"

I laughed, but it sounded forced even to me. "You could say that."

Taka's smile faltered, and he went uncharacteristically quiet.

"What?"

He flinched. "What do you mean, *what*?"

"What do you want to ask me?"

"Nothing." He shook his head emphatically. "I mean...I don't want to pry."

"You don't?" I scoffed.

"Hey, give me a break," he said with a pout. "My mouth gets ahead of my brain sometimes. I don't do it on purpose."

I laughed and waited patiently while he fiddled with his haori himo.

"It's just...when I met you, you seemed…"

"Seemed what?"

"So unhappy."

My steps faltered as the shock turned into a lightning storm. Sadness settled over me like a heavy blanket. "We're just going through a hard time right now, that's all. We'll get through it. We always do."

A crease formed between his brows, but he nodded and gave me a small smile. "Do you love him?"

My mouth went dry. The parade had drawn closer, shamisen and pipes joining the throbbing drumbeat, an old song that touched off something familiar in me. I peered between heads in the crowd, spotting the dancers.

"Oh, I know this." I put Taka's question aside and hummed along to the tune, my hands mimicking the movements I'd learned as a young man.

Taka stopped in his tracks, eyes wide. "You're kidding."

"It's easy. Look." I closed my eyes and let muscle memory take over. One foot in front of the other, hands raised over my head. A slow pivot on my front foot, and then my right hand came down like a blade. My knee came up to meet it with a little hop, my arms churning the air in graceful, sweeping motions. Taka giggled, and I cracked one eye open.

"You look like a crazy person," he said.

"Come on, I'll teach you." I grabbed his wrist, pulling him into an open spot in the crowd, and he yelped in protest. Hands on his hips, I maneuvered him into the proper starting position.

"This is stupid," he groaned.

"Where's your Yamato spirit?" I asked, poking him in the ribs before taking my place beside him. I demonstrated the first move, a wide sweep of the arms, before turning back to him, eyebrows raised. He copied the move, swinging his arms awkwardly around his body and triggering a stream of snorting laughter.

"I look like a wounded seagull," he huffed, dropping his arms to his sides.

"No, you don't," I said. "Try again. This time with less...flapping."

He tried again. He was truly awful, but smiling, and the pain in my chest felt like a distant memory, replaced by something softer, warmer. The dance ended with a spin. Taka pushed his tongue into the corner of his mouth and, wobbling on his wooden geta, threw himself into the move with all his might. His hakama flared out, wrapping up his legs, and he went tumbling out of control. I rushed forward and wrapped my arms around him before he fell face-first in the pavement, and we both went down in a stream of curses and wild laughter.

"That was perfect," I said, sides aching.

"That's me. Graceful as a ballerina," he replied, grinning up at me. Our eyes met, and I became abruptly aware of his body sprawled over me, how his small frame fit exactly into mine, warm and soft and delicate.

His ears turned red and he scrambled into a more upright position, punching me in the gut in the process. "God. Sorry." He tried to get to his feet but stumbled. "Aw man, my shoe."

The strap on his geta had come unfastened, and the wooden base flopped awkwardly around his foot. "It's okay, we can fix it." I gestured to a bench a few feet away. "Let's head over there."

I stood up, offered him my arm, and together we hobbled to the bench. I plucked the broken shoe off his foot and set to retying the bindings. He leaned on my shoulder to watch. A knot rose in my throat when I leaned back and he didn't pull away. Like we weren't strangers who met in a ramen shop. Like we'd always been this way.

"You fixed it," he said, a dreamy look in his eye.

"Yeah." I had to clear my throat to keep my voice from cracking. I slid out of the bench and onto my knees in front of him. He inhaled sharply when I took his foot in my hand. "Are you hurt?"

He shook his head. I ran my fingers over his ankle just in case, afraid he had twisted it. No bruising, no swelling, everything in place. I slipped the shoe back onto his foot and adjusted the straps.

"All done. You're good to—"

"Does he know?"

My throat seized and I froze, hands still curled around his foot.

"Your boyfriend," he continued. "Does he know you're having lunch with me almost every day?"

I blew out a long breath and rose stiffly, settling onto the bench beside him.

"He doesn't, does he?"

I shook my head.

"Why not?"

The back of my eyes burned, and I squeezed them closed. "I don't know."

It wasn't true. I did know. I knew he would be angry and would disapprove. I knew he would be jealous. Worse, he'd see it as some kind of dereliction of duty, and I just wanted someplace I could be something other than "Hiro, King among Demons."

I didn't want to lose this.

"Listen, if you need to…" The bench creaked as Taka shifted his weight toward me. "I mean…I know I talk a lot, but I listen pretty well too."

Warmth slid through my extremities and curled up in my chest. I opened my eyes and found his hand resting over mine on my thigh.

"Not a date, huh?"

We both jerked away from each other as Maia appeared in front of us, smirking like the cat that got the cream.

"Stop it, Maia."

Maia balked at his tone, her playful expression dropping, and I couldn't shake the feeling that I'd broken something special.

SEVEN

Nostalgia

SPRING 1994

I ALMOST DIDN'T GO BACK. IN FACT, I STAYED AWAY FROM THE RAMEN-YA and Takanori for two days. Two whole days of relative silence, though his voice still rang in my ears.

Does he know?

I burned with guilt every time I thought of him while sitting on the porch with Hideyoshi drinking wine, or at his table practicing calligraphy just an arm's reach away. I could have told him. We weren't doing anything wrong. Just a shared meal and pointless conversation. But every time I tried, I imagined Hide's face reddening in anger as he forbade me to see him again, and my gut would twist like a wrung rag. Everything about our relationship felt so fragile. What if this was the thing that broke us?

So I stayed silent. And I stayed away.

I stayed away from home too, volunteering to run every errand no matter how much I hated it as long as it got me away from my guilt. Which is how I found myself standing in a train station in front of a garish poster advertising domestic travel. Stylized polaroid photos of scenic locations scattered across its surface: the summit of Mt. Fuji, the hot springs of Hokkaido, the tile roofs and flame-colored maples of Kyoto.

A longing opened up in me so deep and wide I could hardly breathe. Kyoto. The start of everything, for better or for worse. No matter how long I spent in Tokyo, Kyoto would always be my home, but I hadn't set foot in it since I left with Hideyoshi all those lifetimes ago. My only remaining connection to the place I grew up was Hanagawa. The person was long gone, of course, but the legacy she built remained in the form of Hanagawa Home for Boys, built on the site of our okiya and supported by a trust I'd set up in her name. I still wrote to her as if she were there and sent gifts for the boys, and they always wrote back. I had a shoebox at home full of photos—some sepia-toned and faded to almost nothing, others in bright, hyper-realistic color—of the boys who lived there, all of them victims of one tragedy or another. Hideyoshi thought me foolish and soft-hearted, but I held it as the one truly good thing I'd done in my long life.

"Hiro-san."

I snapped out of my reverie and turned to find Matsudaira Takeru, the great-great-something of Matsudaira Tsuketada, the daimyo Hideyoshi had served under before he lost his sword. We helped him rescue his father-turned-youkai from abduction and torture by Hunters, and in return he'd pledged a sort of fealty to us. Now his ancestor stood well out of arm's reach behind me, begrudgingly carrying out his obligation. He was a long, severe-looking man, bearing only the faintest resemblance to his predecessors. He stood with his back straight, shoulders squared, everything perfect down to the unbroken crease in his pant legs. Even his face looked starched and pressed. He regarded me with a wary and impatient eye, hands clasped primly in front of him.

"Matsudaira-han." I acknowledged him with a small bow. I took a step toward him and he stepped back, his scowl deepening. He had let me know in many ways his distaste for our dealings and that our relationship extended only to his family's obligations and no further. He hadn't even had children, something Hideyoshi took as an act of defiance. The Matsudaira's deal with monsters would end with him. "You know, I could come to your office instead of meeting in the train station like criminals."

"I'd rather you didn't."

I released a huff of a laugh and extracted a small envelope of cash from my jacket pocket, the rent for our unfinished office building. "Your compensation."

He stepped just close enough to pluck the envelope from my fingers before stepping back again.

"Have you ever been to Kyoto?"

He stopped his retreat short. "Excuse me?"

"Kyoto," I repeated. "Ever been?"

"Yes."

"What's it like now?"

"Loud," he said. "Many tourists."

I nodded and he took that as his chance to flee, leaving me alone in the terminal. I turned back toward the poster, eyes drawn to that idyllic photo. *It won't be the same.* But I couldn't stop thinking about it, about the samurai I met there and fell in love with and couldn't seem to find anymore. I missed him so bad it felt like bleeding. I wanted him back.

EIGHT

Change

SPRING 1994

I HAD A PLAN. AT LEAST I THOUGHT I DID. I GOT ABOUT HALFWAY HOME before I started second-guessing everything about it and tying my thoughts into such a knot, I couldn't see the end anymore. I needed to talk it out, for someone to tell me I was doing the right thing—or at least, that it would be okay if I wasn't.

I needed to talk to Takanori.

As I turned my feet toward Nakano, my stomach flipped for a different reason. My non-date with Taka had ended strangely to say the least, and the silence that followed only made it feel stranger. I'd headed toward the ramen-ya in Nakano assuming he would be there, but what if he wasn't? What if he'd been avoiding it just like I was? What if he took my absence as rejection and stopped going altogether? Or worse, what if I showed up to find him talking the ear off some other guy? The last thought bothered me more than it should have, and I shook my head to free myself of it. We were hardly even friends, practically strangers. If he wasn't there, I would just go home and carry on with my life. It was probably for the best anyway.

But he was there, sitting at the bar with his bowl of noodles. The puffy coat and sweaters had been traded out for a thin, cotton T-shirt that clung to his back and light-wash jeans with holes in the knees. Not exactly the salariman uniform, but comfortable enough for someone who worked from home.

He was alone. For a moment I just watched from the other side of the glass door, watched his sneakered feet swing just above the floor and his nervous fingers flick at the corner of his placemat, always moving.

He looked up when I walked in, brows lifted and eyes wide. For a heart-stopping second, I thought he was angry, but then his mouth curved into a bright smile.

"Hiro!"

I nearly melted with relief. He waved me over, and I crossed the small space in three long steps, nodding to the cook as he got to work on my usual order. Taka patted the stool next to him, and I settled onto it.

"Everything okay?" he asked, studying me as I stared at the countertop.

"I'm okay. I just...I thought..." I glanced up at him out of the corner of my eye. "...you might be mad at me or something after how we left things at the festival."

He burst out laughing, and I startled so hard I nearly fell out of my chair. "Me mad at you? Come on." He dismissed the idea with a wave of his hand. "For what? Not divulging every detail of your personal life to a stranger? If anything, you should be mad at me for sticking my nose where it doesn't belong."

"You're not a stranger, Taka."

"Even so." His cheeks went a little pink. "You don't owe me that. Don't owe me anything, really. Honestly, when you didn't show up for lunch like usual, I thought I'd scared you off for sure...What?"

I didn't realize I'd started laughing. "Nothing. I just missed your voice, that's all."

The red in his cheeks rose all the way to his ears. "Don't worry," he said with a giggle, "you'll get sick of it in no time."

My meal arrived soon after, and we fell back into easy conversation as if nothing had ever happened. That knot inside me loosened to the point I'd almost forgotten about it. It felt good. Really good. So good I waited until Taka's bowl was nearly empty and we had settled our bill to ruin it.

"Can I ask you for advice?"

His eyebrows lifted over the edge of his bowl as he tipped the remaining broth into his mouth. "Sure."

I cringed. "Relationship advice."

"Oh." He shrugged and laughed. "It may not be the best advice, but I'll give it a try."

I pulled in a long breath, held it for a moment, then let it out before reaching into my pocket and pulling out a pair of train tickets. "I bought train tickets. To Kyoto."

Taka swiveled in his seat to face me. "Okay."

"Hide and I…"

"That's the boyfriend?" he asked.

I nodded. "We met when I was still living there."

"You moved here with him?"

"Yes." I frowned down at the tickets in my hand, guilt cooling in my gut as I picked around the truth. Why was this so hard?

"When was the last time you went back?"

"We haven't."

"Not even to visit family?"

"I don't have any family."

"Oh." He drew out the word as if that meant something. Perhaps it did.

"When I was in the train station today, I saw an advertisement and got this crazy idea. What if we went back? Just for a visit. It's been so long and…" I rubbed a hand over my eyes. "I don't know. Sometimes I think we've forgotten why we got together in the first place. Maybe if we saw it again, all those places that used to mean something, we'd remember."

Taka nodded, his brows lowered in a look of sympathy.

"Is that stupid?"

"No, Hiro," he said gently. "It's not stupid."

"I can't help but worry that I'm just setting myself up for disappointment," I said with a dry laugh. "Hide is about as far from a romantic as they come."

"But you are, though," Taka said. "A romantic, I mean."

"Am I?"

He gestured to the tickets in my hand. "I'd say so."

I took another breath, held it, let it out.

"What are you really afraid of?"

I jerked as if he'd poked me in the ribs. The fear and doubt I'd refused to acknowledge filled me up. It pressed against my skin from the inside until I thought I would split at the seams.

"I'm afraid…" I started, my voice thin and brittle. "I'm afraid we'll go and nothing will change."

The confession pressed down on my shoulders until they nearly touched the countertop. Taka released a breath and laid a hand on my back. It was so warm and gentle, it made my eyes burn.

"I understand," he said. "But you *know* nothing will change if you don't go. So what do you really have to lose?"

I squeezed my eyes shut and let the truth roll over me. He was right. I knew he was right. But somehow, doing nothing still felt like the better solution, the easier solution. If I did nothing, then I could pretend that we were okay, that we weren't still together out of some ancient obligation. That maybe under that mask he wore, he loved me even if I couldn't see it. How long had it been since I'd caught a glimpse of the heart he kept locked away in a box? I couldn't remember.

I opened my eyes and found Taka still there, waiting patiently, his fingers stroking small circles on my back. I straightened and his hand dropped, but the warmth remained, as if he'd left a piece of himself there and I felt a bit stronger for it.

"Okay," I said on a long exhale. I slipped the tickets back into my pocket and dropped out of the stool. "Thank you, Taka."

"Of course," he answered. I turned toward the door, and he called after me. "Hey, Hiro."

I stopped just inside the door and turned.

"Whatever happens, I'm here for you."

NINE

The End

SPRING 1994

THE HOUSE APPEARED EMPTY AT FIRST AS I PUSHED THROUGH THE FRONT gate. The shoji were all open, and the fresh, warm air cut an unimpeded path through the main room. Brushes and sticks of ink were laid out on the chabudai beside a stack of papers already dripping with Hideyoshi's graceful vertical script and held down by a brass paperweight. I knew without reading it would be poetry, verses memorized and copied a hundred times over the years. Even if the words weren't his, I used to take the practice as a hint at Hideyoshi's deeper feelings. I even had a few copies of my favorites tucked away inside a drawer where he didn't know I had them. I used to fawn over them like love notes, the words of great masters written in my lover's hand, a feigned intimacy.

"Hideyoshi?"

I pulled my eyes away from the papers and slipped down the hallway toward his room. I was about to poke my head inside when I heard a familiar, sharp whistle from the back garden. I changed direction and headed toward the already open back door. Hideyoshi stood at the far end of the engawa, eyes upturned to a pair of goshawks perched on the eaves. A warm flush of nostalgia washed over me as I watched him with the birds, tossing up scraps of meat and cooing gently.

Though we presumed the goshawks that returned every year were descended from the first, they were wild-born and slow to trust. It didn't stop Hideyoshi from trying to win them over. He'd stand outside for hours, holding meat in a leather-gloved hand and whistling until he was hoarse. I was ashamed to admit that I'd found myself jealous of them more than once over the years, jealous of Hideyoshi's effort and attention.

One of the hawks turned its amber eyes on me and barked as I crossed the engawa behind Hideyoshi. I laid my hand between the ridges of his shoulder blades, and his cotton dress shirt whispered beneath my fingers as I slid them down the line of his spine. I closed my eyes and let myself drift back to an earlier time, a simpler time, when his mere presence was all I needed. I leaned forward and pressed my nose into the back of his neck, breathing in the sharp, herbal smell of him. No matter how much time had passed, my heart still beat faster when I was near him, and as I slipped my arms around his waist and pressed myself against his back, I was sure he could feel it.

"Stop it, Hiro. You'll scare away the birds."

Cold rushed through me as he shrugged me off, followed by a heat of a different kind, fiery and volatile. For half a minute, I just glared at his back before turning and stomping into the house. I made it as far as the kitchen before his heavy footfalls followed me.

"What is it, Hiro?" he asked with a tinge of exasperation.

"Nothing." I avoided his glare by fetching a cast-iron teapot, the same one I'd used for at least a century, and filling it under the tap.

"You are angry with me."

"I'm not."

"You are," he said. "Are you going to tell me, or do I have to guess?"

I dropped the heavy teapot onto the electric range with a loud bang and flipped it on. "Forget it. I don't know what I was expecting anyway."

For a long moment he just stood there, eyes narrowed as I focused on making tea, before finally disappearing with a muffled curse. A headache brewed behind my eyes, and I scrubbed at the space between my brows. I wasn't angry at him, not really. I couldn't blame him for being who he'd always been. But I couldn't deny I'd hoped for something different.

I let the comforting, meditative practice of brewing tea smooth the sharp edges of my disappointment. The train tickets sat heavy in my pocket, and I remembered what Taka said. *What do you really have to lose?*

Carrying a teacup in each hand, I drifted down the hallway and back out to the main room. Hideyoshi had resumed his calligraphy practice, his brush flicking over the paper in quick, expert strokes. He didn't look up as I knelt opposite him and placed a teacup next to his papers. I waited until he finished, set down his brush, and reached for the cup before slipping the tickets out of my pocket and laying them on the table.

"What's this?" he asked, eyeing the green envelope bearing the Japan Railways logo.

"Train tickets."

"I can see that." He took a long sip of his tea. "Going somewhere?"

"Kyoto."

He blinked, and his fingers did a strange little twitch around his glass. "What is there for you in Kyoto?"

"I thought *we* could go. Together." His brows knotted, and I fumbled forward before I could lose my nerve. "It's been...so long. And I thought it could be...I don't know...nice."

"Nice?" One eyebrow quirked up.

"Yes. Nice." The words came out edged, and I took a breath to calm my temper, a practice that grew more difficult every day. "Don't you miss how we felt back then? Back when everything was new?"

He frowned, put his teacup aside, and picked up his brush again. "We can't just pick up and leave, Hiro. We have responsibilities."

"Responsibilities that will still be here when we get back," I said. "I'm only talking about a few days."

He didn't respond, the only sound the scrape of his brush against the thin rice paper.

"Please, Hideyoshi. I know you don't...feel the same as I do, but I need this. I miss it. I miss us." Nothing. "Hideyoshi."

"After over two hundred years, what would be the point?"

His brush never paused its movement. He didn't even look up. I may as well have not even been there. Anger flared behind my breastbone again and I slapped the table, sending ink splashing out of its dish and across his papers. He sat back with a huff, a scowl twisting his features. I jumped to my feet, hands clenched into fists, and made to storm off.

"What on earth is wrong with you, boy?" he growled, grabbing for my arm as I passed. "Sit down."

"The time I've spent with you is not pointless," I said, jerking out of his grip, eyes burning. "I am not pointless."

"That's not—" He stood up to follow as I turned away again. "Would you just stop? If you want to go to Kyoto, we'll go to Kyoto."

"It's not about Kyoto." I pushed the words through gritted teeth, blinking hard to keep tears from falling. "I love you, Hideyoshi. I've given my whole life to you. And you can't even pretend for one day, *one day*, that you love me."

He froze, eyes wide, reeling as if I'd struck him. But then that familiar mask came down, turning his expression unreadable, and it made me want to scream or cry. I turned away again, this time not stopping until I reached my room.

"Hiro, stop." His voice boomed behind me. "Don't walk away from me."

Snap!

He was right behind me, and I shut the door so fast I nearly took off his nose. His footsteps vibrated the floorboards as he paced in front of my door. I stepped back, expecting him to barge through it, but he never did. With a grumbled curse, his steps retreated back down the hall, leaving nothing but the sound of the wind.

My knees shook and my chest constricted. Silent tears wet my cheeks. When Taka asked me what I was afraid of, I'd never considered this. Hideyoshi's complete and total indifference cut me down to the marrow. I looked around the room with blurry eyes as if it could give some hint as to what went wrong. My shamisen sat in the corner, freshly strung but unplayed. A shelf of music magazines organized in numbered order propped up a set of string-bound, handwritten manuscripts. A cell phone charged next to a two-hundred-year-old oil lamp. A confused amalgamation of a too-long life.

Maybe he was right. What *was* the point? The dark thing inside me surged to the surface, bringing with it a bloodlust that promised to drown these too-human emotions and bring relief. I caught sight of myself in the brass mirror leaned up against the wall. My eyes were white.

I had to get out.

I pulled a duffle bag out of the closet and started throwing things in. I had no plan. I didn't know how long I would be gone or where I would go, I just knew I couldn't be here. I grabbed clothes and the box of letters from Hanagawa. While rummaging through a drawer, my hand fell on one of Hideyoshi's poems. For a long time I stared at it, the words blurring and the paper crinkling in my grip. Part of me wanted to tear it into little unrecognizable pieces, but instead I folded it into a neat square and tucked it into my pocket before slipping out the back door.

TEN

Starting Again

SPRING 1994

I WALKED FOR HOURS BEFORE LANDING ON TAKANORI'S DOORSTEP, sweating and shaking and more scared than I'd been in my whole life. The navy blue sky pressed against the roofs off the close-packed buildings, showing itself only in starless slivers. The duffel bag hung like an anvil off my arm, all that remained of what I was before.

"Hiro!" Taka answered on the second knock, his bright smile dropping the moment he saw me. His gaze bounced over my face, down to the bag in my hand, and back up again. I kept my eyes lowered, afraid of what he would see there. "What happened?"

"I left." The words slammed against my fragile composure, and I shattered into great, hiccuping sobs. Taka pulled me inside by my shirtfront, slammed the door behind me, and threw his arms around my neck. Face buried in the crook of his neck, I clung to him. For a brief and terrifying moment, the monster inside me noticed his pulse tapping against my nose, but the warmth of his embrace chased it away.

He held me without comment or question until my sobs died down to a sniffle. He then led me gently by the arm to the sofa and lowered me into it. He stood over me a moment, his own eyes glassy and hands clenched, as if he wasn't sure what to do with them.

"I'll make some tea," he said and sped off to the kitchen. I melted into the sofa, exhausted down to my soul. Two minutes later a microwave dinged, and Taka shoved an over-hot mug with a tea bag floating in it into my hands and perched on the edge of the couch next to me.

"Do you want to talk about it?" he asked.

I shook my head, gaze focused on the water as it slowly changed color. The truth was I did want to talk about it, but I didn't know how without also telling a string of lies, and I couldn't bring myself to do that to him. Not when he was being so kind to me.

"Okay." He settled back next to me, shoulders close but not quite touching, and rubbed his hands on his thighs. "I'm so sorry, Hiro. What can I do to help you? What do you need? Do you need a place to stay?"

A place to stay. I hadn't managed to think ahead even that far. I didn't know a single person who wasn't somehow connected to Hideyoshi. Word of my leaving would get around soon enough, but I didn't need to shame him that way, and anyone who housed me could be perceived as choosing a side. Our domestic break could easily turn into a political one, dividing an already fickle community of monsters down the middle. I nodded, pressing a hand against my eyes as tears threatened again.

"It's okay. That's okay," he said quickly, waving his hands in the air. "Stay as long as you need...as long as you don't mind the couch."

He jumped up and disappeared again, reappearing seconds later with an armload of pillows and blankets. He dropped them on the far end of the couch, forcing us closer as he wedged himself back in beside me. Our shoulders did touch this time and our knees knocked together, and it took everything in me not to mold myself to his side. Something told me he would have let me, and a bit of the fear I'd felt standing on his porch faded.

"I'm sorry to barge in on you like this," I said. "I just..."

"Don't be sorry. I told you I'm here for you and I meant it."

I forced a weak but grateful smile. "I'm so tired," I said on a sigh, wiping a hand over my face. "I feel like I've been chasing after him my whole life, but instead of getting closer, he's only gotten farther away. I don't know what I've done wrong."

"Nothing. You've done nothing wrong," he said with such genuine conviction, it made my throat tight. "If he can't see how incredible you are, he's the one who's wrong. I've known you five minutes and I can see it."

He gasped and turned his face away, his ears going very red. Something fluttered deep in my belly. Whatever this new emotion was, I had no room for it, so I pushed it aside.

Taka cleared his throat. "You must be exhausted. I'll let you get some rest."

"Wait." I grabbed his wrist as he started to stand. "Can you just...talk to me for a while?"

"About what?" he asked with an awkward laugh.

"I don't know. Something. Anything. The weather or the cost of rice." I swallowed around the rising lump in my throat. "Anything but this."

He smiled softly and settled back into the sofa. "Sure. I can do that."

He must have talked for hours. About what, I didn't know. It didn't matter, really. I simply found comfort in the rhythm of his voice. I let it fill all my empty spaces until I didn't feel quite so fragile. At some point I fell asleep, waking slumped into the corner of the couch with a blanket thrown over me as the gray light of morning seeped in through the curtains. Confused and groggy, I almost forgot where I was, until the memories of the day before pounced and I fell into despair all over again.

Taka treated me with the utmost care and patience, conducting his day around me and not even commenting when I hardly moved from my pile of blankets on the couch. He slipped out at some point in the afternoon, returning about an hour later with a copy of his key. I complained profusely when he handed it to me, swearing on every deity I could think of that I would make other arrangements as soon as I got myself together. One day. Two tops. He simply smiled softly and pressed the key into my hand.

"As long as you need."

Two days turned into a week, a week into a month, and still he didn't push. On the contrary, he bought new bedding and cleaned out a coat closet for me to store my meager belongings. Taka and I fell into an easy rhythm. I would read or watch television while he worked from a small desk in the corner, the clacking of keys providing a pleasant soundtrack to an otherwise mundane life. Around midday, he would grab me by the arm and drag me off the couch and out to the ramen-ya. He never seemed to notice when I slipped out at night. It was boring —good boring, the kind that felt normal and safe, almost like a human life. Every day I missed my life with Hideyoshi a little bit less.

ELEVEN

Threat

SPRING 1994

SIX WEEKS PASSED. TAKA WAS WORKING AWAY AT HIS DESK WHILE I MADE tea, hunched and squinting through round, wire-framed glasses that I'd long decided were the cutest thing in the world. I'd begun to notice all sorts of cute things about him I wasn't quite ready to process, like how his shirtsleeves were always just a little too long and how his nose crinkled when he laughed. He'd been like this all day, all his manic energy hyper-focused on his task, stopping only to throw insults at the faceless client on the other side of the computer. I blew the steam off a fresh cup and slid it under his hand. His left hand groped for the handle while his right continued typing. He took a long sip, pausing long enough to release a groan of approval.

"Have I told you that you make the best tea in the world?"

I laughed. "Yes."

"Well, it bears repeating."

He returned both hands to his work, eyes red-rimmed and bleary. "You need a break."

"I don't have time for a break," he huffed. "I've gotta have this back to my client by two p.m., which will take a small miracle as it is."

"You have to eat at least," I said. "Come get ramen with me."

"I can't."

"Taka…"

"Hiro," he echoed, annoyance creeping into his voice.

"Okay, okay." I sighed and leaned back against the wall next to his desk, arms crossed over my chest. "If I go pick it up for you, will you at least stop long enough to eat it?"

His fingers slowed on the keys and he frowned, his eyes flicking up to me. I flashed an innocent smile, and he rolled his eyes.

"Fine. Okay. Yes," he said, throwing up his hands.

With a triumphant whoop, I popped off the wall and headed for the door before he could change his mind.

"There's money in the—"

"Keep your money," I said. "I'll be back in ten."

"You're a lifesaver," he called after me.

The irony.

It took almost no time to walk down to Nakano Broadway, and I was on my way back with Taka's usual order in hand when a cold finger slipped up my spine and stopped me dead in my tracks. The monster inside that I'd been ignoring since my stay with Taka slid to the surface, its senses tuned to the deep shadows cut by the electric lights. A hundred hearts beat around me in little pulsating balls of light, but one was different. Darker, deeper, with the reverberance of a kettledrum. My head jerked toward the snap and sizzle of a lighter, and a familiar square face materialized in the alleyway across the street, skin made golden in its reflected light.

No.

Kyo touched the lighter to the end of a cigarette, face lowered but eyes never leaving mine. His hair was short, bleached blond, and looked like it had been cut with garden shears. Black and gray tattoos crawled up his arms and peeked out of the collar of his navy blue work shirt, the sharp lines of which made his small, hard frame look even harder. He snapped the lighter closed and took a long drag off the cigarette, before jerking his head over his shoulder and melting into the shadows of the alley.

My gut turned into a block of ice, and my skin went cold despite the heat. Fear and anger battled inside me. He shouldn't be here. We had a deal. My gaze jerked over the sea of faces between us. Were there others? Would I follow him into that alley only to get a silver knife in my back?

Palms sweating, I crossed the street with heavy steps and ducked into the alley. Kyo stood at the far end, leaning against the wall under a security light. Despite his dress, he appeared anachronistic under the harsh orange glare, like a ghost out of time, here but not here.

"Hisashiburi," he said around his cigarette. I ignored the greeting, hands clenching around the bag I carried making the plastic creak. "Relax, Hiro, I'm not here for a fight."

"Then why are you here?"

He shrugged. "Just checking in. Perhaps offering condolences."

My stomach lurched with a wave of nausea. He'd heard.

"You've done a fine job here up to now," he said after another long drag. The smoke pooled around him, turning the garish light milky and blurring his features. "Population is steady, death toll is down, even the typical theatrics—"

"I did none of it for you."

His lips quirked. "And yet it benefits me."

"What's your point?"

"I'd like you to continue doing it."

"You think because I'm not with Hideyoshi that I've stopped?"

"Haven't you? Is it even possible to be, as your friend so aptly put it, a king among demons in your current...situation?" His gaze drifted down to the bag of ramen in my hand, and my heart seized. "You haven't been seen among youkai in over a month. There are rumors you've left the city and abandoned them entirely. I wonder how they would react if they knew their king was pretending to be human."

I sucked in a breath, and it caught behind my breastbone. A small smile tugged at his lips, and he dropped his cigarette to his feet, crushing it under his boot. The smoke parted before him as he stepped forward, laying a hand on my shoulder as he passed me, then disappeared into the crowded streets.

I released an explosive breath. My legs went limp as noodles, and I sank against the wall at my side, gasping, heart pounding. That crack in my mind opened up wide, and clawed fingers scratched at the edges. Flashes of broken and bloodied bodies blurred my vision. A pair of fangs in a box.

Break off the parts that scare you.

My ears thundered with the sound of heartbeats, and their glaring presence whited out my vision, promising relief, promising answers. I squeezed my eyes shut against them and pressed the heels of my hands against my temples.

"Get it together, Hiro," I whispered between gritted teeth as I struggled to regulate my breathing. This was what he wanted, to push me, to make me lose it in this very public place where it would both create fear among humans and erode the confidence of my youkai followers. What was it he'd said before? *Isseki nichou.*

I opened my eyes slowly, my gaze falling on the ramen containers going cold at my feet. I'd grown too used to my almost-human life with Taka. Kyo's words may not have been a threat, but they were most certainly a warning. How long could I pretend before the beast had its way?

But I wanted this life. Wanted it so bad, the thought of leaving it hurt like bones breaking. Hide's words from so many years ago echoed in my ears.

Your presence endangers them.

With one last, deep breath, I forced myself upright. The walk back to Taka's apartment felt like miles instead of blocks as I tried to reconcile with what I knew I had to do.

"That was more than ten minutes," Taka called out the second the door opened.

"Sorry, I...got held up." I wiped at the sweat on my brow and dripping down my temples before fully entering. Taka was still at his desk, nose centimeters from the screen, and I scooted past him into the kitchen before he could see what a wreck I was. "I'm afraid your ramen may have gone cold. I'll rewarm it for you."

He gave a grunt of acknowledgment, his key taps slowing as he wound down to a stop. I dumped his ramen into a pot on the stove, jumping when his arm brushed against mine as he reached into a cabinet for a bowl.

"Are you okay?" he said laughing, though his brows pulled together with concern.

"I'm fine. You just startled me." I forced a smile. "Go sit. I'll be there in a second."

He gave me a long, questioning look, his round glasses perched low on his nose.

"Seriously." I pushed his glasses up with the tip of my finger, making his nose crinkle in that way that made my heart skip. He shook his head and retreated to the dining room table. I followed shortly behind with the rewarmed ramen and dumped it into his bowl before settling into the seat across from him.

"Itadakimasu!" he sang before plunging in. I watched, really watched, with hungry, indulgent eyes as he ate, taking in everything from the curl of his lips around the noodles, to his restless fingers, to his angry little huff as the steam fogged his glasses.

"I'm moving out."

Taka froze, limp noodles hanging from his chopsticks.

"I've been here for over a month…" I picked at the edge of my fingernails, eyes on the scratched surface of the table.

"You don't have to leave."

"I know. And you've been so kind to let me stay this long."

"I like having you here."

Warmth flowered in my chest, followed by a deep sadness. "I like being here. But I think it's time."

"Oh." Taka nodded, gaze dropping to his bowl. He poked listlessly at his noodles before forcing a laugh. "Gosh, I'm really going to miss you."

"Me too."

"Will you at least teach me how to make tea before you go?"

"Of course," I said with a tight smile. "As long as you promise never to buy anything that comes in a bag."

"Deal."

He swirled his noodles around again before releasing a deep sigh and pushing away from the table. "I've got to get back to work. You can have the rest of this if you want."

Taka crossed the few steps to his desk and sat down, his back to me. The tapping resumed, though at a slower pace than before, and silence fell over us. Not the comfortable silence we were used to, but one heavy with the knowledge that things were about to change.

TWELVE

Worth the Risk

SPRING 1994

TAKA FINISHED HIS PROJECT JUST BEFORE HIS TWO O'CLOCK DEADLINE, threw a laptop into a beat-up briefcase and a blazer over his shoulders, and bolted out the door. The silence closed in hard around me, making it difficult to move. I cleaned the kitchen, alphabetized the bookshelf by author then by title then by author again, and drifted around the apartment until there was nothing left to do but the thing I was avoiding. I found the newspaper folded up into a neat rectangle on the coffee table, sat down cross-legged on the floor in front of it, and spread the paper open.

Taka came home to me surrounded by crumpled pages full of housing ads, a felt-tip pen in one hand and my head in the other. "Looking for an apartment?" he asked. He kept his tone light, but there was a crack in his voice.

"Mn." I nodded and squinted at the page in front of me.

"How's it going?"

"I'm a bit overwhelmed, honestly. Can you believe I've never done this before?" I gave a dry laugh. "What exactly is an LDK?"

"Living, dining, kitchen." Taka dropped his briefcase by the door and threw his blazer over the back of the couch. "Need help?"

I groaned and Taka laughed. "I'm glad you find this amusing."

"Scoot over."

I shifted a bit as he shoved aside a pile of my discarded pages and dropped down next to me. He leaned in close, his fingers trailing over the few circled listings on the page in my hand. Our bodies touched from shoulder to knee. He smelled of citrus and ink from that ballpoint pen that was always leaking on his fingers, and for a moment I forgot what I was doing.

"This one's no good," he said, plucking the pen from my hand and scratching a big, black X over one of my circled listings. "I know this neighborhood. There's a pachinko parlor right on the corner. You'll be up all night with the noise."

He pursed his lips and pressed the end of the pen against them. His fingers skipped to my next circled listing, and his jaw dropped.

"This much rent for an eight-mat room? It's a scandal!" He shook his head and made another black mark. "You have to be careful of some of these companies, Hiro. They'll really take advantage of you if you let them."

One by one he scrutinized the listings, and one by one he marked them off. He'd pressed himself so close to me that one of his legs draped over mine, and if I turned my head, my nose would brush his cheek. It burned a fire through me until it was all I could think about, and I had to move away.

"Keep this up and there'll be nothing left," I said with a hoarse laugh.

"Hmm…" he said, voice almost imperceptibly soft. "Maybe we'll have better luck tomorrow."

"Taka…"

"Don't leave." His eyes shot up to mine, wide and glassy. He grabbed my arm and pulled himself close again. His heart pounded where his chest pressed against my side. "I don't want you to leave."

My mouth went dry. I opened it to voice an objection, but it got stuck somewhere behind my ribcage.

Taka gasped and pulled back again, covering his face with his hands.

"I'm sorry. I'm acting like a lunatic." He laughed a tight, embarrassed laugh. "You're just moving house. It doesn't mean we won't be friends anymore."

"We'll always be friends, Taka," I assured him, though it felt like a lie.

"It's just...I like you. I *really* like you." His shoulders sagged, and he dropped his hands into his lap. "I have for a while now and I know you're not ready and that's okay. But when you told me you were moving out, I had this horrible feeling like I might never have the chance to tell you."

He'd delivered his entire confession without looking at me, his attention firmly focused on a scuff in the tabletop. He scraped at it with his fingernail and tipped his face ever so slightly in my direction, watching for my reaction out of the corner of his eye. His cheeks were bright red. I could only stare in stunned silence, my heart in my throat and my stomach in my knees. That bone-breaking pain ripped through me again. I knew what I should do, for his safety and mine, but I couldn't bring myself to do it.

"I could be bad for you," I said, my voice raw and broken. "There's...a lot about me you don't know..."

"I can learn."

"I don't want you to get hurt."

He shrugged, a little smile tugging at his lips. "Maybe I think you're worth the risk."

Just like that my resolve shattered. I didn't know how it started or who moved first, all I knew was his fingers curled in my hair and his lips on mine. A soft sound vibrated through his throat, somewhere between a whine and a sigh, sending a wash of desire through me. I pulled him into my lap and he came willingly. With his chest pressed against mine, I could feel his heart. Its light blinded me, but unlike others, I had no desire to consume it. I wanted to protect it, bask in it, bathe in its warmth for as long as it could last.

Taka pulled back just enough to catch his breath, my jaw cupped in his hands. "Does this mean you're not leaving?"

The threat of Kyo's appearance still itched at the back of my mind, but it was nothing compared to Taka in my arms, Taka's wide, pleading eyes looking down on me, Taka's light enveloping me. I couldn't, *wouldn't*, let him take that away from me.

"I'm not going anywhere," I said breathlessly. I slipped my hand around his waist, up the line of his spine, and he shivered.

"Good," he said and took my lips again with a hunger that stole my breath. Teeth clashed and tongues fought, and I devoured another stream of whines as they tumbled between them. "Wow, you're an incredible kisser. Why haven't we been doing this the whole time?"

"Good question."

I wrapped my arms around him and hoisted him up onto the couch. Cheeks red, lips wet and swollen, he released a peal of joyous laughter that awakened something long dormant inside me—happiness. The realization rang inside me like a bell. I was happy, truly happy, something I hadn't been for a long time.

Taka's smile dropped a little and his brows pulled together. "Everything okay? We don't have to...you know, if you're not ready."

I shook my head, blinking back the sudden haze in my eyes. "It's not that. It's just...I didn't expect..."

"What?"

"You."

He released a deep breath and his smile returned. With a tug on my collar, he pulled me up to him and I molded my body to his, marveling at how we fit together. He let his head drop back as I traced feather-light kisses down the column of his throat, and by the time I reached his collarbone, he was panting.

"Hiro, not to distract from what you're doing," he mumbled between ragged breaths, "but my bed is right over there."

"My bed is right here," I said, slipping my hand underneath the hem of his shirt and pinching his collarbone between my teeth.

"Good point," he said, arching into my touch. His nipple pebbled under my thumb and he hissed at the contact.

"Sensitive?" I asked, grinning against his sternum.

"Well, I have been dreaming about this for almost two months."

"Really?" I lifted my head and arched an eyebrow at him. "What kind of dreams?"

"What kind do you think?" he answered, punching me in the shoulder.

"Tell me," I growled against his ear and his body rolled beneath me.

"The short version, you tease me until I come so hard I forget my name." I released a dark chuckle against the crook of his neck and he shuddered. "Hey! That wasn't a challenge."

I lifted my head and pouted.

"Two months, Hiro! I think I've been teased enough."

"Well in that case…"

Taka squealed in delight as I unbuttoned his pants and whipped them off in one quick motion. He responded with equal enthusiasm, peeling off his shirt and throwing it aside before clawing at mine. Limbs tangled and hair got pulled and I'd never had so much fun getting undressed in my life.

There we were, bare in front of each other for the first time. I should have been nervous. I hadn't been like this with anyone but Hideyoshi in centuries, and even that had faded into the background, our once vigorous sex life reduced to the occasional early morning quickie. But when Taka looked at me, pupils blown and eyes wide with wonder, I felt safe, adored, maybe even loved.

He ran a hand over the planes of my chest, leaving goosebumps in his wake. "You're beautiful," he said, voice breathy.

I traced my thumb over the line of his jaw and lower lip. "So are you."

Devouring his lips again, I pressed him back into the couch. He was small but strong, tectonic plates of lean muscle creating mountains and valleys under his skin as he hooked a leg around my waist. A wave of tingles burst through my pelvis as our hips slotted together and he pressed hard and hot against me.

"I like it like this," he said against my lips. "Do you like it like this?"

I groaned and grabbed his thigh, pulling him tighter against me. Sparks turned into fireworks as our bodies rolled together in unison. Every moan and sigh that vibrated through his chest and slipped between our lips went straight to my head, like being blood-drunk, only lighter, softer, a high shared not taken.

A shudder ran through me as the heat in my pelvis built to almost unbearable levels. "Taka...I'm..." I gasped.

"Give it to me, Hiro," he murmured against my skin, pinching my earlobe between his teeth. One hand gripping the arm of the couch over his head, the other hooked around his knee, I snapped my hips against his hard and fast, almost out of my control. He pressed his fingers into my back and arched into me as I came with a guttural cry. He continued to grind against me, sending electric shocks of pleasure through my already wrecked body, until with a splash of sticky warmth, he shuddered and stilled.

I fell into his chest, overwhelmed by an emotion I couldn't quite name. His light surrounded me again, and I pressed my lips against his chest where it glowed most intensely.

"You're so bright," I said, words slurred together.

Taka laughed. "What does that even mean?"

"It means..." I closed my eyes, trying to find the words in my muddled mind and failing.

Taka swept his hand through my damp hair, fingers snagging in the curls. "Did you forget your name?"

"No." I chuckled, lifting my head and giving him a devilish look. "Wait, who are you?"

He slapped my shoulder and pulled me into a deep, slow kiss, smiling into it. All my doubts melted under that kiss. We were taking a risk, one greater than even Taka understood, but he was right.

We were worth it.

THIRTEEN

Forever

FALL 1994

I WOKE EARLY WITH TAKA'S BODY WRAPPED AROUND ME. SIX MONTHS had passed since I'd almost moved out and he'd made his awkward confession. Things moved so fast after that, I felt weightless, like catching a wave—overwhelming and thrilling at the same time. I still worried, of course, that I'd made a mistake, that a cruel reality was lurking in the shadows just waiting to pounce. But then the morning would come, I would wake with his bright light all around me, and I knew I'd made the right choice. Whatever Kyo had planned to set in motion by confronting me in that alley couldn't touch us here. Even the monster inside me I'd grown so afraid of had stilled, the crack in my mind almost imperceptible. The world of demons had nothing to do with us.

Taka moaned and stretched his legs, causing his body to press and rub against me in tantalizing ways. He had his face burrowed into the crook of my neck, and his breath tickled across my skin.

"You awake?" I whispered into his hair, voice scratchy with sleep.

"No," he groaned, burrowing deeper into my chest. His even breathing resumed before he emitted a half-growl, half-moan.

"What?"

"I'm hungry."

"So get up and eat something."

"Don't want to."

I laughed and unwound his arms from around me, triggering another long whine. "Relax. Stay here. I'll make you something."

Taka pressed his face into a pillow as I extracted myself from his grip. I tucked the blankets in tight around him, pressing a kiss to his forehead before slipping quietly out of the room and into the kitchen. With a smile on my face and a song in my heart, I clicked on the rice cooker and set a kettle of water on the stove. I had my head half in the refrigerator when a weight hit my back and a pair of arms looped around my waist.

"Taka! I thought you were—"

Taka spun me around to face him and pulled my face down to his. His mouth covered mine in a kiss that made my whole body glow. His fingers curled in my hair and his body melded to mine, his lips soft and sweet. He tasted like oranges.

"What was that for?" I asked without pulling away, my head light.

"Just wanted you to know I love you," he said, smiling against my lips.

"I know you do." He told me often, every day, and each time felt like a miracle. Like I'd been living in an emotional desert and finally found the rain. "I never get tired of hearing it though."

We kissed again, lips parting in a gentle caress of tongues. He made that little sound again, the same sound he'd made the first time, and the glow turned into a radiant heat. I loved that sound, like he'd been starving for my touch even though it had only been seconds.

Taka giggled with surprise as I turned us around and walked him backwards, pinning him to the counter. "What are you up to?"

"What do you think?" I asked, sliding my hand over the curve of his ass. He was wearing my boxers, and they hung loose in a way that made my mouth water. He wore my shirt too, and I bit at his exposed collarbone. This had become a thing for him, wearing my clothes, and it made it all but impossible to keep my hands to myself.

"I thought you were making me breakfast."

"You started it."

He laughed and shoved me away with his fists on my shoulders. "Come on, I'm really hungry."

I pouted. "You're a terrible man."

He dropped a kiss on the end of my nose with a cheeky grin before slipping out of my grip and parking at the kitchen table. The kettle had just begun to whistle. I poured the water over a filter packed with leaves. When I handed the freshly brewed tea to Taka, he cuddled it to his chest and inhaled deeply.

"Oh, I love you."

"You already told me that."

"I was talking to the tea."

I shot him a look of mock offense, and he blew me a kiss.

"I heard you get up last night," he said as he blew the steam off his tea. "Did you get any sleep?"

A pin twisted somewhere deep in my heart. Now that we were sleeping in the same bed, it had become harder to slip out at night unnoticed. He'd noticed even before, as it turned out. I told him I sometimes had trouble sleeping and took walks so as not to disturb him, a lie for his own safety and one he readily accepted—but it tasted bitter nonetheless.

"I got enough," I said, focusing on the omelet sizzling in front of me.

"You can take something for that, you know."

"I'm fine. Just restless is all." I slipped the omelet over a pile of rice and set the plate down in front of him. "Besides, I like walking at night when no one's around."

I grabbed a bowl of rice and my cup of tea and sat down across from him. The meal was mostly for appearances anyway. I could eat, but it wasn't necessary for survival. It was, however, comforting in its way and helped maintain the illusion of humanity, as much for myself as for him.

"Don't forget," Taka said around a mouthful of eggs, "we're meeting Maia at the park later."

I nodded, a smile tugging on my lips. I'd grown to adore his sister, in no small part because of her close relationship with Taka. She was barely half his age, a difference which could make some siblings strangers, but she worshipped him and he doted on her in a way that made my heart warm.

"Be warned," he said, an ominous glint in his eye. "She's a photographer this week."

"Oh?" A nervous flutter started in my stomach. The ability to capture a perfect representation of a person, to freeze a moment in time, still felt mystical to me. Not to mention the danger of exposing my unchanging nature.

"Apparently, Mom bought her one of those cameras that doesn't use film, and now she won't put it down." He shook his head, a sad, wistful look in his eye. He always got like this when he spoke of his parents. I didn't know why, but I could guess.

"That's nice. Who knows, maybe it will become her calling."

"Right, like painting was her calling or fashion design was her calling…" He rolled his eyes, but affection lightened his tone.

"She's just a kid trying to figure things out," I said as I cleared our plates and flashed him a mischievous smirk. "Maybe I'll teach her shamisen and that will become her calling."

"Wait, you play shamisen?" I nodded and he shook his head with a click of his tongue. "Sometimes you're like a very old man."

"Say cheese!"

Taka cringed as yet another flash went off in his eyes. We'd met Maia at Yoyogi Park and just as he had warned, she hovered around us with her new camera, snapping photos as we sat on a blanket in the grass. I managed to duck my head or hide behind Taka for most of them, but she was relentless so eventually I gave up.

"Maia, please," Taka whined. "Can you give it a rest for five minutes?"

"This thing is so cool," she said, squeezing herself between us and vibrating with excited energy. "It can hold over a hundred pictures in one go, and you can look at them instantly. Look!"

She turned on a screen on the back of the camera and tipped it toward each of us in turn, scrolling through the photos she'd snapped.

As our faces flashed across the screen, once again I was in awe of what people could do.

"We need one of all three of us," she declared, hooking an arm around my neck and holding the camera out at arm's length. "Like a family photo."

Taka cringed. "Maia…"

Family. It had been so long since I'd been part of one, I'd forgotten what it felt like, the safety and the love. And my love for both of them was overwhelming, so much that it scared me at times. But every time I looked at Taka and saw that love reflected back to me in his eyes, my fear melted away.

His annoyed expression softened when I found his hand behind Maia's back and gave it a squeeze. The flash went off and Maia checked the result on the screen, her eyes warm and cheeks a little pink. A perfect moment frozen in time.

"I'm going to take some pictures around the lake," she said, popping up from her seat. "Be back in a minute."

Taka and I laughed as she ran at full speed toward the lake in the center of the clearing, camera pointed at the fountain of water piercing the sky. The maples surrounding it had just begun to turn, framing her silhouette in bright orange and red. Taka shook his head and sighed, his eyes warm.

"Finally," he said. "A little peace."

"She's cute," I said, scooting closer and dropping a discreet kiss on his shoulder.

"She's a pest," he countered with a good-natured groan. "But I love her."

"Me too."

I released a deep breath, my heart dancing in a way I hadn't quite gotten used to. I dipped my hand into my jacket pocket, and the dance turned into a nervous hop as it closed around the small box inside. I'd bought it over a week ago on a whim and had been carrying it around ever since, wondering, doubting, hoping. It was crazy, really, a thing modern people did, not old relics like me. But I didn't feel so old lately, and with the warm sun and the cool breeze, with the maples flaming over our heads and Taka's wonderfully annoying sister flitting around us, it felt like the perfect time.

"I have something for you," I said, keeping my voice as casual as possible through the tightness in my throat. He turned back toward me, eyebrows lifted in surprise. I took a deep breath and pulled my hand out of my pocket, the box concealed in my hand.

"Wait," he said, pulling back. "Did I forget something? Is today some kind of couples holiday, because I didn't get you anything."

"It's not a holiday."

"This isn't some weird however many months since we first slept together thing, is it?"

I laughed. "You're ridiculous."

"I'm not in trouble?" he asked, eying the box with suspicion. I laughed again, shaking my head. "Are *you* in trouble?"

I clicked my tongue. "Can't I just give you something because I want to?" He squinted at me, and I held the box out in my palm. "Do you want it or not?"

One corner of his mouth lifted, and he snatched it out of my hand. My heart thundered in my ears as he flipped the top open, revealing a thin silver band.

He gasped, eyes shooting back up to mine. "Hiro, this is...this looks like a wedding band."

"Yeah," I said with a shrug, though I couldn't breathe. He plucked the ring out of the box, his hand going to his mouth when he read the inscription.

Love you forever.

"I know it's...a lot," I stammered. My cheeks heated and a flicker of doubt returned. "I know it's only been six months and it's probably too soon. And if you're not ready to wear it, that's fine, really, I just..." I took time to choose my words, careful not to make promises I couldn't keep. "I love you. I love our life. I am grateful every day that I get to share this time with you. And I just wanted you to know that I will be here beside you for as long as you'll have me. So just keep it, and when you're ready—"

He didn't even hesitate. With a giddy laugh, he slipped the ring on his finger.

FOURTEEN

Starting Over

SPRING 2004

"RED-EYED HARPY." HIDEYOSHI WAITED FOR ME ON THE SIDEWALK, grumbling and shaking his jacket as if to rid himself of some contagion. I avoided his eyes as I emerged from the stairwell behind him. The air around us was thick with words unsaid, so we stayed silent for fear of suffocating.

We both jumped as my phone rang, a jarring melody from who knows where. I fished it out and flinched at the name on the screen.

"Let's get out of here." I silenced the phone and jammed it into my pocket, turning my back on Hideyoshi before he could ask who it was. "I need a shower to get that stench off of me."

We started home, me in front and Hideyoshi a step behind. I hadn't walked ahead of Hideyoshi since...well, ever, but I was afraid of what I would feel staring at his back. Truth was, I didn't want to feel anything. I didn't want to feel the sting of Asagi's words, didn't want to need the comfort of a man who had none to give.

Hunger scraped at the inside of my skin, and I gritted my teeth so hard my jaw ached. It wasn't real. What I'd taken the night before with Hideyoshi should have been enough to sustain me for at least a day or two. It wasn't the blood I craved, but the blankness that followed, a psychosomatic need for relief.

I focused on the feel of the wind and the pavement under my feet, trying to forget about the name on my phone. Hideyoshi pushed past me when we reached the house, stomping up the steps and through the door before me. I slipped out of my shoes and walked into the house without raising my eyes.

"Come here, Hiro." He sat down at the table and dumped the contents of the envelope. I took a deep breath and sat down beside him. Paperwork, passports, IDs, everything one would need to live as someone else covered the table. He picked up a passport and handed it to me. I opened it and saw my picture next to the name Yamaguchi Akira.

"What's this?"

"That, for all intents and purposes, is you." he said, handing me the matching IDs.

"How did you know I—"

"I was watching."

Ice crystals formed under my skin. He'd been watching. Watching when Taka got sick, while I struggled with guilt and indecision. Watching when he died. "Of course you were," I said with a wry laugh.

"Are you angry?" he asked, meeting my eyes for the first time since we left Asagi's bar.

"No," I answered, though I didn't know what I felt.

"Good," he said, sliding a small packet of papers out of the envelope and putting them in front of me. The deed to the house. On the bottom line were two names: one I didn't recognize—presumably, Hideyoshi's new alias—and Yamaguchi Akira.

"You put me on the deed?"

"This is your home too, isn't it?"

I opened my mouth to speak, but no words came. I may have lived here, but the house had always been his. The lovestruck geisha boy in me wanted to scream with happiness, but I wasn't that boy anymore. All I could do was stare.

The phone went off in my pocket again. I scrambled to my feet and fled to the porch. Grateful for the distraction, I hurriedly fished it out and pressed it to my ear.

"Hello, Hiro? It's Maia."

I pinched the bridge of my nose and squeezed my eyes closed. I slid the shoji closed behind me and closed my eyes against a wave of dizziness. Hearing her voice brought everything I'd been struggling to suppress rocketing to the raw surface.

"Oh. Hey, Maia." I let my body drop heavily to the porch and rested my head in my hands. "How are you?"

"I'm okay. Worried about you. You don't answer your phone."

"Yeah…sorry about that. I just…"

"Yeah, I know," she said, letting me off the hook. We hadn't spoken since the funeral, and I sagged with guilt, but her voice was soft, reassuring and without judgment. I leaned against a post and sighed deeply.

"So the reason I called…" she started gently.

"Oh, right."

"Your building manager contacted me."

"What? Why?"

"About your apartment." She paused. "They've been trying to reach you. You haven't been around…"

"Yeah, I just...can't be there."

"…and you haven't paid rent. For two months."

"Oh…" I must have forgotten. When Taka's health turned for the worse, I'd begun ignoring all the mundane aspects of living and focused entirely on him. I'd even forget to shower if it weren't for Maia's prompting.

"They heard about Taka, and they aren't unsympathetic," she said. "They'll give you until the end of the week to catch up, but if the rent isn't paid, they'll consider the place abandoned and re-lease. Whatever's not cleared out, they'll take to the dump."

My heart sank. I pictured all our most precious moments packed away in boxes, all the surfaces he'd touched wiped clean, and the void sucked the air from my lungs.

"I know it's hard, but—"

"Hard doesn't even cover it."

"So that's it, then?" she asked after a long pause. When I didn't answer, she sighed and continued. "Fine. I'll be down there packing up what I can. If there's anything you want—"

"I don't want anything."

"Well, if you change your mind, you know where to find me."

A long pause, then a click as she hung up. I dropped the phone and pulled my knees to my chest. It felt like being torn in two. One Hiro ending, another one starting again. Maia was in our apartment dismantling my life, and my new name on the bottom of Hideyoshi's deed was like the final nail in the coffin. Dying didn't hurt this much.

FIFTEEN

A Demon Inside

SPRING 2004

I MADE IT ALL THE WAY HOME WITHOUT LOOKING UP. I DON'T KNOW when I made the decision to return to the apartment I'd shared with Taka. I just knew I couldn't stay on Hideyoshi's porch with his cold presence looming over me. Asagi's words rang in my ears: *He'll never understand.* Hideyoshi with his heart of ice, who never loved anything, not even me. My mourning was a nuisance to him, my hesitation to return to our life together an affront to his pride. Bitterness rose like bile in the back of my throat. I had to get away.

So I let my feet take me where they would and soon found myself in a quieter part of town. Narrow streets stood lined with condos and small, walled-in homes. Greenery poked out from flower boxes and over walls, lending the air a floral scent. The houses around me became familiar, and I planted my eyes on the road under my feet. Without even realizing it, I'd become caught in a terrible forward momentum taking me to the last place I wanted to go, and I was powerless to stop it.

One of our neighbors spotted me on the stairs and rushed over to me, taking my hand and offering tearful condolences. "Such a sweet, wonderful man. It's not fair. Just not fair." I brushed her off as politely as I could, pain ringing through me like a tuning fork, and by the time I reached our door, I was shaking.

I fumbled with my keyring and took a deep breath before unlocking the door and swinging it open. The familiar smell of home rushed my senses, knocking me off-balance. I braced myself on the doorway to keep from falling. Everything was just as we'd left it: shoes in the doorway, books lying open. Even the not-so-pleasant reminders of his illness—pill bottles and medical devices—lay scattered across countertops. So much the same and yet so different, like the color had leached out with his passing—a faded photograph of a happy life.

I closed my eyes and took a long, slow breath before stepping out of the genkan and making my way through the apartment. I ran my hands over tabletops and across bookcases, stopping when I found a book sticking out and not in order. I plucked it up and reshelved it in its proper place, trying not to think about the thin layer of dust that had gathered on it.

Quit fiddling with the books, Hiro, and come sit with me.

My heart seized, and I whipped my eyes to the couch. I could see him there, like the afterimage of a light that shone too bright. A mist formed over my eyes as I drifted over to the couch and lowered myself into it. I closed my eyes and could almost feel the warmth of his hand on my back, comforting me the same way he did when I left Hideyoshi. A smile pulled at my lips despite the tears in my eyes as I found myself longing for tea out of the microwave. I touched the ring hanging over my chest. My neighbor was right. It wasn't fair and even the fondest of memories ached.

A faint rustling from deeper in the apartment caught my attention. I stood and moved toward the bedroom, stopping short at the sight of a body in the bed. Maia. I'd forgotten. Dozing on top of the sheets, surrounded by empty cardboard boxes, she looked so much like Taka it hurt to look at her. Old photos littered the floor around the bed. She must have been looking at them, and they slipped from her hands as she slept. I bent down on one knee and gathered them up, trying to ignore the smiling faces beaming up at me.

I stopped when I came across one with all three of us. Maia must have been no more than seventeen. She had an arm around my neck and a broad smile on her face. Takanori looked apologetic as I tried not to laugh. I remembered this day. I sat on the floor, my back against the bed, as the memory washed over me—warm sun and laughter and family.

"You came." I turned my head at the sound of Maia's voice. Her eyes were red and puffy from crying.

"Yeah," I said, running a finger along the salt trails on her cheeks. "You okay?"

"No. You?"

"No." I sunk back against the bed and flicked the edges of the photo with my fingertips.

"I remember this," she said, reaching her arm around my neck and tapping the photo. Her head practically rested on my shoulder. She even smelled like him. "You two just couldn't keep your hands off each other."

"It was our honeymoon period," I said with a chuckle.

"Well, your honeymoon period lasted a decade," she said, laughing. "You guys were disgusting." We both laughed before falling into a solemn silence.

"I'm sorry," I said, "for disappearing on you like that."

"It's okay, really—"

"No, it's not," I insisted, rotating on my hip to face her. "You lost him too."

She was silent for a moment, her eyes glistening. "I can't imagine what you've been going through these past months. You took such good care of him through everything, and I'll always be grateful for that. I just…" She swallowed hard, her voice thickening. "I just want you to know that I think of you as my brother too. I'm here for you. Just because he's gone doesn't mean you don't have family."

A dam broke inside me. Her statement, while well-meaning, shone a bright light on everything I feared—not only the loss of a family I had grown to love and depend on, but the loss of my humanity, upon which I had a tenuous grasp at best. That dark thing scratched around inside me even now. My time with Taka, while devastatingly short, reminded me of so many things I had forgotten, that had been buried, neglected, and almost lost over three centuries among monsters. But that humanity was a double-edged sword, and now that I suffered the back end, a dark voice inside begged the question.

Was it worth it?

Maia wrapped her arms around me as a violent sob wrenched its way out of me. I clung to her, shaking, disoriented. I felt like I was bleeding, my very soul leaking out of me in fat drops. I buried my nose in the crook of her neck, and something dangerous slid to the surface, bringing with it a cold numbness.

If she looked like him, smelled like him, did she taste like him too?

"Hiro?" Her voice held a note of concern as my grip on her tightened, shifting into something more dangerous. "Hiro, what are you doing?"

I made a sound like relief as the searing pain receded and my focus shifted to the blood pulsing just beneath her skin. The background faded away until the light inside her filled my vision. I pulled my body into the bed next to her. Need sizzled through me as her racing heart thumped against mine. No love, no pain, only hunger. The crack widened. The demon crawled out.

"Hiro, stop!" Her panicked voice in my ear broke through the fog, and I jerked my head up. She shoved me hard in the chest, sending me tumbling out of the bed. The ground tilted under me as I scrambled to my feet. What had I done? Dizzy, delirious, I steadied myself on the dresser and caught sight of myself in the mirror, white-eyed, fangs bared.

I looked like a monster.

My stomach lurched. I hid my face behind my hands and turned away before Maia could see the beast I'd become. Hunger still raged inside me, tearing at the inside of my skin. All I needed was one drop, one swallow, and everything would make sense again. My pain would fade into a blissful nothing. The temptation to give in, to throw away my grief and succumb to the darkness, was nearly overwhelming. It would feel so good to let it go.

I had to get out.

"Hiro, what just happened?" She was out of the bed and standing beside me, her hand on my arm.

"I can't do this," I said between wheezing gasps. "I don't belong here."

"No, don't run away," she said as I jerked my arm out of her grip and stumbled toward the door. "Please, Hiro, just talk to me."

Head down, eyes closed, I fled. How could I tell her I had a demon inside me that wanted to eat her? That what she took as a momentary lapse caused by grief could have been the end, maybe for both of us? Visions of cages and screaming madness ending in piles of dust filled my mind. Ignoring her desperate pleas, crashing into every piece of furniture on the way, I ran away from my human life.

I needed to kill something.

SIXTEEN

Emotional Eating

SPRING 2004

I DIDN'T SEE PEOPLE, I SAW HEARTBEATS, BUNDLES OF VEINS COURSING with liquid gold. My pulse quickened and pupils dilated as I spotted my target. A young man, beautiful and careless, drunk already or still drunk from the night before. He wore a rumpled black suit with an open collar that exposed the bright, pulsing veins underneath. Long, bleached-blond hair fell into bleary eyes as he stumbled through the street, falling into me as he passed.

The smell of him hit my nose like a line of cocaine. My fingers tightened around his arms as I caught him. Animal lust boiled inside me, making my skin hot. I wanted to tear into him, rip his throat open, and devour him right there in the bright light of day. But I resisted. I let him go but followed him, keeping a small but safe distance between us as he wove his way through the crowded station and onto a train. His head lolled as he stood draped over a support bar.

I thought he'd fallen asleep until a tinny voice announced the stop for Roppongi. He snapped upright and waded into the crowd again, heading toward the currently dozing club district. Bars that in a few hours would be bursting with light and life and noise lay quiet, holding their breath in wait for the night to come. I followed him through the back door of a host bar. Judging by his familiarity with the place, he was one of the host boys. The bar was empty, save an old man with a mop who seemed to deliberately ignore our entrance. I waited for the young man to disappear into a back room before slipping the old man a ten-thousand-yen note and suggesting he take the day off.

My skin tingled as I slipped silently through the club, my white eyes darting through every hallway, around every corner in search of my prey. The place was nothing but dark corners with hard lines of LED track lighting leading from one table to the next. Come sundown, the place would be filled with women and young girls, drinking and throwing money at handsome young men whose attentions they could never hope for in the real world. It felt like a perversion of something familiar.

I found him in a dressing room, rummaging through a leather duffel. I saw myself stalking him, my cold expression reflected over and over in the bank of mirrors along the wall. He saw me too and jumped to attention.

"Who the fuck are you?" he said, a tremor in his voice.

"That's a good question," I answered with an evil grin, showing my teeth. I advanced on him, and he fell back against the mirrors. "Aikawa Hiro? Sakurai Hiro? Yamaguchi Akira?" I curled my nose at the last one, leaning in close. "What's your name?"

He pushed me back and tried to flee, but I caught him easily by the throat and shoved him up against the wall. I would use no magic to calm him. I wanted him to fight, struggle, scream. I wanted to feel like a monster as I stole his life from him. Monsters don't feel grief, guilt, regret. Love.

I didn't want to feel human.

I growled and plunged my teeth savagely into the young man's throat. His light poured over my tongue and down my chin in a euphoric rush. He kicked, pushed, clawed at me as his blood gushed over my lips and down the front of his shirt. But I was immovable, something made of stone pressed against him, draining him. His screams wove a dark melody with my moans as I took swallow after swallow, my fingers digging into his flesh where I gripped him.

Just as his fighting started to weaken, I let him go. He fell to the floor, bleary-eyed from blood loss. He struggled to escape, crawling on hands and knees, his legs too weak to carry him. I watched with perverse pleasure as he reached for the door, blood still leaking from his wounds.

A flash of hope entered his eyes as he pulled himself to his feet by the doorknob and fell through the doorway, only for that hope to be crushed as I grabbed him by the collar and tossed him backwards into the dressing room. His body struck a mirror and it shattered, glass cutting into his arms and shoulders before he fell to the floor. He whimpered and begged as I slowly approached him. I went down on one knee and locked my eyes on his.

"Stop. Please," he begged with tears in his eyes. "Whatever I did to deserve this..."

"You don't deserve this," I said. "I don't deserve this."

Grief pushed ever so briefly against the numbness. Taka didn't deserve to get sick. Maia didn't deserve to lose her brother. I didn't deserve...what? To lose him? To have him in the first place? A sharp pain cascaded through me like my skin being peeled away. I just wanted it to stop.

The numbness returned, and I plunged my teeth into him again. He choked as I ripped open his windpipe. Blood spilled from his mouth. Ecstasy pooled in my gut and shot through my limbs with orgasmic force, making me tremble. I pulled harder on his veins and his heart skipped and stuttered, struggling to keep beating. My knees went weak. One more long pull and he went limp in my arms. It was over.

I slumped against the opposite wall on the floor, the young man's corpse going cold across from me. The high of the blood permeated through me and I sank into it, letting it wash away what remained of my pain. It felt good to be brutal, to be shameless, to think about nothing but feeding the need burning inside me. But my human parts lingered just outside of the buzz, carrying all my guilt and shame with them, and I knew it was only a matter of time before they returned.

The distinct click of high heels reverberated through the silence, piercing the fragile fog around me. Asagi appeared in the doorway, their tall, broad form filling every bit of it as they glared disapprovingly down their nose at me. They clicked their tongue and shook their head as they surveyed the mess.

"What a wasteful beast you are," Asagi said, using my pant leg to wipe a bit of blood from their shoe. "But then it wasn't about the blood, was it?"

"How did you know…"

"I have eyes in surprising places," Asagi answered.

I gave a dry laugh. "The janitor."

Asagi's lips quirked in affirmation. Their scowl returned as they bent at the waist to examine the body opposite me. "You nearly took his head off. Perhaps we can blame it on a dog." They swung their red eyes back to me. "Feel better?"

I didn't answer. Still panting and woozy, I let my head fall back against the wall and closed my eyes. The haze was lifting, and I wanted to hang onto it just a little longer. Asagi released a tired sigh. Their heels clicked around me, and they laid a gentle hand on my forehead.

"I just wanted to…breathe."

"I know."

"What do I do now?"

"Go home," they said, pulling a random shirt off a hanger and dropping it in my lap. "I'll take care of this."

I pulled myself up off the floor and found my way to a bathroom. I stared in the mirror, struggling to find a trace of the man I was before in the blood-soaked beast before me. The young man's voice whispered through my veins, almost lost in the din of a thousand others. What would Taka think if he could see me now? If he knew what I was?

I stripped out of my stained shirt, washed the blood from my face and hands, and left the bathroom with heavy feet. The club was empty, a missing mirror the only evidence of my recent activities. Even the old man was back at his mop.

Go home, Asagi said.

SEVENTEEN

Goodbye

SPRING 2004

DRUNK ON BLOOD, I WEAVED MY WAY BACK TO HIDEYOSHI'S HOUSE. THE monster, the demon, that other part of me I'd repressed for so long, slithered up to the surface again, bringing with it a pleasant nothingness. It would wrap itself around my heart if I let it, blocking out everything but the hunger and the thrill. I often wondered if that's what happened to Hideyoshi. If sometime long before he met me, he'd made a deal with his devil to feel nothing. Could I do the same? Could I find some place just short of insanity that could bring me relief without ending up in a cage?

He was waiting for me when I stumbled through the gate, like the temple guardian, Agyo, chest puffed out and wrath in his eyes. Wrath. The only emotion he showed freely. He stomped toward me but I held my ground, not stopping until he practically ran me down.

"Where have you been?" he snarled.

"I went home," I answered, my voice steadier than I felt.

"*This* is your home." Eyes flaring white, he grabbed me by the front of my shirt and dragged me the rest of the way up the path and into the house, tossing me through the door. My drunken legs were unable to cope with the sudden change of pace, and I fell onto my hands and knees. His bare feet slapped the tatami around me as he grabbed me by the shoulder and flipped me onto my back. "I've indulged you long enough. The time for playing human is over. And whose blood is on you? Hers?"

"What? What are you—"

"*Aikawa* Maia." His lips curled around her surname as if it were toxic. He pressed my phone against my nose, and it lit up with her name. I must have left it on the porch when I left.

A mad laugh bubbled up from somewhere inside me, and he balked. "You'd enjoy that, wouldn't you?" I said. "One less Aikawa to compete with."

"Why did you even come back here?" he asked, throwing the phone down hard enough to crack the screen. "Leaving once wasn't enough for you? You had to disgrace me further?"

"I didn't want to come back!" I spat the words in his face, and he jerked as if I had slapped him. "I told you I wasn't ready, remember? I told you, but you didn't listen. Because you don't care. All you care about is that your toy is back on its shelf where it belongs."

He pulled away from me, and I scrambled to my feet. Bitterness pushed its way up through the darkness, hot enough to make me sweat.

"I gave you everything." He paced, fists clenched, voice strained in a way I'd never heard before. "You wanted power, I gave it to you. You wanted revenge, I gave it to you. You wanted to be some kind of youkai savior, I gave it to you. I gave you a life."

"You killed me."

"I *made* you. And I only asked for one thing in return. What could he possibly have given you that I haven't?"

"He loved me." Tears flooded my eyes, and I let them fall unchecked. A stillness fell over Hideyoshi, and the white receded from his eyes.

"Are you suggesting I don't love you?"

"I don't know," I said, throwing up my hands. "You've never told me. Not once. I lived by your looks, and all you did was take from me. I was nothing to you. A doll. A piece of furniture in your life you hardly noticed until it was gone."

"That's not true."

"Then why didn't you chase me?"

A bitterness poured out of me I wasn't even aware I had. Memories of the days just after I left, curled up on Taka's couch and miserable, invaded my mind. As much as I feared it, I wanted so bad for Hideyoshi to come looking for me, to show up at Taka's door and drag me home, something to show that my leaving meant anything to him. But all I got was silence and loneliness and doubt.

His shoulders slumped. Hideyoshi's mask slipped, and a trickle of regret leaked out around the edges. A second later it was gone, burned away by the anger I knew so well.

"Why didn't I chase you?" he repeated, fangs bared. "Because I was pissed off, that's why. Because you left when you decided you didn't need me anymore."

"I left because I *did* need you," I cried, voice raspy. "I still need you. I need you to ask me if I'm okay, even when you know I'm not. I need you to hold me when I'm hurting, even if the cause makes you jealous. I need to know that you love me, because I can't love enough for the both of us anymore."

Shaking and unable to bear the distance any longer, I reached for him. I clutched at his shirtsleeves and dropped my head on his chest, half-expecting him to shove me away. Even worse, he didn't move at all. It was like leaning against a stone monument, the only sign he lived the rapid beating of his heart.

"Please, Hideyoshi." I struggled to breathe as the demon inside me spread its dark wings, threatening to envelop my heart, held back only by the small, flickering light he put there. "Please, tell me. I need to hear it. Tell me you love me."

A terrible silence fell over us. My tears dried, my skin went cold. I lifted my head slowly to find his eyes pinned to the wall behind me, his face hard as marble. I took it in my hands, pulled it down, and when his eyes met mine, they jerked as if waking from a trance. I ran my fingers over the lines of his face, his brow, his cheekbones.

Fine. If you can't tell me, show me.

I kissed him, a deep, exploring kiss. His lips were dry, but they moved against mine, and he gripped my waist. He pressed me against him, deepening the kiss until it bruised. Possessive. Wanting. All the things I used to mistake for love. I gave into them as I had in the alleyway.

But it wasn't real. It was a cheap substitute, a knockoff that didn't hold up after having the real thing, and instead of giving me comfort, it only highlighted my loss.

I pulled back, and his grip on me tightened. "Don't go," he said against my lips. He knew my intention before I did. I laid my hands over his, untangled his fingers from my clothes, and allowed my heart to slide into the cold as I took one long, backward step. It was the only way. The only way I could face the great, yawning hole inside me that he could never fill.

"Hiro…" his voice cracked, but it was too late.

"Goodbye," I said, my voice so flat I hardly recognized it. "Sakurai Hideyoshi."

EIGHTEEN

Hideout

SPRING 2004

DIZZY, HEAD POUNDING, EMOTIONS JUMPING FROM SOUL-CRUSHING despair to giddy indifference, I stumbled away from Hideyoshi's house as fast as my legs could carry me. I weaved through the crowded streets like a drunk, leaning heavily on every solid structure I passed in an effort to steady myself. People laughed and stared. A whispered comment about *his lenses* prompted me to slip on a pair of shades to hide my monstrous eyes.

I took again. A woman this time, young and sweet. I didn't even know I'd done it until the fog cleared and I found myself in a dark corner booth of a windowless bar, her head resting on my chest like a sleeping child. I felt sick and guilty, but grateful that there was no sign of struggle, that I had taken her gently when I could have torn her apart.

I was losing it, the two sides of myself at war with each other. The monster inside offered a tempting refuge from grief, but it also frightened me—what it could do, what it would cost. But the heart that loved Takanori was the same heart bound to Hideyoshi, and the further I got from him, the more it bled.

I needed to lay low, someplace that was safe, but also safe from me.

My stomach turned as I headed toward the one person I knew who understood what it was like to live in two worlds, to be something in-between.

Asagi.

I practically fell down the stairs and through the door of the now-bustling Bar Sakura. Ryo was tending the bar, winking and smiling with half his face at a pleasantly inebriated crowd. Salarimen with their ties undone leaned on the bar and whispered in the ears of fashionably dressed ladies. He slid among them with a liquid grace, keeping conversation light and glasses full. His daytime awkwardness was gone, and his hands flew over the bottles with the dexterity of an athlete and the poise of a dancer. It was no wonder Asagi liked him. His strange beauty fit in well here.

His smile dropped when he saw me take a seat at the end of the bar, hunched and trembling like a junkie. He approached cautiously and poured me a whiskey. I wrapped my hands around it but didn't drink. It was all for appearances anyway.

"You shouldn't be here," he said in a low voice.

"I need to see Asagi."

He hesitated, finger tensing around a bar rag. "They're not here."

"You're lying," I said, downing the drink and slamming the glass down on the bar. Ryo reached for it, and I grabbed him by the wrist. His breath caught as I pulled him toward me with a flash of fang. "I doubt they'd let a beauty like you out of their sight."

A heavy hand grabbed my shoulder from behind and squeezed—hard. I released Ryo, who staggered backwards, gasping a moment before collecting himself and going back to his patrons. I turned my head to see red eyes glaring down at me.

Asagi pulled me roughly out of my seat and away from the bar. I almost didn't recognize them. They looked shockingly masculine in a finely tailored black-on-black suit and tie, their long hair swept to one side and falling neatly over their shoulders, and I found myself suddenly intimidated by their sheer presence.

"What are you doing here, *Sakurai* Hiro?"

I hadn't heard my name paired with Hideyoshi's in so long, it made me flinch. "I need your help."

"I think I've helped you enough for one day."

"Please. I feel like…" I couldn't bring myself to say it. The implications were too great. "I don't want to do that again. I have nowhere else to go."

Asagi looked me over, their eyes narrowing as they slipped my shades down my nose. I could tell by the press of their lips that my eyes were still white. "What about Yoshi?"

I shook my head, eyes burning. "You know what he'll do to me."

Asagi huffed in frustration, arms crossed tight over their chest. They tapped their foot, a touch of empathy leaking into their eyes. "Fine. Come with me."

We retreated into a private room at the back of the bar. I fell into a leather sofa, and Asagi pulled up a chair across from me. We sat in silence as they studied me, their eyes hard and unreadable. They pulled a pack of cigarettes from their inside jacket pocket and popped one between their lips. I pulled off my shades and rubbed a hand over my tired eyes.

"So?" Asagi said, taking a drag off their cigarette and filling the room with sweet-smelling smoke. "What have you done?"

"I left Hideyoshi." Asagi's lips pulled into a long smile. "That pleases you?"

"Immensely," they answered. "But that's not really it, is it?"

"Is that not enough?"

They flicked at the end of their cigarette with a long, manicured thumbnail, and their smile quivered around the edges. "It takes a special kind of pain to drive a man into the dark."

"I've loved two men in my life and I've lost them both," I said from between my teeth, nails digging into my palms.

"Loss is an inevitability when you live as long as we do," Asagi said, eyes darkening. "You wouldn't have lasted half a century if that was enough to push you over the edge." They took another long drag, holding it in their lungs before releasing it through pinched lips. "No, it must be linked to something else. Fear? Guilt?" I cringed, and their eyes flashed. "Tell me."

"No."

"Then I can't help you." Asagi stood, arms crossed over their barrel chest. "Get out."

"Dammit, Asagi, what do you want from me?"

"I can't risk an out-of-control monster under my roof," Asagi snarled. "This is a *human* establishment."

"Do you think I'd have come here if I had anywhere else to go?"

"Then tell me," they growled, pinning me to the couch, one hand on either side of my head and their nose millimeters from mine. Smoke curled around my face from the cigarette between their fingers, and it made my nose itch. "If you want me to protect you, I need to know what you're hiding from."

My heart thundered in my ears. Hiding implied I was afraid. Objections piled up in my throat, but I choked on them. Asagi wasn't wrong. I *was* afraid. Afraid of facing what I'd done. Afraid of being alone. But the demon threatening to swallow my heart scared me too.

I took a deep, shaky breath and gripped the edge of the couch until my fingers stung.

"I killed Takanori."

NINETEEN

Fall

FALL 2003

I slid a cup of tea under Taka's hand where he sat—or rather, slouched—at his desk, eyes squeezed shut and pinching the bridge of his nose. Blue light reflected off his cheekbones from a screen filled with densely packed rows of figures, and shadows settled in the lines around his eyes. He'd been sitting in the same spot since early morning. His round glasses perched haphazardly on the top of his head, and I plucked them off, running my fingers through his tousled hair. There was a bit of gray in it now, a thing I chose not to think about.

"Another headache?" I asked.

"Mn," he answered without moving.

I dropped my hand to the back of his neck, massaging slow circles with my thumbs, and he leaned back into me. "That's almost every day this week."

"I'll be okay. I just need a break." He slipped his fingers around the tea glass without opening his eyes. It trembled a bit as he lifted it to his lips. It wasn't just headaches. He was irritable, he hardly slept, and when he did, he curled into a ball and clenched his fists tight in his pillow as if he were trying to hide from something. I did everything I could think of to comfort him, even singing softly in his ear to help him relax, but it only got worse.

"I think you should maybe talk to a doctor."

"It's just eyestrain." The muscles under my fingers tensed. "I have an appointment with an optometrist in a couple of days."

"Taka—"

"I'm fine!"

I jerked back, shocked at his sharp tone. We'd been together over nine years, and he'd never once snapped at me that way. The line of his back went momentarily jagged, then he slouched again.

"I'm sorry. I just...sorry." He released a deep sigh and pushed out of his chair. He seemed a little wobbly, but it could have been my imagination. "You're right. I think I need a break. Splash some cold water on my face or something."

I squeezed his hand as he walked by, and he squeezed back before vanishing into the bathroom. A knot formed in the pit of my stomach as I listened to the water run. The headaches started about a month before, small ones that left him irritable and uncomfortable for a few hours. We'd written them off as everything from stress to allergies, but their frequency and severity steadily increased. Taka still insisted they were no big deal, but like any caring partner, I worried. I'd managed to get through nine years without dwelling on his mortality, but now it was all I could think about. Where once I had seen the lines in his face as something beautiful, like the worn cover of an old book, now I saw them as cracks in the walls of a decaying building destined to fall, and it made me angry, sad, and profoundly afraid.

Pushing my worries away, I drifted into the kitchen and started filling a dish towel with ice. I had just finished when a crash sounded from the bathroom. My lungs seized. I dropped the makeshift ice pack and ran toward the sound.

"Taka?"

I slapped the closed door, my heart in my throat. I smelled blood. Panic zapped across my heart. When he didn't answer, I yanked the door open. Taka lay on the floor, groaning and barely conscious. There was a splash of blood on the edge of the counter and a deep gash just over his brow. I dropped to my knees and pulled him into my lap.

"Taka! Come on, look at me," I said, tapping him lightly on the cheek. Blood ran down the side of his face from his wound. I pressed a hand towel against it. His eyes rolled around in their sockets before finding me. "What happened?"

"I...don't..." His brows pulled together in confusion as he pressed the heel of his hand against his forehead. "My head hurts."

"You fell." My mouth went dry. "You don't remember that?"

He groaned and squeezed his eyes shut.

"That's it," I said firmly. "We're going to the hospital."

Taka floundered around in an attempt to sit up. "No, Hiro. I'm—"

His skin went white, and he clapped a hand to his mouth before lurching for the toilet. I rubbed his back as he heaved, waiting patiently until he sank back into my arms.

"You at the very least have a concussion," I said. "Please, no more arguments."

Shivering and pale, he finally relented with a weak nod. His wound had mostly stopped bleeding, and I cleaned him up as best I could, resisting the urge to cut into my own hand and heal it with my blood. But he didn't know.

Nine years together and he still didn't know.

I pushed the guilt aside and helped him to his feet. Once outside, I tucked him into a cab and directed the driver to the nearest emergency room. I held him tight against me, giving him the occasional shake to make sure he stayed conscious, all the while berating myself for not doing more, for not insisting he see a doctor sooner. I'd sworn to myself to protect him, and I couldn't even get this much right.

The taxi dropped us at the entrance of Tokyo General and a thankfully uncrowded ER. A nurse took one look at Taka's head wound and directed us to an exam room, where we were soon joined by a female doctor. A foreign woman with a soft face and a long, brown ponytail slid into the room, clipboard in hand. I balked a bit, and Taka jabbed me in the ribs with an exasperated headshake.

"My name is Dr. George," she said in lightly accented Japanese, her attention on her clipboard. She jerked a little when she looked up at me, her eyes widening and lips parting in a gasp. She shook it off quickly, making me question whether I'd seen it at all, and turned her attention to Taka with a smile. "Aikawa-san. I hear you hit your head."

"I fell in the bathroom," Taka said. His voice was less slurred than before, but his eyes still had a glassy sheen to them along with a constant squint. His head hung low and at an odd angle, as if it were too heavy for his neck.

"He's been having headaches," I said, earning a glare from Taka.

"It's no big deal," he insisted. "He just worries."

Dr. George nodded and made a note on her clipboard before extracting a penlight from her pocket and shining it in Taka's eyes. "Did you lose consciousness?"

"Yes."

"Before or after you hit your head?"

Taka opened his mouth to answer but stopped, a blank look on his face. The doctor looked to me.

"I was in another room. He had just come to when I got to him."

"You were having a headache at this time?" she asked Taka.

Taka sighed and nodded.

"Dizziness? Nausea?"

"A bit dizzy. Like I had water in my ears." He glanced up at me, and I squeezed his shoulder.

"Okay." She put away the penlight and made another note on her clipboard. "A nurse will be in to clean up that wound for you, Aikawa-san. In the meantime, I'll schedule an MRI to check for a concussion." She turned to me, her green eyes startling, and gestured toward the hall. "Can we…"

I gave Taka's arm a squeeze before slipping out into the hall with the doctor. As soon as the door closed, she turned on me with hard eyes. "How long has he been having headaches?"

"They started about a month ago."

"How frequent?"

"At first, maybe once a week. Now almost every day."

Her lips tightened. "Is there a reason why he's withholding information about his symptoms?"

I released a deep, tired sigh. "I don't know. I think he's scared."

"Of what, exactly?"

"Of being sick." The hardness of her expression sent a spike of irritation through me. "What are you implying?"

She was silent for a long moment, her green eyes studying me. Finally, she blew out a breath, and her face softened. "Nothing. I'm sorry." She ran a hand over her long, brown ponytail and shook herself as if to rid her mind of whatever suspicions about me clung there. "I told him the MRI was to look for a concussion. That's not entirely true. We'll also be looking for any abnormalities that could cause pressure in the brain."

My stomach twisted. "Like what?"

"The list is long and most of it is treatable. It could also be as simple as a migraine."

"But he...forgot..." Fear had tied my tongue into knots, and I was barely able to get the words out without choking.

"That's not unusual with a head injury," she assured me. "It's very possible he just tripped on a rug and hit his head. I don't want you to worry until we know more."

"Earlier, before he fell," I started, my mouth dry and sticky, "he snapped at me. He never does that."

Her lips pressed into a thin line. "Pain can affect a person's mood."

"But you don't think that's it, do you?"

She sighed and closed her eyes a moment. "Go be with him. There's no use making yourself crazy until we have all of the information."

I nodded, gaze dropping to the floor. Every part of me felt heavy as if I'd been wrapped in a lead blanket. A cold knot formed in my stomach, and I had to suppress the urge to grab Taka by the arm and run as far from the hospital as we could get. For all my urging, I shared his fear, as if the knowing would make whatever was happening inside him real.

The doctor leaned forward like she wanted to touch me, to provide some kind of comfort, but she held back. With a tight smile and a curt nod, she turned and walked away, her shoes squeaking on the tile.

TWENTY

Diagnosis

FALL 2003

ATLAS OF DIAGNOSTIC ONCOLOGY. THE BIOLOGY OF CANCER, SECOND Edition. Clinical Radiation Oncology.

"Hiro…"

PET/CT in Cancers. No, that's not right. Head and Neck Cancers: Evidence Based Treatment. That one goes first. Practical Radiation Oncology Physics goes after.

"You know, this OCD stuff is cute when we're at home, but in someone else's office, it's kind of rude."

Still not right. Maybe by authors. Arthur T. Skarin. Robert A. Weinberg. First name or last? These Western names. I can never get them right.

"Hiro, stop," Taka said from behind me, a sharper edge in his voice.

"But they're out of order," I said, not taking my eyes off the spines of the books lining the built-in shelves in front of me. If I focused on them, I didn't have to see the rest.

"Look at me."

I froze, *The Emperor of Maladies* by Siddhartha Mukhergee tipped forward under my finger. My chest tightened and my heart struggled to beat.

"I know you're scared…"

"I'm not scared. Everything's fine. You're going to be—"

I turned to face him, and it was as if the air had been sucked from the room. Taka sat in a hard-lined, straight-backed chair across from a wide metal desk. Harsh fluorescent lights cut dark shadows under his eyes and made his skin look thin as rice paper. Spidery lines spread out from the corners of his mouth and eyes, the natural marks of age cut deeper by weariness. Shoulders hunched, hands clasped in his lap, he looked so small.

"It *is* going to be fine." He smiled, but it trembled around the edges. "Now stop fiddling with the books and come sit with me."

He held out his hand and wiggled his fingers in my direction. I took a deep breath and slipped my hand into his, allowing him to pull me down into the chair beside him. A thread of guilt slipped through me as he pressed his lips to the back of my hand. He shouldn't have to be the strong one. He should be the one panicking, not me. He's the one—

I pushed the thought from my head. *He's fine. He's going to be fine.* I'd seen modern medicine perform miracles I would have never thought possible, people given new limbs, new organs. They could fix this.

We both pivoted in our chairs as the door to the office swung open. Dr. Ishihara, a thin, severe-looking man with silver hair, strode in without looking up, his short, hooked nose buried in the file in his hands. A large manila folder dangled from his fingers and knocked against the desk as he made his way around it. Though his expression was blank, every part of him moved as if it were weighted down. Two days had passed since Taka's MRI. When the hospital called to give us the results, they didn't say much, just referred us to Dr. Ishihara and set an appointment. I knew it couldn't be good news.

Taka and I flinched as he slapped the file down on the desk. "Aikawa-san," he said, eyes still on his desk. "How are we feeling today?"

We? I already wanted to punch this guy in the nose.

"Um…fine, I guess," Taka answered in a small voice.

"Any new symptoms? Blurred vision? Cognitive issues?"

"Cognitive…?"

"Trouble thinking," the doctor said, making a mark on the file.

Taka's gaze jumped down to the doctor's pencil, and he swallowed thickly. "No."

"How are the headaches?"

"About the same."

"Look, can we just get on with it?" I snapped, slapping the arm of the chair. Taka gave my hand a warning squeeze, and I closed my eyes a moment to gather myself. "Just tell us what's wrong and how we can fix it."

Dr. Ishihara's eyes lifted for the first time, cold and distant. They stopped on me, our clasped hands, the corners of his mouth twitching in a way that made my teeth grind. With an impatient sigh, he snapped the file closed and grabbed the large envelope. He stood, slipping two sheets of translucent, black plastic from the folder, and flipped a switch on the wall-mounted light box behind his desk.

"This," he said, snapping the films onto the light box, "is an image of your brain."

The films lit up with images in grey and white. They didn't even look human, and part of me latched onto the idea that this was all a mistake. He gestured to a pair of fuzzy blobs with the end of his pen.

"Your headaches are a symptom of intracranial pressure caused by a glioblastoma here and here." He tapped each of the spots in turn.

"A glio...what?" I asked.

"A tumor," he answered bluntly.

"I have cancer...in my brain?" Taka asked in a small voice.

"Yes."

My vision went fuzzy around the edges, and I struggled to catch my breath. Taka's hand tightened around mine and it felt clammy.

"So what do we do?" I asked, a lump of ice forming in my stomach. "Can't you cut it out or something?"

Taka exhaled loudly from beside me, and I looked over to find him with his head down, fingers massaging his brow, a habit that started with the headaches.

"I'm afraid in your case surgery is not a viable option," Dr. Ishihara said, dropping back into his chair and clasping his hands in front of him. "Glioblastoma is an invasive cancer, meaning it grows into the brain tissue itself. Removing it completely, even under the best circumstances, is almost impossible."

"And in these circumstances?"

"The smaller of the two tumors," he said, gesturing over his shoulder with his pen, "is sitting right on the brain stem, which controls all the autonomic systems of the body. Breathing, heartbeat, all the things you do without thinking about it. Like a switchboard between the brain and the body. It's a very complex and dangerous area to cut into."

"You're saying I could end up a vegetable?" Taka asked in a hoarse voice.

"Yes," Dr. Ishihara replied. "And you would still have cancer."

The blood drained from Taka's face. Anger and resentment simmered beneath my skin as he shrank even further into his chair, his eyes fixed to a point on the doctor's desk. I thought about the books on the shelves, the machines in the next room, all those miracles of medicine. What good were they if they couldn't save Taka?

"That's not to say we don't have options," Dr. Ishihara continued, pulling a card out of his breast pocket. "I've made you an appointment with the radiologist."

"How long?" Taka asked, expression hard.

Dr. Ishihara's expression softened around the edges. "With treatment, maybe a year."

I doubled over as if I'd been punched in the gut.

"And without?"

The doctor shrugged. "Weeks."

Taka's eyes filmed over with tears, and he closed them before they could fall. The temperature dropped, and I shivered so hard my teeth clacked together. Taka squeezed my hand so tight it hurt, but I didn't let go.

"Taka—"

He stood abruptly and darted out the door before I could stop him. I took one desperate look at the doctor, who stood unperturbed as if this happened all the time, before chasing after him. I caught him halfway to the elevator, both of us panting as if we'd run a kilometer.

"Stop, Takanori," I said, grabbing him by the arm.

"I'm sorry. I can't do this," he said, tears streaming down his cheeks.

"Can't do what?"

"*This*," he said, gesturing emphatically at the hospital around us, his voice taking a hysterical pitch. "Surgery, treatment, any of it."

"You have to do the treatment," I said, voice trembling. "If you don't—"

"What? I'll die? I'm dying anyway." The truth of it fell like a lead weight between us, and I nearly collapsed under it. This was it. I was losing him. "My grandfather on my mother's side got lung cancer when I was a boy. He spent over a year bedridden and in pain, kept alive on machines because our family was unable to face the truth. I don't want to live like that. I won't."

"So you're just going to give up?" I asked, resentment flaring once again.

"It's my life, Hiro."

"And mine too."

Taka flinched as my voice boomed off the walls. I shook with anger born from desperation, undercut by a hard line of guilt and grief. I leaned against the wall to keep from falling, hiding my face behind my hands as tears forced their way out of me. I had dreams of our life together, of watching him grow old, of being mistaken for his son and laughing about it together. He'd know everything about me and accept it all, the good with the bad, and keep me up all night with detailed questions about historical events. And when he did die, it would be with the comfort of a long life filled with happy memories and few regrets. Now, with the heels of my hands pressed against my eyes, I watched those dreams pop like brightly colored balloons and drop shredded and destroyed at my feet. I was selfish. All I could think about was *my* loss, what I'd given up for the life I would no longer have.

He touched my arm and I crumbled. I pulled him into me and held him tight. I'd known all along, deep in my heart, that this day would come. With every new line in his face and streak of gray in his hair, I knew. But not now. Not like this, like a candle blown out in a storm. Maybe if I could hold him tight enough, he wouldn't have to go.

"I'm sorry," I said through a hard sob. "I'm sorry. I just...it's too soon."

"It will always be too soon," he said. "Whether it's a week, a year, fifty years from now."

"I don't want to lose you."

"I don't want to leave you. But it's out of our hands."

Something dark tickled at my subconscious. Out of our hands? Out of *his* hands. Not out of mine.

WE DIDN'T TALK ABOUT IT AFTER THAT. WE SPENT THE REST OF THE night in each other's arms, just being together. We cried until we were exhausted, then watched stupid movies and laughed until our sides hurt. But as much as I wanted to focus all my thoughts on him, I couldn't shake the temptation to tell him everything, to spill the biggest secret I'd ever kept from him.

I am an immortal monster. I can change you. I can save you.

Romantic images of a life together, an *eternity* together, were enough to make me swoon. But they brought with them images of something else—Takanori with his hands dipped in blood, sharp fangs and white eyes.

It was wrong, obscene. The fact I was even considering it made me nauseous. I'd spent our entire life together struggling to keep my demon at bay, and now I would allow it to devour his gentle heart. And for what? So I could hold his hand for one more day?

I was no better than Hideyoshi.

"I'll do it."

"Do what?" I asked, groggy and punch-drunk. We lay curled up on the sofa, the rising sun making the curtains glow.

"The treatment," he answered. "Radiation or...whatever."

My breath caught. My heart skipped. I wiggled myself into a more upright position so I could look at his face. "You're doing that for me?"

"Yeah," he said with a sad smile.

"Why?"

"Because I love you, you idiot," he said, laughing and knocking me on the head. Fear leaked into his eyes, and his expression turned serious. "But you have to promise me something."

"Anything."

"No hospitals. No machines. No...hoping for miracles." He took a deep, shaky breath, his fingers curling in the front of my shirt. "I'll fight this for as long as I can, but when it's over, promise you'll let me go."

My heart broke with an almost audible crack, and all my immortal fantasies dissolved. He answered the question I had yet to ask. He didn't want to die, but he was prepared to. Our natural conclusion. He'd offered me a compromise, and while a part of me still felt cheated, I had no choice but to accept.

TWENTY-ONE

Progression

SPRING 2004

FIVE MONTHS PASSED WITH RELATIVELY MINOR SYMPTOMS. A LITTLE nausea, mostly from the treatment, some weakness, a few small lapses in thought here and there. The worst were the headaches, some so bad he could hardly lift his head. But we were making it, making the best of the good days and weathering the bad together. Until five months and three days after his diagnosis, Takanori forgot my name.

It was just for a second, but I would never forget the terror in his eyes. How could he forget my name? *My* name. The person who loved and cared for him most in the world and who he loved in kind. Every lapse after that took on new meaning. What else could he forget? What if the next time, it didn't come back?

His senses went next. Within a week, he was deaf on one side and could barely see past his nose. He suffered violent mood swings, uttering strings of vulgarity the likes I'd never heard from him before. When I spoke to Dr. Ishihara about it, he simply shrugged and said it was the progression of his disease, something about hormonal imbalances and loss of impulse control, and not to take it personally. It was hard not to. Resentment simmered deep in my gut, not against Takanori, but against my own inability to do anything except watch him disappear piece by piece.

"Chikushou." The hissing of a pot boiling over snapped me from my stupor, and I jumped to remove the okayu from the burner. I hadn't slept in four days. Every second was spent caring for Takanori, comforting Takanori, worrying about Takanori. There was no space for anything else. Maia was on her way over, determined to give me a break. How could I possibly take a break?

I ladled the rice porridge into a bowl, thankful it at least hadn't burned, and loaded it onto a tray with a cup of tea and a pill bottle before shuffling into the bedroom. Taka lay curled on his side in our bed. He'd lost a devastating amount of weight, and his small frame barely disturbed the plane of the comforter. I set the tray down on the bedside table before squatting beside the bed, my face close to his where he could see it.

"Hey, sleepyhead," I said, giving him a soft pat on the arm. He stirred but didn't open his eyes, his face pinched. He reached a hand blindly toward the drawer. Painkillers. I stopped him halfway, pressing his hand between mine. "Sorry, you're maxed out. Gonna have to wait a couple hours. Your sister's coming over. You think you can make it to the couch today?"

He groaned, whipped his hand out of mine and rolled away, turning his back to me.

"Oh, it's gonna be like that?" I tried to keep my tone light, but inside I was bleeding. "Well, try to eat something at least. I brought you some—"

"I'm not hungry," he said in a raspy voice.

"Can you just try?"

"I don't want it."

"You know if you take your meds on an empty stomach, it will make you sick."

"I said, I don't want it!" His arm swung around faster than I could stop it, and he swiped the tray off the table, sending porridge across my lap and the bowl skittering across the floor.

I sat in stunned silence, rice seeping into my pants and dripping from the ends of my hair. I tried to remember what the doctor told me

—*Don't take it personal*—but the bitterness of the action sent guilt slamming down on me, crushing me to the point of suffocation. He was suffering for me because I had asked him to stay and fight an impossible fight he was destined to lose. I couldn't help but wonder how much his love for me had eroded as the pain got harder and harder to bear.

A knock at the door startled me out of my despair. Maia. Gathering myself as best I could, I stood up and went to answer. Maia pushed her way in with hardly a greeting, her hands loaded down with plastic bags. She smiled brightly as she passed, but her eyes held the same tired, raw look I saw in the mirror every morning.

"What the hell happened to you?" Maia asked after dropping the bags off in the kitchen and taking in my sorry state.

"Your brother hates me."

"What makes you think that?"

I gestured bitterly to my stained clothes.

"He doesn't hate you," she said as she unloaded a bag of groceries into the fridge. She'd been great about these little things. It was so hard for me to leave the house, she always made a point to bring something when she visited, which was often, and she never once commented on how much went to waste.

I snatched a towel off the rack in the kitchen and scrubbed at my pants. I was angry. Not at him, of course. It wasn't his fault. But it didn't stop me from wanting to punch a hole in the wall.

"You look tired." She stepped up beside me, laying her palm against the side of my face, and for a moment I just soaked in that small comfort. "You should sit down."

"I can't...the mess…"

"I'll take care of the mess." She snatched the towel out of my hand and steered me by my shoulders toward the couch. "For crying out loud, take a nap."

Ignoring my protests, she pushed me down onto the couch and threw a blanket over me, not letting up until I was flat on my back and wrapped up like a burrito. We laughed, and it felt good to laugh. Sometimes she was the only thing that kept me sane.

"Need anything?" she asked, tucking a pillow under my head.

"Get him to take his medication and you'll be my hero."

"You know he can't say no to me," she said with a wink. My eyelids drooped as she squeezed my shoulder.

Next thing I knew, the light had shifted and the house was quiet, save for the gentle sound of running water from the kitchen. I groaned and untangled myself from the blanket, blinking the sleep from my eyes. I didn't even remember falling asleep.

"Hey," Maia appeared from the kitchen, a dishrag in her hand.

"What time is it?" I grumbled, pushing myself upright.

"Almost four. You've been out most of the day."

"Shit, I'm sorry." My eyes swept over the living area, which had been tidied around me. "You didn't have to…"

"Don't apologize. You needed it." She dropped down onto the couch beside me, laying her hand on my arm. "And it's okay to accept help once in a while."

My lips tugged upward in a grateful smile. "How is he?"

She shrugged. "He told me to tell you he's sorry about the bowl."

My chest warmed, his face flashing before my eyes. How he was before—cheeks flushed, big, round eyes blinking up at me as he apologized for some imagined awkwardness.

"Two days ago was our anniversary," I said, hands clutched on my lap and eyes on my knees. "Ten years."

"That long?" Maia said with a whistle. "It feels like you've always been in our lives."

"You were just a kid when we got together," I said, pinching her cheek and making her giggle.

"I never told you this but, he called me the day after you…you know…." She blushed a little, and her eyes glistened with nostalgia. "He said, 'I think I could spend my whole life with him.' He was so happy."

A warm silence settled over us. We leaned on each other, holding one another up under the weight of impending loss.

"Mom asked about you," she said slowly, eyes on her hands clasped in her lap. "About Taka."

Bitterness crawled up my throat like bile. "She asked you?"

"Don't hate her, Hiro."

"We have a phone too," I said through clenched teeth. "She could have talked to him."

"You know how it is, Hiro. With my father—"

"Their son is dying. They can't put aside their homophobic nonsense long enough to make a phone call?"

I pressed the heels of my hands against my eyes as I struggled to maintain my temper. Maia could paint it over with all the sweet words she wanted, but I would never forgive them. I couldn't stop thinking of the day I came home to find Taka sitting on the couch, head hung low, with the phone clutched in his hands. It was a few days after his diagnosis, and he'd called to tell them. "He wouldn't even talk to me," he'd said in a voice so small I hardly recognized it as his. They hadn't visited once.

Maia rubbed slow circles on my back until my breathing returned to normal. I wondered what Dr. Ishihara would say about *my* hormone levels.

"Does he ask about them?"

"He used to," I said. "Not anymore."

A hard silence fell over us. I don't know what I expected. The one time I met Taka's father, a random encounter on the street, he'd looked me up and down with unveiled disgust, as if I were a worm that had infected his son. The look he gave Taka wasn't any better. I could never understand, *would* never understand.

"I've gotta go," she said with a long sigh. "You gonna be okay?"

I nodded, and she gave my hand a squeeze before standing and letting herself out. I sank back into the couch with a deep sigh. I did feel better. Her presence, her cheerful strength, had a way of making me feel like things weren't falling apart.

"Hiro…"

I jerked up straight at the sound of Taka's voice, weak but unmistakable. He stood in the doorway of our bedroom, leaning heavily on the doorframe, eyes unfocused and searching.

"Taka! What are you doing—" Something in his face made me draw up short. I stood and his eyes snapped to the movement. They were wide and red-rimmed. I ran to his side, and he clung to me. "You okay? What's wrong?"

He took my face in his hands and cupped it gently, running his thumbs over my cheekbones. Tears gathered on his lashes as he pulled me down into a kiss. His lips were dry but warm, and like every kiss before it, it made me feel light. I returned each soft caress with equal tenderness, my hands pressed against his small back. His body melded to mine. Every moment of our lives was there in that kiss, and I savored its sweetness.

Just wanted you to know I love you.

His muscles went rigid and he felt heavy in my arms. A seizure. It wasn't his first, and even though I knew not to panic, my veins still zinged with adrenaline. I lowered him carefully to the floor on his side, head in my lap and arms tucked against him to prevent him injuring himself. "It's okay, I got you," I said, stroking his hair as I waited for it to pass.

Gradually, his muscles relaxed and I was able to breathe again. I cradled him in my lap, wiping away the film of sweat that had formed on his forehead as I waited for his eyes to open.

But they didn't open.

"Taka?" My throat tightened, and I hovered my hand over his mouth and nose. Still breathing. I pressed my fingers to his pulse point. His heart still beat. I gave him a gentle shake. "Come on, baby, come back to me."

No response came from him, no flicker of the eyes, no little sounds. Something was wrong. With a curse, I gathered him up in my arms and bolted out the door. I ran as fast as my unnatural legs would carry me to the Tokyo General emergency room. The desk attendant recognized us on sight. A flock of nurses swept us into an exam bay. I laid him out on a bed, relaying as much information as I could about his condition, his doctors, his medications, all with his hand firmly clasped in mine.

The world blurred as they worked around me, taking vitals, checking airways, shining a bright penlight in his eyes. I went numb to everything but the feel of his hand in mine—warm and soft, but so very brittle. I touched the metal band on his finger, scuffed and scratched but still there.

"Hiro-san, we're going to take Aikawa-san for some imaging," one of the nurses said, laying a hand on my arm. I nodded dumbly, Taka's hand still clutched to my chest. "Hiro-san, I'm sorry, you're going to have to let him go."

Promise me you'll let me go.

Grief slammed through me and I shook all over. *Let him go. You have to let him go.* But I wasn't ready. It was too soon. We were supposed to have a year. I wasn't ready.

With another gentle nudge from the nurse, I released his hand, and the others whisked him away into the bowels of the hospital. "Don't worry, we'll take good care of him." She led me by the arm to a waiting area down the hall. "Is there someone we can call for you?"

"Maia...his sister." I could hardly get the words out. I couldn't even take a full breath. She nodded and disappeared.

Maia appeared in what seemed like seconds. She knelt in front of me, both my hands clasped in hers, looking rumpled and pale. Tears clung to the ends of her lashes, but she held them back, probably for my sake.

"What happened?" she asked, her voice thick.

"He had a seizure. I...couldn't wake him up."

She closed her eyes a moment, calling on a deep well of strength before opening them again. "It's gonna be okay, Hiro. He's gonna be okay."

"I don't think so."

TWENTY-TWO

Letting Go

SPRING 2004

IT WAS TWO HOURS BEFORE WE HEARD ANYTHING. THE HOSPITAL CALLED Dr. Ishihara and he appeared grave as an undertaker to give us the news. The tumor had grown into Taka's brain stem. He was breathing on his own and they were able to control his heart rate with medication, but he was in a coma.

"W-when will he wake up?" Maia asked, her lips quivering.

"It is unlikely Aikawa-san will regain consciousness," Dr. Ishihara answered. His words were matter-of-fact, but his eyes held a surprising amount of sympathy. "I'm sorry."

I thought I knew what numb felt like. Like waking up after falling asleep on your arm— pins and needles and a limp, disembodied feeling. It was actually more like walking out onto a frozen lake and falling through the ice—a shock of pain that takes your breath away and then nothing. Life slowed to a stop.

Dr. Ishihara escorted us to his room, and my stomach dropped. It was everything Taka was afraid of—a sterile, white hospital room, his small body lost in a forest of wires and plastic tubing. Monitors clicked and pinged all around him, the sound ricocheting off the walls like ball bearings.

A whimper escaped Maia as I lowered myself down onto the edge of Taka's bed. His hand was cold in mine.

He doesn't want this.

Dr. Ishihara cleared his throat. "He'll remain here until we can get him a room in a long-term care facility—"

"No."

"Hiro…" Maia gasped.

"I want to take him home," I said, my eyes never leaving his face. The light inside him that used to burn so bright had dimmed to almost nothing, a pale shadow of Takanori.

"I would strongly advise against that," Dr. Ishihara said. "If he stops breathing outside of a hospital—"

"I know the consequences."

"Hiro, please!" Maia clung to my arm, her eyes wet and pleading.

"He doesn't want to live like this, wasting away in a hospital hooked up to machines."

She made a sound between a hiccup and a sob. "But—"

"Look at him, Maia," I said, my voice breaking, tears streaming down my cheeks. "He's already gone. We have to let him go."

She crumpled under my words. Tears glistening in her eyes, she studied her brother's face, searching for evidence that he was still with us. My heart broke for her, for all of us, and I wanted to rage at the unfairness of it all. She closed her eyes, and two tears fell in vertical lines down her cheeks. She looked up to Dr. Ishihara.

"You're his next of kin," he said, shrugging his shoulders. "It's your decision."

She took a deep breath, squeezing my arm.

"Discharge him. We're taking him home."

THE HOSPITAL ACCOMMODATED US SURPRISINGLY FAST, AND WE WERE soon back home with Taka tucked back into his own bed. Part of me was afraid Maia would be angry, resentful of my unwillingness to wait for a miracle, but if she was she hid it masterfully. Once we had Taka settled, she groaned and rubbed her eyes.

"I'm exhausted." She ran a hand over her face and let out a long breath.

She looked thinner somehow, as if she'd been emptied out. Even her skin hung on her strangely. "Mind if I sleep on your couch?"

I could tell she didn't want to leave me alone. "Of course not."

She gave me a little smile of thanks before turning her attention back to Taka. "Goodnight, Brother," she said, placing a kiss on his forehead. On her way out, she stopped and threw her arms around my neck. "He's lucky to have you," she said, tears in her voice.

Lucky. This was my fault, wasn't it? I took him to the hospital, the last place he wanted to be. I could have saved him months ago. This didn't have to happen.

The door clicked shut behind her just as my numbness began to thaw, starting with a squeezing pain in my chest.

"I'm sorry," I said, barely above a whisper. "You fought so hard for me. Now look at you."

I sat on the edge of the bed next to him, picked up his hand, and pressed my lips against the silver band he'd worn every day for ten years.

"I have a confession to make," I said, voice barely audible even to me. "I wasn't honest with you about who I am. About my past. About...what I do at night." My throat squeezed so tight, I could barely breathe. "About anything at all, really. Except how much I love you. That was always true."

I took a deep breath and wiped at my nose. "The truth is I could have fixed you. I have magic in my blood. Magic that has kept me alive and young for hundreds of years. And I could have given it to you. I could have given it to you, and it would have taken away your sickness and made you strong. But the price is so high..."

I trailed off, unable even now to tell him the whole truth, about the blood on my hands and the dark thing constantly gnawing away at me. Even now it raked sharp claws over the inside of my skin and whispered false promises in my ear.

"I know where you are right now. That terrible in-between place.

I've seen it. I know how unbearable it is and that this body clinging to life is chaining you there." I leaned forward and brushed my hand over his wan cheek. Tears fell unchecked down my face and made a wet spot on the bed clothes. "But I can set you free. I can elevate you, make you part of my immortality."

I slipped into the bed next to him, my head on his chest. Not yet. One more night. He could forgive me for that, couldn't he? One more night warming the bed next to me. One more night with his heartbeat in my ear and his breath against my cheek. And then I could do the thing I promised when this all began. I could let him go.

I spent that night curled up against him. As the sun rose the next morning, my monster rose with it. I didn't fight it. I needed it to help me bear the weight of what I had to do. It wrapped itself around my heart as I lifted my head to look into Takanori's face. So peaceful as if in a deep sleep, a small crease in his brow the only indication of the pain he suffered.

Tears rising in my throat, I gathered him up and cradled him in my arms. I placed one last lingering kiss on his lips before tipping his head back to expose his slim throat. He gave an involuntary twitch as my fangs pierced his skin, and I took the first gentle pull. His blood hit my throat like needles, and I struggled to swallow. My fingers told him *Love you forever* as I timed each drink with his heartbeat. My soul shattered as I felt it stutter.

And then, he was gone.

TWENTY-THREE

Distraction

SPRING 2004

Tears dropped off the end of my nose onto my clenched hands. I didn't even know I was crying. I glanced up at Asagi who sat very still across from me, brows low over their red eyes. They were the first person I'd told the whole story to—not even Maia knew what happened that last night—and a paradoxical relief fell over me. Finally, someone knew. Someone would hold me accountable. Someone would point their finger at my hypocritical tears and call me a murderer.

But they didn't. When Asagi finally moved, knocking the long ash off the end of their cigarette, there was no blame. They leaned forward in their chair and placed their hand on my shoulder.

"You did the right thing."

I blinked in surprise as they stood, pulling their long frame straight and releasing a breath as if to expel the sour mood. They crossed their arms over their barrel chest, studying me down the end of their nose.

"Okay, I'll help you," Asagi said with an exaggerated sigh. They leaned forward, jabbing a finger in my face. "My humans are off-limits to you, do you understand? You will do your killing out on the street. I will not have death here. And if you so much as LOOK at Ryo again…" I nodded quickly, their murderous glare finishing the sentence for them. "Good. Now come with me."

"Where are we going?"

Asagi answered with a coy smile over their shoulder as they exited the VIP room. I followed them through the crowd toward the back of the bar. Ryo's eyes followed as we approached, wide and tinged with concern. Asagi gave him a quick wink as we passed, leading me down a back passage lined with kegs and liquor crates until we reached a locked door. They fished a small brass key out of their pocket and slipped it into the lock.

"What's this?" I asked, suspicion creeping into my voice.

"This," Asagi said, "is distraction."

The door swung open on a small, windowless dormitory, not nice but not entirely unpleasant, with a dresser in the corner and a bed pushed against the back wall. The walls were bare, except for a mirror hanging over a white porcelain sink. It was the kind of place used for quick naps during a long shift, or for a live-in handyman.

A young man sat on the edge of the bed—small, fit, and stylishly dressed like he belonged in a counterculture magazine. Chains hung from his belt loops, and heavy silver rings knotted his small fingers. His hair stuck out all over in manicured spikes, and his right ear hung heavy with tracks of silver jewelry. Despite his ostentatious appearance, he sat with a hunch, eyes wary and muscles twitching, as if not quite comfortable in his own skin.

"This is Rui," Asagi said, gesturing grandly into the room. The boy stood up, shuffled his feet around, and bowed. His eyes remained lowered even after he straightened, his hands shoved in his pockets.

"I don't get it."

Asagi sighed and moved to Rui's side, draping an arm over his shoulders. Rui flinched but didn't pull away, his prominent Adam's apple bouncing with a hard swallow. "Do you know what it is that drives us crazy, Hiro? What really makes a monster go mad? The things that are missing."

"I still don't understand."

Asagi rolled their eyes and pointed a long-nailed finger at me. "You have a desperate, insatiable need to be loved. It's why, no matter how much you love Yoshi, you are destined to be unhappy, because he will never give you that validation. He isn't capable of showing you the love you need, at least in a way that you understand. You found it for a while with Takanori, but now that he's gone…"

"Make your point."

"Yoshi loves to judge me for the humans I keep and call them *slaves*, but do you know what our relationship is really based on? Mutual need." Asagi hugged Rui closer to their side, making him yelp. "My need is…well, obvious, but theirs can often be more existential. Maybe they need adventure, maybe they crave the secret, maybe they just need to know that magic is real, no matter the price. Do you know what Rui needs? Escape."

"From what?"

"My life," Rui said in a gravelly voice, a deep crease forming in his young brow. His dark eyes were molten like the leading edge of a lava flow. His shoulders pulled inward, and his fists made two big lumps in his pockets as if his whole body were working to contain it.

Asagi chuckled. "It seems you have something in common."

"Okaaay," I drawled. "I still don't understand what this has to do with me."

Asagi grinned before taking Rui by the chin and tipping his head up. "Look at me," they purred. Rui's eyes locked on theirs, and a shiver ran through him. The lava cooled and the dark tension he'd carried melted away, replaced by hazy-eyed adoration. Asagi spoke to him gently, the way one would to a beloved pet, running a finger over the line of his jaw. "This is Hiro. He will give you what you need. But you have to show him you love him. Can you do that for me?"

Rui nodded dreamily, his gaze turning to me. Eyes the color of dark chocolate locked on mine. Something twisted inside me and I stepped back.

"You can't make him fall in love with me," I said, pulse quickening.

"Of course not. We both know our influence only goes so far." Asagi took Rui by the shoulders and nudged him in my direction. "Your bite will do the rest."

Need surged up in me, dark and urgent, knocking away everything but the warm glow of Rui's blood. I shook my head as I struggled to focus.

"I thought you said your humans were off-limits," I said breathlessly.

"They are." Asagi grinned. "I'm giving him to you. I'd appreciate it if you don't kill him."

Rui stepped closer, reaching out a hand to touch me. I grabbed him by the wrist, and the warmth of his skin burned through me like fire.

"This isn't right," I said in a thick voice.

Asagi clicked their tongue, offense sharpening their red-eyed glare. "What do you take me for? This is completely consensual. He knew what I was and what he was asking for when he came to me."

"But Hideyoshi...he said—"

"Forget Hideyoshi," they growled, making Rui flinch. "If he did a half-decent job of caring for you, you wouldn't be in this state."

"You hate him so much, why help me at all?"

Asagi's lips curled. "We don't choose our makers, Hiro. They choose us. What he is is not your fault, nor is what he's done to you." A strange expression flickered across Asagi's face, quickly hidden behind a seductive smile. "Think of this as a bandage for your broken heart."

My heart pounded in my ears. Rui looked up at me from under a cloud of dark lashes. The hunger sang in me as he leaned in close.

I licked my lips and swallowed hard. "It won't be real."

"Real enough if you let it," Asagi said, expression strangely blank.

Gently, I took the boy's face in my hands. He was beautiful, with soft cheeks and deep, sad eyes. In another time, I would have been drawn to his darkness. Maybe I was. A tuning fork rang inside me as I brushed a sticky lock of hair from his face. Maybe we could save each other.

Just the smell of him made me dizzy as I lowered my face into his neck. Like brown sugar and fresh laundry. I lingered there, numb to everything but that smell and his distinctly human warmth. He curled his fingers in the front of my shirt, urging me closer, short, gasping breaths brushing against my ear like a moth's wings.

"Do it. Please," he said in a barely audible whisper.

I pressed my teeth to his skin, and the first shot of blood hit my tongue like molten light. A gentle pull and the boy moaned, not in pain, but pleasure. His head fell back as he wrapped his arms around me and pressed his lean body to mine. An electric tingle crawled across my scalp as he laced his fingers into my hair. His body warmed and breath quickened as I hummed into his neck.

What did Asagi do to him? Not only did he not fear my bite, he was aroused by it.

It took every ounce of strength in me to release my hold on him. The thing inside me roared in protest, and my head spun as I watched twin trails of light leak from the holes I had made. I lost my balance and fell back against the wall. Rui came with me, his body pressed against mine. Our noses brushed. Our breath mingled. Those deep, dark eyes held mine, alight with adoration, and my sinuses burned. Asagi was right. I hated that they were right. If I let myself, I could believe he loved me, I could fall into those eyes like freshly tilled earth and never return. My skin ached. I craved this closeness like I craved blood. It wasn't the same, nothing would ever be the same as what I had with Taka. But it made the hole inside me seem not quite so dark and deep and wide.

I caught Asagi's gaze briefly where they sat on the bed, chewing the end of their cigarette stem with a self-satisfied smile. Demanding my attention again, Rui pressed blood-coated fingers to my lips. I took them gladly, running my tongue over them and sucking every drop of sweet liquid from his skin. As soon as I released his fingers, he brought his face close and pressed his lips to mine. He had bitten his tongue, filling his mouth with blood, and I devoured him. Every sigh and moan I made only seemed to heighten his pleasure, and he ground his hips into me, slipping his hands under my shirt and raking his nails over my back.

Show him you love him.

I pushed him backward into the bed, eliciting a squeal from Asagi. The wound on Rui's neck had cut a river of red along his porcelain skin. I pulled his shirt over his head, searching for the river's end. It ran nearly to his waist, and I followed it up from there with my tongue, making him shiver and moan. I bit him again and again on his collarbone, chest, abdomen, repeating the process until my tongue had traced almost every part of him.

My body ached for more than this. Pants heavy with studs and chains clanged to the floor as I slipped them off his small hips. I threw his leg over my shoulder and pressed my teeth to his inner thigh. I drank lazily, letting his heart do the work as I ran my fingers over the ridges of his pelvis. I lost myself in the taste of him, in the feel of his light sliding through my veins.

"Enough, Hiro," Asagi said, their hand on my shoulder. Rui had gone still, his breathing shallow, his flushed skin pale. I didn't care. I wanted him, all of him. "Stop! You'll kill him!"

Asagi yanked me off him and threw me onto my back on the bed. Blood-drunk and blind with lust, I thrashed and snapped at them. They pinned me easily, straddling my hips and pressing my wrists over my head into the mattress.

Rui's blood raged through me, my mind awash with the power of it, the pleasure of it. It drowned my human heart, replacing grief and guilt with carnal need. I throbbed with it, the beast roaring as I strained against my captor's grip.

"Control your heart, Hiro," Asagi said, their face close to mine. "It is the only thing that is truly yours. Don't let the monster blind you. Control it, or it will control you."

But I didn't want to control it. I wanted to devour it, to throw it in a deep, dark pit where it wouldn't hurt. I snapped at Asagi's neck and they pulled back, shifting their grip to my throat instead. Something shifted in them, something subtle but profound. Their shoulders lifted, back straightened, mannerisms became more fluid. Their feminine self peeking through the masculine exterior.

"Do you want to end up in one of Yoshi's cages?" Asagi asked, voice thick with disdain.

Ice shot through my veins, and my vision blurred with images of fluorescent lights, steel bars, and an ash-covered floor. My thrashing limbs went stiff as steel beams. I couldn't breathe. I closed my eyes, causing tears pooled in the corners to fall down my temples as I shook my head.

Asagi's grip loosened. "I know it's hard. Believe me, I know." They released my throat, cupped my face in their hand, and swept the tears away with their thumb. "But you are stronger than you know."

The monster slunk back into its hole, leaving me raw and empty. I didn't feel strong. I felt broken, hollowed out, and tired beyond all reason. I opened my eyes to find Asagi looking down on me with surprising tenderness. They blinked and jerked upright, clearing their throat before shifting their weight off of me and their attention to Rui. Sweeping a hand over his forehead, Asagi peeled his eyelids back and squinted into his face.

"Is he okay?"

Asagi nodded with a deep sigh before tucking a blanket around him. "What now?"

"Now?" they asked, pulling up straight. "I'm going back to work."

I lifted myself up onto my elbows. "But Hideyoshi…"

Asagi sneered and rolled their eyes. "That's your problem, Hiro," they said, wiping the dust off their suit. "You cling to him in the hope that one day his heart will magically open to you. Well, it won't. What's left of his human heart, if he ever had one, is gone. He will never understand you." Asagi pulled on their lapel, pointing out a particularly deep crease. "This is Armani, by the way."

Asagi moved with long strides to the sink and studied themself in the mirror. Their tie had pulled loose in our scuffle. They tugged it off with an annoyed huff. Pulling a comb from their inside jacket pocket, they smoothed their long hair back into a more dignified arrangement.

"And Ryo?" I sat up straight. "Does he understand you?"

Mid-stroke, Asagi's comb stopped, and their expression hardened in the mirror. Tucking the comb back into their pocket, they took a deep breath and schooled their features back into their usual smug arrangement before turning toward the door.

"Does it ever stop?" I asked.

Asagi pulled up short. "Stop what?"

"Hurting."

For a long time, Asagi was silent before releasing a long breath. "No. But you get used to it."

The strength drained out of me and I fell backward onto my back, making the bed springs squeal.

"Take it easy on him, would you?" Asagi said, gesturing to Rui.

The door clicked shut behind them and I closed my eyes, allowing the post-blood fuzz to settle over me. Asagi was right, after all. I'd let Hideyoshi take control of my heart, allowed myself to get lost in the waiting and the desperate need for his approval that would likely never come.

Some small noise drew my attention back to the young man on the bed. Rui. I had to hand it to Asagi—he was beautiful, but I'd made such a mess of him. Still feeling soft around the edges, I pulled myself up and leaned over him. His eyelids fluttered as I peeled the blanket back and trailed my fingertips over his pale chest, tracing the edges of the wounds I'd left on him. I punctured my thumb on one of my fangs and, with a little of my blood, sealed them one by one.

I stopped when I reached his inner thigh. The wound was deep and angry and would surely leave a scar. Something dark in me thrilled at the thought that I had marked him, that every lover he had from here forward would see it and know that I'd been there.

He would be bound to me forever through the power of that bite. When I looked up at his face, at the pink rising in his cheeks and the glaze in his hooded eyes, I saw it there. He would live for my happiness at the expense of his own and that shallow, artificial affection felt better than none at all.

TWENTY-FOUR

Lost

HIDEYOSHI

SPRING 1994

"I LOVE YOU, HIDEYOSHI. I'VE GIVEN MY WHOLE LIFE TO YOU. AND YOU can't even pretend for one day, *one day*, that you love me."

The door snapped closed between us with the finality of a dropped bomb. I stumbled backward, seething with anger. It rose up hot, burning off all the messier emotions I didn't know how to deal with. Guilt, disappointment, shame evaporated in a cloud of smoke and ash. I clung to it, wrapping it around my heart like armor.

The one major concession I'd made for him when I moved him to Edo was his room, his own space. It was a place for him to hide when my temper became too much to bear. A symbolic gift, really. I still expected him to spend his nights with me, but as time wore on, he used it to punish me. Not an undeserved punishment, but hurtful nonetheless.

It was not as if I couldn't follow him in. Like in every traditional house, the door was made of paper and didn't even have a lock. But I'd trampled over so many lines in the course of our relationship, and this was one I dared not cross. I clenched my fists and pressed my knuckles against the doorframe until they ached and then, cursing and snorting like a bull, turned and trudged back down the hall, one razor-sharp thought cutting through my mind.

He thinks I don't love him.

Hiro loved me. A wild, irrational love. I knew that. In our early days, it shone like silver in firelight. Hiro wore his heart on the outside, and while that was a big part of what attracted me to him, it also made him vulnerable. He needed to be treated delicately, with great care. I was not delicate nor careful, and while over two hundred years was enough time to tarnish anything, I was afraid I'd put such dents in his heart that no amount of polish could bring back the shine.

Our tea had of course gone cold, so I bypassed it in favor of a bottle of wine I had stashed in the kitchen. Stupid boy. He didn't know how good he had it. I may have been hard, but I'd given him everything he could ever want—position and power, a roof over his head, and a closet full of fine kimono. Spoiled was what he was, pouting in his room like an insolent child.

The first glass of wine went down so fast I hardly tasted it, chased hard by the second. I took a couple of deep breaths before pouring a third and taking it with me out onto the engawa. The sun had burned off most of the morning chill, leaving the air pleasantly warm and clean. Fresh leaves lent everything a new brightness, and birdsong drifted through the garden as the world shook off the blanket of winter. While the weather and the wine did their work softening the edges of my foul mood, I let my mind wander.

Warm tendrils curled through me when I thought of the day I met Hiro. Or maybe it was the wine. He seemed so young, so naive, and *mattaku*, that voice. I walked around under a cloud my entire life, but when he sang, it brought out the sun. He was wasted there among whores and brutes. When he came to me asking for help, I was powerless. I had to take him away, make him mine, my light to chase away the dark.

When was the last time I heard him sing?

The wine turned sour in my gut, and I set aside my glass half-drunk. He'd changed so much in our time together. Older, worldlier, yes, but also more cynical. I scrubbed at the space between my brows as an ache started there. When Hiro was young, he was constantly at my elbow, clinging, touching, batting his eyes, and it pained me to realize he didn't do that anymore. He'd given up. Perhaps we both had to a degree, falling into a tense orbit around each other, close but never touching. I glanced back over my shoulder where the train tickets still lay on the table. There might still be time to fix this. With an annoyed groan, I pulled myself to my feet, snatched the tickets off the table, and marched head down to Hiro's room.

"Hiro." My voice cracked, and I cleared my throat before trying again. "I don't want to fight. Let's go to Kyoto. I want to go. With you. I don't have to...pretend."

I rubbed at my sternum as if I could loosen the tourniquet binding my lungs. This was hard. Why was it so hard? These kinds of things always came so easily to Hiro. Love poured out of him like water, a seemingly endless wellspring. For me, it was like a glacier, slow and destructive.

I tapped on the doorframe, tipping my ear toward it. Silence thrummed on the other side. Frustration hardened under my skin. "Come on, Hiro. Just talk to me. Tell me I'm a monster and you wish you never met me." Still nothing. I clenched my fists, paced down to the end of the hall and back. "I'm trying here, Hiro. What more do you want from me?"

I glared at the door with such intensity, I thought the paper would catch fire. Every second of silence made my anger burn hotter. I was cutting myself open and he was ignoring me.

"Dammit, Hiro, I am your maker. You will show me some respect." I wadded his train tickets up into a ball and threw them at the door, sweating with the heat of my wounded pride. I had to go in. It was the only way to make him face me. I laid a shaking hand on the door. If I went in, there would be consequences. But if I didn't...

With a growl, I threw open the door and it slid into the wall with a loud *snak*. Wind whipped through the room, slapping me in the face and leaving me momentarily disoriented. The outer door that led to the back garden was open. The room was empty.

Hiro was gone.

My body felt heavy, as if gravity itself had changed with his absence. My breath came in shallow, raspy gasps. He was angry. I'd hurt his feelings and he stormed off, that was all. He'd be back once he cooled down. At least that was what I told myself, despite evidence to the contrary. The open closet, the missing bag, the drawers where he kept his special things he didn't think I knew about thrown open and emptied.

He wasn't coming back.

My knees went weak, and I had to grip the doorframe to keep standing. I'd been among the last of a losing army, outnumbered five to one and covered in my own blood, but I'd never felt panic like this. It cut to the marrow.

I closed my eyes and pushed it down, letting anger rise in its place. Anger was useful, familiar, something I could mold and control. More importantly, it was something that would quickly burn out, leaving my heart hardened like tempered steel. I slammed my fist so hard against the doorframe, it splintered, and then I stomped back into the house and straight to my bottle of wine.

I downed another glass without even tasting it. Fine. Let him leave like an ungrateful brat. It would only be a matter of time before he saw how cruel the world could really be. Then he'd be back, pounding on my gate, begging to come home.

And if he didn't?

Panic threatened again, and I drank what remained of the bottle. I didn't even bother with a glass. It sanded down the sharp edges, leaving me simmering in my own dread.

I spent days like that, three quarters in the bag and struggling to maintain a routine that no longer included Hiro. I'd underestimated how much space he took up. The ghost of him was everywhere, in the teacups organized by season and the long, curly hair I found stuck to my clothes. My house now felt vast and empty—so much so, at times I wanted to burn it to the ground.

My heart jerked as my front gate swung open. I sat on my knees in front of a chabudai, an ink brush hovering over a sheet of rice paper. The shoji were thrown open wide, giving me a full view of the front garden. My chest tightened with a disappointment bordering on despair when Asagi appeared on the path. I refused to acknowledge why.

He stopped just short of the engawa and studied me with pursed lips. He looked like a movie from the 1950s, his black A-line dress falling neatly around his calves. A black parasol and large, dark glasses hid him from the sun, the only color some small, silver glints in his hair and the red splash of his lips.

"What do you want?" I barked, careful to keep the slur out of my words.

"To see if it's true." He slipped his glasses off his nose, exposing another shock of red. His gaze bounced from the very empty wine bottle beside me, to the piles of crumpled papers surrounding me, then back to my face. I pulled myself up straighter under his scrutiny.

"To gloat then?"

Asagi gave a small sigh, his expression guarded. "No. To ask you an important question. Are we still safe?"

"What are you implying?"

"Don't play coy with me, Yoshi," he said, irritation slipping into his controlled demeanor. "I know you don't care about us. You care about Hiro. He's the only reason you even pretend to protect us. If he's gone—"

"You think I'll shirk my responsibilities over a domestic dispute?"

Asagi gave a little shrug, eyebrows bouncing.

"I won't." I bit off the words. "Besides, he'll be back."

Asagi's expression softened around the edges, and I jerked my attention back down to my calligraphy. A large, black spot had bled onto the page. I crumpled it up and threw it against the wall with the others.

"Perhaps you're right," he said. "It is...difficult being away from your maker. As it is being away from one you made."

A hysterical laugh burst out of me, making him frown.

"That's funny to you?"

"Quite."

Asagi jerked his face away and shoved his glasses back on before pivoting on one dangerously high heel. "I'll leave you to your misery then."

"I'm not mis—"

The slamming of the front gate sent a sizzle up my spine. I'd had about enough of slamming doors.

TWENTY-FIVE

Found

SPRING 2004

HE LEFT.

He looked me right in the eye and he left. What's worse, he told me exactly what to do to make him stay. All I had to do was tell him I wanted him, I missed him, that I'd counted every day he'd been away in blood and empty sake bottles. Every cell in my body screamed the words, but I couldn't make them come out of my mouth. I couldn't even be mad at him. He told me what he needed. It was my fault. I let him go. Again.

Goodbye, Sakurai Hideyoshi.

I stood lifeless where he left me, drenched in unfamiliar emotions. My fingers twitched at my sides as if reaching for him. Every time I blinked, I saw his eyes searching, yearning, pleading. I shivered as that glacier shifted and groaned inside of me, struggling to carve its way through the rock.

A dull vibration across the floor shook me out of my daze. Hiro's cell phone. I lowered myself down to one knee, picked it up, and stared at the cracked screen. Aikawa Maia. According to the log, she'd called three times in the last five minutes. I don't know why I answered.

"Hiro, where are you?" Hysterical crying came from the other end. "Hiro, please talk to me. Just tell me what's wrong."

"He's not here." My voice cracked as I spoke the words. A sharp intake of breath and the line went silent.

"Who is this?" she asked quietly.

"Sakurai Hideyoshi," I answered robotically. Why was I even talking to her?

"I'm looking for Hiro. Have you seen him? I think something's wrong with him."

"I know."

"Well, where is he?" she asked, panicked.

"He...left." My hand started shaking and I nearly dropped the phone.

"Sakurai-san..." she said after a long pause, "what's going on?"

I didn't know how much to tell her, how much she already knew. His monstrous life had collided with his human one, leaving rubble in its wake. The girl sounded scared—not of him, but for him.

"Did he...do something to you?" I asked hesitantly.

"No. Yes. He...grabbed me. Hard, like..." Her voice wobbled, and she took a breath to compose herself. "I don't know. He's never done anything like that before. I know he would never hurt me, but it..."

"Scared you."

She released a long, shaky breath. "He was confused. I think he thought I was someone else."

My skin went cold. He'd been drunk when he returned. He didn't think she was someone else. It didn't matter who she was. The darkness was rising in him, pushing him to drown his pain in blood. What she'd felt was a python wrapping his coils around her.

She had no idea.

"I have to find him," she said, breathless with panic.

"No. Stay away from him."

"But—"

"If you see him, call this phone."

"What are you going to do?"

"I'm going to find him," I said, that hard shell of anger hardening once again around my heart.

"I'm going with you," she said, her voice steady.

"Absolutely not. It's dangerous. He's—"

"He won't hurt me. He would never hurt me."

"Then why did he scare you?" She answered with a sharp intake of breath and then silence. "I understand that you care about him, but you don't really know him."

"How dare you," she spat. "He's my family. I don't even know who you are."

"He's sick." The admission broke something inside me. Every time he'd used violence to fight against despair played like a newsreel in my head. How long had I been ignoring this?

"He's *grieving*," she said, tears leaking into her voice again. "He's alone and in pain. I will not abandon him, so are you going to help me or not?"

I released a long breath, pinching the bridge of my nose. Stupid, stubborn girl. Going after Hiro could get her killed. Who knew what state he was in after leaving here, bleeding from the fresh wound I dealt him? Hurting her would put him over the edge for sure, and I couldn't let that happen.

"Fine," I said. "Where are you?"

"At Taka and Hiro's apartment. It's—"

"I know where it is." Silence stretched long and brittle between us. "Are you sure you want to do this? You don't even know who I am. Maybe I'm the one who's dangerous."

"Do you care about Hiro?" she asked.

"Yes." It came so easily now.

"That's all I need to know."

MAIA OPENED THE DOOR ON THE FIRST KNOCK. IT WAS LIKE LOOKING AT a ghost. She had Takanori's face, only softer, plumper. Jealousy went off like a firework and I tamped it down, a reflex when it came to anything Aikawa. Big eyes wide and tearful, she studied me with a quiet intensity that made me squirm.

"Sakurai-san?"

I nodded.

"Want to come in?" she asked, gesturing to the apartment behind her.

"No."

"Oh...okay." She shuffled her feet, pulling her lower lip between her teeth. "I guess we'll just...go then."

She ducked back inside to fetch her bag, leaving the door open. Despite myself, I took a peek inside. Hiro's human life. I'd spent ten years making a conscious effort to avoid picturing it. He'd left his mark on everything, shoes sorted by color, pens and pencils laid out in perfect rows, carefully ordered books, their edges worn from constant reshuffling. His little compulsions. His face smiled back at me from a framed photo on the wall, his arm hooked around Takanori's waist. He looked so happy.

I huffed as Maia appeared in the doorway again, falling into her shoes and fumbling with her keys. With an exasperated sigh, I turned and stomped down the stairs. This was ridiculous. How was I supposed to find Hiro with this clumsy girl in tow?

"Wait, where are we going?" she asked, running to catch up.

"Roppongi."

She wrinkled her nose. "Roppongi? Why?"

"To find Hiro. Isn't that what we're doing here?"

"You're kind of a jerk, aren't you?" she asked, narrowing her eyes and crossing her arms over her chest.

"So I've been told."

"Why would he go to Roppongi? There's nothing but bars and foreigners down there."

"To find something to eat," I answered, my eyes on the street.

"Are you serious?"

"You know him so well, where do you think he went?" I snapped.

Her expression fell, and her arms dropped back to her sides. "I don't know. Anytime I wanted to find him, I just looked for my brother. Cemetery, maybe?"

"You think he could face Takanori after what he did to you?" She didn't answer, her eyes dropping to her toes. "Roppongi then."

We walked in silence for a while, watching the lights of the city grow brighter in the distance. I could feel her eyes on me, sizing me up, and it made my blood boil. A million questions hung in the air around her head, buzzing like flies in the silence.

"What?" I barked.

"Nothing," she said, flinching a little. "I was just...wondering."

"Wondering what?"

"Are you him?"

Something jerked inside and I stopped, squaring myself to face her. Did he tell them about me?

"Him?"

"When he and Taka first started hanging out," she started, kicking at the pavement and avoiding my eyes, "he said he was with somebody. When it ended, he was pretty torn up about it. Hardly moved from Taka's couch for weeks."

Anger and regret cut through me like a heated blade, and I turned my back to hide my flush. *He* was torn up? *He* left *me*. I continued up the road, frustration lengthening my strides until she had to run to keep up.

"It was you, wasn't it?" She was practically giddy, her face lit up with the pride of discovery. I didn't answer, my face twisting into a scowl. "So, what happened?"

"If he didn't tell you, why should I?"

"Oh, come on. It's been ten years. Surely you're over it by now." She skipped a few paces ahead, bouncing backwards on her toes in front of me. I shot her a venomous glare, and her gleeful expression sobered. "You should know, if this is all just some ploy to win him back, he's not ready."

"I know that."

"Do you?" Her eyes were hard but not devoid of sympathy, and something about it made my throat clench. "What he and Taka had was special. I've never seen two people more in love." She swallowed around a lump in her throat and her lips trembled. "He spent the last six months watching Taka die, and his loss blew a hole inside of him the size of a planet. He may never be ready."

The truth of her words was not lost on me, but a smell on the wind stole my attention. Metal and smoke. Blood. Faint but unmistakable. Maia squealed in surprise as I took a hard left turn down a narrow alleyway, my nose tuned to the air. Details emerged as I drew nearer the source. The sweet smell of blood drawn slow from a still-beating heart slid through my lungs and raised bumps over my skin. He was breaking his own rules. He'd taken once today already. I forced myself not to think of the carnage he may have left behind. He wasn't satisfying a need, he was chasing a high.

Son of a bitch.

"Where are you going?"

I had to get rid of her, that clattering girl behind me, but no matter how fast I walked, she kept pace. I burst out of the alleyway into the arterial flow of bodies that made up the jerk and pulse of Roppongi. Head down, I shoved my way through the crowd and the familiar maze of lights. I knew I couldn't protect her. I didn't even know if I wanted to.

Whoever Hiro was taking was still alive. Dread curled like a black snake in my gut. The direction of my feet told me why.

I plunged down a familiar set of stairs and into a cloud of smoke and booze. My eyes burned as they struggled to adjust to the sudden change in lighting. What had been an empty hole in the ground a day ago now rattled with activity. Music blared from overhead, something bright and fast. People bumped into me from every side, their hearts drumming in my ears like hoofbeats.

"Sakurai-san!" Ryo's voice, shrill with panic, rose above the din of the crowd. Led by the smell, I pushed my way toward a door behind the bar, and he threw himself in my path. "Don't go back there."

"I will break you in half, boy," I snarled through clenched teeth. An ember deep inside my heart, one I'd spent centuries trying to snuff out, glowed brighter with every step.

Ryo paled at the fire in my eyes. "I...I know I can't stop you, but—"

A sharp cry drew my attention back to the door behind me. Maia had fallen on the last step and crashed into the back of one of the patrons, sending his drink splashing onto the woman beside him. She muttered a tight apology and bowed before stumbling and pushing her way through the crowd toward us.

"You want to do some good?" I said, grabbing him by the front of his shirt and pointing him toward the girl behind me. "Stop her."

He blinked at me, then at her, before giving me a sharp nod and scurrying off to intercept. I waited long enough to see him take her by the arm before throwing myself through the back door.

There stood Asagi, leaning against the wall of a long corridor, his collar unbuttoned and a cigarette dangling from his lips. Smoke made a lazy curl around his nose and brushed against his cheek. His red eyes flicked up at my entrance, and the corners of his mouth lifted ever so slightly.

"Where is he?"

Asagi's smile dropped and he pushed out a long stream of smoke. "This is quite a mess you've made here, Yoshi."

"I know he's here. What have you done with him?"

"You want the play-by-play?" he said with a snide smile. I grabbed him by the front of his shirt and shoved him into the wall, causing him to drop his cigarette. He clucked in annoyance. "I'm protecting him. You should be thanking me."

"Protecting him from what?"

"From you."

I balked, and my grip loosened just enough for him to shake me off.

"You live in the dark, Yoshi," he said, his lips curling as he straightened his collar. "It's easier for you. Comfortable. But it is no place for that boy. What he needs now, you can't provide."

"He's mine. My responsibility."

"Then stop being selfish for once in your worthless life," he sneered. "Do the right thing. And maybe for once, I won't regret—" He bit off the words, jerking his eyes away from me.

My jaw clenched. I knew what he would say, but I asked anyway, like a dare. "Regret what?"

He turned back to me, teeth bared and pain in his eyes.

"The day I made you."

TWENTY-SIX

Asagi

YOTSUYA 1630

THERE WAS SOMETHING STRANGE ABOUT THAT WOMAN.

I sat at a table in my usual teahouse, positioned along the edge facing the street where I could catch the weak breeze through the open shoji and avoid the sweaty press of bodies inside. I watched her pass by over the rim of my sake glass. She was tall, almost as tall as the dappled grey gelding she walked beside, her height accentuated by her heavily ornamented topknot. Dressed in a bright red kimono, she looked like the lady of a fine house. But she had no escort and none of the bearing —shoulders rolled forward and eyes downcast, except when they flicked up to stare wide-eyed at shop signs and squint into windows.

She pulled herself up as a man approached from the opposite direction and dipped her head in a polite bow of acknowledgment. I hid a snort behind my glass. It was all a show, affectation, like a little girl playing dress up. The corners of my mouth lifted as I watched her crumple back into her more natural posture after the man passed.

I leaned out on my hip, and a tingle crawled up my spine as she moved through my field of vision. There was a broken sort of elegance to her, like a teacup dropped and repaired with gold. Beautiful but fragile. It had been awhile since I'd been so enthralled by another person.

"Okyakusama?" The server, a small, mouse-like girl, a fresh sake bottle in her hands, caught my attention just before I tipped over entirely.

"Do you know anything about that woman?" I asked as she set the bottle in front of me. She leaned out the doorway to follow my eyeline, a strange expression on her face. When she turned back to me, her face was pinched as if she'd just bitten into a strong umeboshi.

"Oh, pardon me, Okyakusama." She leaned closer and lowered her voice. "That's Arakawa Asagi."

"Arakawa?" I knew the name by reputation. A once-samurai family turned merchants, but no less powerful. It explained the displayed affluence, but something was off. This person didn't move with the confidence of an heiress of a prominent family, but the caution of a pretender one false move away from being outed. Arakawa Asagi was hiding something.

I leaned out again to find her tying her horse, then snapping open a fan and ducking through the doorway of the teahouse. She moved with a practiced grace, one that knew she was being watched, judged.

And she was. Half a dozen pairs of eyes dragged over her as she stepped inside. Her back stiffened as if she wanted to hunch to mask her height. Her too-broad shoulders strained against the urge to curl inward as she met the gaze of her onlookers with a defiant glare over the top of her fan. Asagi's eyes landed on me for the briefest of moments and sent a prickle over my skin. It must have been a trick of the light. Even her eyes were red.

I tugged on my server's sleeve as she started to move away. "Invite her to join me."

The girl gave me a strange look before bowing and moving away. The server conveyed my invitation and Asagi stiffened, thin brows pulling together. Asagi bowed lightly before pulling herself up tall and drifting toward me.

"Have a seat," I said, gesturing to the space across from me. She wrinkled her nose, glaring at the mat as if it were booby trapped, before snapping her fan closed and dropping down onto the mat. She arranged herself carefully, broad hands smoothing the lines of her kimono. She pulled a long pipe out of her obi and packed the bowl, casting me a questioning glance before lighting it. The server appeared again to drop off a second sake cup and I filled it, pushing it in her direction.

Asagi peered at me through a cloud of sweet smoke, eyes narrowed, corners of her painted lips slightly lifted. It wasn't a trick. Her eyes were red, a deep red like blood pooled on dirt.

"Pardon me, O-Samurai-san," she said after a long silence. Her voice was soft and low. An effort to hide its pitch, perhaps. "Why am I here?"

"Safer than sitting alone, I expect."

She laughed a deep, short laugh. "I don't need your protection."

I shrugged and sipped from my sake.

"O-Samurai—"

"Sakurai."

She blinked. "Excuse me?"

"My name," I said around the rim of my glass. "Sakurai Hideyoshi."

"My, what a mouthful," she said with a sly smile.

"A gift from my father and my daimyo."

"Your daimyo?"

"Toyotomi Hideyori."

Asagi's eyebrows lifted, and she sucked in a breath. I was a young man when Hideyori suffered his great defeat in Osaka under Tokugawa Ieyasu. My father, Sakurai Yoshinori, served him before I did and had given his life protecting what remained of his meager holdings just the year before. The character he gave me should have been a mark of shame, one I would labor under forever as the soldier of a vanquished army, yet I bore it with pride, a small act of defiance against the shogun who fancied himself an emperor.

Asagi eyed the sword leaning against the table. "Now you serve under Tokugawa."

"Mn."

"That makes you either a traitor or an opportunist."

"It makes me a realist," I said, a curl of offense souring the wine in my belly. "We rarely get the chance to choose our leaders. I chose to neither die with my daimyo nor hang my head in shame for having served him. I choose instead to continue to serve."

"And if the one you serve betrays you?"

"Then I'll have another choice to make, won't I?"

Asagi released a huff of a laugh, knocked the coal out of her pipe, and tucked it back into her obi. "Well, *Yoshi*-san, I appreciate your concern, but if you don't mind—"

"You're leaving?"

"Yes."

"But you haven't even drunk your sake."

A wrinkle formed on the bridge of her nose. It was disorienting looking at her. What from afar appeared to be a beautiful woman was up close so obviously something else, and yet no less alluring. Her eyes never left mine as she lifted her sake glass, and I choked back a surprised laugh when she tossed it back in a single swallow. I admired her. She gave no ground, even to me.

"Now if you'll pardon me, Yoshi-san." Asagi gave a curt bow before pulling herself to her feet and stomping out of the teahouse. A dozen pairs of eyes followed, and people whispered behind their hands.

I let her get all the way out the door before I jumped up to follow. She'd just reached her horse when I emerged. She didn't bother to hide her annoyance.

"You're going to follow me now?" she huffed.

"You put me in an awkward position."

"You put yourself in an awkward position."

I laughed. "You see, as samurai, I am obligated to certain noble families—"

"I am not of a noble family." She yanked at the horse's tether, managing only to knot it tighter.

"No? Aren't you Arakawa?"

Her hands froze on the knot. Her lips trembled, and she pulled in a shaky breath. Her eyes went momentarily glassy, and my chest tightened. She shook herself, releasing that held breath in a huff before working the knot again. The horse whinnied as she finally pulled the reins free and yanked the animal back toward the road.

"If you need help, you can call on me."

She paused, only her eyes and her elaborate topknot visible over the neck of her horse. "Why?"

I shrugged. Her brows lowered, and the horse chuffed between us as Asagi released an exasperated breath.

My belly warmed. Probably the sake. I bowed without breaking eye contact. "I hope to see you again, Arakawa-san."

She tugged on her horse's reins, disappearing behind the horse. "Sayonara, Yoshi-san."

I SPENT ALL OF MY SECOND BOTTLE OF SAKE AND HALF OF A THIRD completely occupied with thoughts of Asagi. The way she moved, the way she spoke, as if the weight of all the stares and whispers pressed down on the words. She'd learned the manner of the nobles, but it was like watching a performer in a play—shallow, two-dimensional, and fragile as glass. One tap in the wrong place and it would all shatter.

Part of me wanted that, wanted to pound on that barrier between us and expose her true self. Idle curiosity? Maybe. Or maybe I just wanted to hear her say my name again. *Yoshi.* The stain on my reputation removed.

The sky was dark when I finally left the teahouse and made a slightly wobbly path toward my rented room. Paper lamps on poles painted with the marks of the local trade jutted out from the squat, wooden buildings, highlighting everything in a soft, shuddering light. They swayed in the wind, giving life to the ink-black shadows. People lingered in pockets around restaurants and izakayas, voices loud and faces flushed with drink.

My sandals scraped against the hard-packed earth as I wandered past, gravitating toward a dark recess flanked by lamps on stone pillars. A shrine sat tucked away against the side of an inn, its small garden a haven of quiet against the usual bustle of the street. A wooden torri no taller than a man marked the entrance to the shrine itself. A miniature building with a sloping roof decorated with paper chains sat atop a plinth guarded by a weathered stone fox, a shrine to a local deity whose name I'd never heard.

I tossed a coin into the offering box, clapped my hands together in front of my nose, and let my heart go quiet. The sounds of the world dropped away one by one, until it was just me and the spirit that inhabited that place. Or so I thought, until a light sniffling broke the silence. A figure hunched on a bench in the farthest corner of the garden.

"Arakawa-san?"

At first I thought I'd been mistaken, as a man in a deep-green kimono jerked to his feet, wiping his face with his sleeve. But there was no mistaking those red eyes. The same tingle I had felt in the teahouse slipped up my spine. The difference between the girl I met that afternoon and the man before me was striking. His hair had been brushed out and pulled into a simple knot at his crown, his face washed and pink. All his earlier ornament was gone, save for a leather strap tied around his wrist decorated with delicate beads that caught the meager light in flashes of orange and white. His wide-eyed gaze skipped over me, and his cheeks colored as if I'd caught him doing something scandalous.

"What are you doing here?" Even his voice was different, deep and rough with a crack in it. He tried to pull his shoulders straight, but they trembled as if under a great weight. "I told you," he said after a shaky breath, "I don't need your protection."

"I'm not here to protect you." I took a step forward and he flinched, eyes narrowed as he watched me make a path to the bench and sit. He frowned down his nose at me as I sat in silence, hands tucked into my sleeves.

"Please don't stare," he said, shifting his weight away from me.

"You have unusual eyes."

"I have a condition." He bit the words off quickly, leaving no room for further questions. I huffed a laugh and turned my attention back to the shrine. Silence settled around us, broken only by the occasional call of insects and the clinking of the beads around Asagi's wrist.

"What are you up to?" he asked.

"Who says I'm up to something?"

"Why else would you be here?"

I gestured to the torri. "It is a shrine."

He scoffed, crossing his arms over his broad chest. "You pray to spirits? For what? A long life?"

"What makes you think I don't?"

"You're a killer," he spat, eyeing the sword at my hip.

"I'm a soldier."

"Is there a difference?"

Heat sizzled up my spine. "Are you always so rude?"

He opened his mouth to respond but clapped it shut before the words could escape, his cheeks flushed. He released a long breath through his nose. "Only when I'm hungry."

I laughed and reached into the folds of my kimono, pulling out a bag of dried plums I'd purchased from the teahouse. I held them out to him on my palm, but he balked.

"Go on. I didn't poison them."

Asagi blinked, his brows lowering. With the wariness of a stray cat, he stretched out his fingers and plucked up the little bag. Rolling the fruits around with his fingers, he sank down onto the bench beside me. His shoulders sagged forward, as if whatever had been holding up his anger had collapsed. A dense silence gathered around us that I dared not break.

"I'm not Arakawa," he said finally, teasing the bag open with his fingertips. "Not really."

"Oh. All right."

He pulled a plum out and held it under his nose before dropping it back into the bag with a shaky breath. The warmth in my belly rose to my chest, and I swallowed it down.

"Are you praying for a long life?" I asked.

"What?"

I pointed with my eyes to the shrine.

"Oh." He swallowed hard, eyes glistening in the dark. "I'm here for a friend."

"A friend in need of guidance?"

"He's dying."

His words hit like a punch to the heart. "I'm sorry." He took a shaky breath and closed his eyes. "Is he sick? Are you in need of a doctor?"

Asagi shook his head. "He's very old. His time is simply coming to an end."

"Then what do you pray for?"

"To ease his pain." He opened his eyes, the red irises molten in the sparse light. His fingers slipped into the sleeve of his kimono and ran over the strap on his wrist. A few of the beads had worn almost completely smooth. This raw, unguarded version of him made my head spin. I thought of the sharp-tongued woman I'd met in the teahouse and wondered which version was real. Perhaps he wore her as armor, the stronger person he wished to be, the person better equipped to handle such tragedy.

"You're scared."

He pinned me with a hard glare. "I'm not scared."

"Lonely then."

Asagi's brows lifted, and his stern expression unwound into something gentler. I saw it there, the sadness, the longing slipping and sliding just beneath the surface. I leaned toward him, transfixed by the play of shadows over his cheeks and across his nose. The warmth in my chest burst into a flame, and my hand twitched with the urge to brush those shadows away.

"I was married once," I said, pulling my gaze away from him and back to the shrine. "When I was young. Barely seventeen. It was arranged by my father. The daughter of another samurai family. I resisted it at first with all the bile of a teenage boy, but when we met…"

"You fell in love with her," Asagi finished softly.

"Mn." I rubbed my hands together in my lap as a creeping ache started in them. "Barely a year later she was pregnant. We were scared, excited, happy. But then she started feeling weak. We called on the finest doctors our fathers could afford, but they hardly knew anything about a woman's body, let alone a pregnant one. She just kept getting weaker and all I could do was watch."

I took a deep breath and blinked back the mist that had formed over my eyes before facing Asagi again.

"People think that mourning starts with death, but that's not exactly true." A heavy feeling started in my chest, and I pushed it away. "You will miss him."

His eyes welled and he looked away, pressing his knuckles against his lips. A single tear slipped down his cheek, and I touched the track with my thumb. Made brave by the drink, I leaned even closer, pressing myself to his side. I would have sworn he leaned back.

"Stop, Yoshi!"

I gasped as he burst out of his seat, slapping the bag of plums against my chest before stomping away. The anger was back, hardening all the sharp angles of him, and he cut the darkness like a blade.

"Stop what?"

"Stop trying to save me." He spun back around on me. "I don't want it. I don't need it."

I jerked to my feet. "Stubborn, prideful woman!"

"I am not a woman, you idiot." He threw the declaration at me like a weapon, but his voice cracked when he said it.

"I didn't mean—" A flash of shame ran through me. In a fit of temper, I'd taken the low road and flung gender at him like an insult. His shoulders shook, and fat drops wet his cheeks. He was falling apart, and all I wanted to do was hold him together. "You don't have to be alone."

He froze. I took one cautious step forward, then another. I reached a hand out. Asagi sucked in a breath and closed his eyes as my fingers grazed his arm. My heart thrumming in my ears, I pulled closer. He swayed toward me. I held my breath.

"Stay away from me," he said in a hoarse voice before brushing me off and disappearing into the night.

TWENTY-SEVEN

Yutaka

YOTSUYA 1630

I FLOPPED AROUND ON MY RENTED FUTON, SKIN SUPER-HEATED AND teeth grinding. I told myself it was the sake. I drank too much. That's why my head was spinning, not because of that strange, beautiful, *frustrating* person I'd met in the teahouse. The one who wore anger like armor over a broken heart, whose vulnerability drew me in even as their volatility pushed me away. But every time I closed my eyes, I saw red and they flew open again.

I gave up as the shoji turned orange with the rising sun. Too much drink and too little sleep made my head throb as I wrestled my way into my kimono and stomped across town to bang on the door of a man who owed me a favor.

"Nakagawa-sensei!" I pounded on the wooden shutters hard enough to make the whole building shake. "Open the door."

A muffled curse followed a crash and then a set of short, stubby fingers appeared around the shutter and wrenched it aside. Nakagawa Jin's bald head appeared, his weathered face scrunched up against the morning light. He blinked and scrubbed his eyes as he struggled to focus.

"Sakurai-sama," he wheezed, a combination of surprise and annoyance. "What are you doing here? The sun isn't even fully up yet." He flinched and pressed his hand under his nose. "Mattaku, did you sleep *inside* the wine bottle last night?"

"I need your help." I shoved the door fully open and forced my way inside. The one-room house was dark and mostly empty, with the exception of a tall apothecary cabinet against the back wall and a disheveled futon on the floor. The remains of last night's fire left a sharp scent on the air, mixing with pungent herbs and incense strong enough to make me sneeze.

"How many times have I told you, Sakurai-sama," he started with a weary shake of his head, "there's no cure for hangover but sleep and time."

"Anything in this cabinet that can help with pain?" I asked, pulling open one of the little drawers and peering inside.

Nakagawa slapped my hand away. "Are you injured?"

"No."

"Sick?"

"No."

"Then I have nothing for you." He pointed at the door and scowled. "The headache will pass on its own. Now—"

"It's not for me."

The doctor squinted at me, mouth twisting with suspicion.

A low heat simmered around my collar and crawled up my neck. "Arakawa Asagi." Nakagawa made a sour face. "You know him?"

"We've met. A very strange, very *rude* person." He scratched his sandpaper chin and crossed his arms over his chest. "I take it this is about the old man? I told Arakawa-san already. His liver is failing. There's nothing more I can do for him."

"So you'll just let him suffer?"

A twitch of sadness crossed his face. "Despite appearances, Arakawa-san is not wealthy. That person is Arakawa in name only, and I can barely keep myself fed. Judge me all you want. I can't afford to work for free."

Anger stewed in my gut as Asagi's tear-streaked face from the night before filled my vision. I took a step toward the doctor, pulled a silk purse filled with coins out of the collar of my kimono, and thrust it into his hand.

"You work for me now," I pushed out between gritted teeth.

Nakagawa blanched and shrank under my shadow, but his color quickly returned as he opened the purse and poked the coins with a finger. With a resigned sigh, he stashed the purse in his own collar before pulling out a canvas satchel and filling it with bottles and packets of medicines from the cabinet. Throwing a tattered haori over his sleep clothes, he tossed me a tired look and stomped out the door.

"Well, come on."

I followed his lead away from Yotsuya, the sun warming our backs, and down a dirt path that culminated in a widely spaced cluster of modest homes. Each sat on a moderate parcel of land. We wove our way through scraggly vegetable gardens toward a house at the back end of the bunch. The one-room farmhouse slouched on its beams, a thin ribbon of smoke crawling out of its crooked roof toward the sky. A line stretched between one corner of the roof to a nearby tree, and for a moment I thought it the only thing keeping the house standing. A small, thin woman stood next to it with a basket of wet laundry, back to us and eyes on her hands.

"Oi!" Nakagawa called out as soon as we reached hearing distance. The woman turned, a damp sheet in her hands and a worried look on her small face. "Is your master home?"

She opened her mouth to answer, but before she could, the front door snapped open and Asagi appeared, hair pulled into a messy bun and dark circles under his eyes. He stopped short when he saw me, a mix of emotions vibrating through his body in waves—surprise, confusion, anger.

"Yoshi." My name came out a curse, and he pulled his threadbare haori tighter around his broad frame. His two sides seemed at war within him, his girlish modesty conflicting with the hardness of his voice. Red eyes darted between me and the doctor. "Why are you here?"

"Because I'd like to get some sleep."

Nakagawa pushed past me and onto the engawa. He reached a hand out to the shoji, and Asagi flung an arm in his path.

"Do you want my help or not?" Nakagawa barked.

Asagi's eyes narrowed, and his voice went tight. "You've already refused to help me."

"Wrong. I refused to help you for free." Nakagawa gestured over his shoulder at me. "I've already been paid, whether you accept my services or not."

Asagi's brows shot up, and he turned wide, shining eyes onto me. I shrugged and nodded, biting back a smile. Slowly, Asagi's arm lowered. Nakagawa whipped the shoji open and disappeared inside. I moved to follow, but Asagi stopped me with a hand on my arm.

"You should know I can't repay you," he said in a thick voice.

"Did I ask for repayment?" I leaned in close. "Next time you need help, ask for it."

His mouth opened to protest, but I pushed past into the house before he could. The one-room farmhouse was nearly bare inside, save for a stack of kimono boxes in the corner and a chest covered with cosmetics and brightly colored accessories. A sword leaned up against the wall, its saya scuffed and battle-worn, though it obviously hadn't seen use in some time. A fire burned low in the brazier, and the incense burning somewhere in the house did nothing to cover the distinct sour smell of sickness. An old man lay on a futon, curled on his side and covered up to his chin in a thin blanket.

Nakagawa was already down on his knees beside the old man, a grim expression on his face as he placed a hand on his pale forehead. The old man's skin was thin and yellowed, his lips cracked and gray. Nakagawa pulled the blanket back a bit, exposing a frail frame. The old man moaned as the doctor poked at his belly, though he showed no real awareness of the rest of us.

"Yutaka-san," the doctor called gently, squeezing the old man's shoulder. He gave no reaction. Nakagawa turned his attention to Asagi. "How long has he been like this?"

"Four days." Asagi made no effort to conceal the pain in his voice. His gaze was locked on the old man, eyes glistening. His fingers found the beads on his wrist again and worried them until they creaked. I ached for him, for the helplessness I knew he felt and the contradictory pain of both anticipating and dreading the end.

"Does he eat?"

Asagi shook his head, causing precariously perched tears to fall, and he swiped at his cheeks. "A little broth sometimes, but that's all."

Asagi stood very close beside me, pressing even closer when the doctor rummaged around in his bag and pulled out a handful of folded paper packets. He tore one open and gently urged the old man's mouth open.

"What is that?" Asagi asked in a stiff voice.

"Does it matter?" Nakagawa barked. I cleared my throat sharply, and he sighed. "Just some herbs. Nothing dangerous. It'll make him more comfortable." He tipped the old man's head back and poured the contents of the packet on his tongue. He swallowed reflexively, face twitching. Nakagawa sat back on his heels, and silence descended over us. Asagi's fingers curled in my sleeve, and he held his breath.

The old man's face slowly relaxed and his eyes fluttered, eliciting a gasp from Asagi. Nakagawa yelped as Asagi pushed him aside and fell to his knees beside the old man. His eyes rolled and struggled to focus. The fog receded a little when they found Asagi. Dry lips parted on a sigh, and he lifted a trembling hand and traced a line down the bridge of Asagi's nose.

Asagi released a tearful laugh before catching the old man's hand in his and pressing it against his lips. My chest ached, and I fought down a ball of emotion that lodged itself in my sinuses. The old man was still dying of course, but we'd given him and Asagi back to each other, even if only for a moment. Suddenly, the money I'd paid Nakagawa didn't seem nearly enough.

Nakagawa slapped me on the shoulder and directed me out of the house. Once outside, we both took a deep, meaningful breath. Even Nakagawa's rough edges had softened, as he raked a tired hand through his matted hair. My mind remained with Asagi on the walk home and on the emptiness he would soon face.

"How long does he have?" I asked.

"Days at most," Nakagawa answered, eyes on the road.

"What is their relationship?"

Nakagawa shrugged. "Don't know. Grandfather maybe? Though I get the impression Arakawa-san doesn't have much in the way of family."

"He'll be alone," I said, more to myself than to him.

"Mn."

Nakagawa gave me a stiff bow as we parted ways. As I returned to my room to sleep off the remains of my hangover, I knew that after today things would be different.

TWENTY-EIGHT

A Mistake

YOTSUYA 1630

I DIDN'T SEE OR HEAR FROM ASAGI FOR TWO DAYS, THOUGH I THOUGHT of him often. I even had the impulse to visit him once, but then I remembered what Nakagawa had told me and it felt like an imposition. *Days at most*, he'd said. I wondered if this was his final day, his final hour, his final minute. Every moment until then was precious, and my appearance would only serve to divide his attention, something he might later come to regret. I hurt for Asagi, this strange person I had met only days ago, yet who monopolized my every thought.

On the night of the third day, I jerked awake at the sound of my door sliding closed. I sprung upright, my hand instinctively reaching for my sword. I fought back the fog of impending hangover and squinted into the dark. Piece by piece, a form emerged, clad all in white and leaning back against the door. Long black hair. Red eyes.

"Asagi?"

He jerked and pressed himself tighter against the door as if about to flee. Something in his expression sent pins through my veins.

"Is something wrong?"

"He's gone." His lips wobbled, and he hid his face behind his hand.

"Oh."

"You're right. I'm scared," he said through a sob. "I've never been alone before. Not like this."

A shiver crossed my heart, and my throat tightened. Asagi's hand dropped from his face, exposing tear-stained cheeks and red-rimmed eyes. After a shaky breath, he took one long step and fell to his knees into the futon beside me.

"Why do you care what happens to me?" Tears still leaked from his eyes, but his expression had hardened into earnest curiosity. "Why did you help me? Why did you...tell me about your wife?"

My heart fluttered like a wounded bird. "I don't know."

"Are you a good person, Sakurai Hideyoshi?"

I opened my mouth to answer but nothing came out. I wanted to believe I was a good person, but could I honestly say it was true? I drank too much, was too quick to anger, and served a leader who killed both my father and my daimyo. Was there really any difference between a soldier and a killer? Asagi took my face in his hands as I tried to look away, forcing my gaze back to his.

As our eyes met, something happened. My pounding heart lurched as if something had latched onto it. I froze, and his red irises swelled to encompass my entire vision. I came unmoored, cast into a red sea and pulled into its depths. A heady rush consumed me, the kind of drunk only attained with the finest liquors.

All at once, the feeling disappeared, replaced with the warmth of lips pressed to mine, a gentle, salt-flavored caress. The rush returned, only this time it started in my chest. It permeated through my skin all the way to the tips of my fingers and the ends of my toes. I melted into it until a splinter of awareness had me pulling back.

"Wait. What are you doing?" I asked breathlessly.

"Something stupid, probably."

Before I could think, he grabbed the front of my shirt and crashed his lips into mine. I grabbed him by the shoulders as our teeth clashed.

"Wait. Just wait a minute," I said, forcing us apart. He clung to me, to my hair, to my clothes. Blood rushed to my skin as his gasping breaths brushed my lips.

"I don't want to be alone."

His words cut down deep inside me, releasing a flood of my own loneliness that made me weak. My empty futon felt cold. How long had it been since another person had warmed my bed? I understood him then, the need to drown his pain, the need to feel alive in the face of death. He'd come to me in his darkest moment looking for comfort, and I wanted to give it to him so bad my bones ached.

That disorienting feeling overtook me again as I slid my hands up the line of his neck and closed the distance between us. His eyelids fluttered closed and he released a sigh. This time his lips were soft, yielding and opening to me like flowers in the rain.

I hooked one arm around his waist and pulled him onto my lap. The way he moved, the sounds he made, were all so much like a woman, yet the body pressed against mine was all man. Broad chest, thick thighs, strong hands. I groaned as he wound them in my hair just tight enough to sting.

"*Mattaku*, where did you come from?" I asked between fevered breaths. I was drunk all over again, and the words slurred together.

"Shut up."

He yanked my head back, pushed his nose under my chin, and inhaled deeply. I thought suddenly of the way he'd held those plums under his nose. Chills ran through me as his tongue flicked over my skin, followed by flames as he pinched it between his teeth.

"Asagi…"

"I said, shut up."

My heart clanged a warning against my ribs as his grip on me changed. No longer sensual but forceful. I tried to pull back, but his arm around my shoulders held me tight, my throat stretched long and vulnerable under his bared teeth. He was strong. Stronger than he should have been.

"What are you—"

My breath caught as a sharp pain ripped through my veins. Every muscle tensed, spasmed, locked. A splash of euphoria colored my vision, and my skin went cold. Bleeding.

I was bleeding. I'd suffered enough battlefield wounds to know what it felt like, and yet I bore no injury.

Except where Asagi bit me.

My vision tilted as I kicked and clawed at him, one hand wrapping around his neck. A purr rumbled through him, and his Adam's apple bounced against my palm—a swallow, drinking. A strange, electric tingle crawled over my skin, almost pleasurable, almost sensual, like it could feel good if I would just stop fighting.

"What...are you?"

The dark closed in, and my limbs grew heavy. I tried to hold on, but I couldn't. I swooned. I fell. Asagi lowered me back down to the futon, and I sank into it as if it were made of smoke, down through the floor and into the ground.

I was dying.

When Asagi raised his head, he had changed again. The darkness under his eyes was gone, his hollow cheeks full and flushed. My blood colored his lips crimson, and he hummed as he ran his tongue over them.

"Look at me, Yoshi," he said, cupping my face in his hands. He stroked my cheek with his thumbs, coaxing my eyes back to his. They met with a snap like a banner on the wind. All my fear, anger, confusion melted away, leaving only blind adoration. My tired heart burst with it, struggled and fought and leaped with the promise of it.

"Now drink."

His lips pressed to mine, and something sweet passed between us. I swallowed, and it burst through my veins like gunpowder, igniting in my muscles. It rushed to my head like the strongest sake. Where I had been buried, now I was floating, flying on wings he'd given me. I didn't know what it was. It didn't matter. I wanted more.

And then it was gone, and I dropped into darkness once again.

TWENTY-NINE

Control Your Heart

YOTSUYA 1630

I WOKE WITH THE WORST HANGOVER I'D EVER HAD. EVERY SOUND TOO loud, every light too bright. My muscles burned and spasmed, wringing cries from me that rang off the walls. I clapped my hands over my ears and squeezed my eyes shut.

Was I dying? Was I dead?

"Pull yourself together. I thought you were a soldier."

That voice. Familiar and yet deeply out of place, as if from a dream. Fractured memories cut through my consciousness like glass—red eyes, strong hands, the taste of blood on soft lips.

I cracked my eyes open. Socked feet paced a circuit of my small room, the hem of a white yukata swirling around them. The tatami squeaked under the balls of his feet with every change of direction, sending an electric shock over my skin.

He was real. This was real.

"What's happening to me?" I asked, flinching at the sound of my own voice. I pressed my nose into the futon, groaning as it cut into my skin. "What have you done to me?"

His pacing stopped, and the air thickened as he hovered over me. "I've made you."

"I feel like I'm dying."

"Maybe you are." He lowered himself to his knees and took me by the chin almost tenderly. "But I've given you the power to turn it away."

Are you praying for a long life?

I blinked up at him, light with a sudden sense of wonder. "Are you...a kami?" I asked, breathless.

His eyes darkened, and his lips pressed into a trembling line. "No," he said, tracing his thumb along the line of my jaw. "Youkai."

His fingers on my skin sent a wash of warmth through me, carrying some of my fear away with it. The wonder hardened into something darker, and I clutched his arm as my eyes made a halting path up to his. Brows low, mouth pinched, he studied me with a guarded expression. He held me just long enough for me to feel the pull of his heart on mine —that terrible, unbreakable bond—before jerking away and getting to his feet. He towered over me, looking down his nose coldly before pivoting toward the door.

"Where are you going?" I asked, voice pinched with panic.

"You need to eat."

"Wait. Don't leave. Take me with you," I said, scrambling across the floor on my knees. I tried to stand, but my muscles screamed in protest, sending me back to the floor.

"Look at yourself," he growled, kicking my hands away as I grasped at the hem of his yukata. "You're a mess. I have a name to uphold. I can't be seen with you."

"Asagi—"

"Control your heart, Yoshi," he spat.

In a rush of fabric and the *snak* of a sliding door, he was gone and I was alone in a dizzying whirlwind of sensations and emotions. *Control your heart.* I wanted to obey him. More than anything, I wanted to obey him, but the world was suddenly too big, too much. The moment he disappeared out the door, it assaulted me with sounds and smells and colors. The familiar perceived with a new clarity. The bite of the tatami on my knees, the sound of the cicadas outside my window, the flicker of an oil lamp.

I squeezed my eyes shut and tried to focus on one thing at a time. I covered my ears and listened only to the sound of my own heartbeat until it drowned out everything else. I sucked in deep breaths, the air thick with humidity and tasting of burned oil and wet grass. I counted each one until they slowed to a more regular rhythm, and only then did I force myself to open my eyes.

It could have been minutes or hours before he returned. He found me with my nose pressed to a painted screen, examining the minute brushstrokes of each pink plum blossom.

"Yoshi." Disappointment curled his lips and wrinkled his brow when I turned to face him, and it crushed me. All my attention focused on the sound of a heartbeat, fast and loud and calling to something dark inside me.

A young man no more than twenty was locked in Asagi's grip. He had a long face and lean frame and was clothed in the typical simple kimono of a tradesman, threadbare at the elbows and ragged at the hem. He wore a drunken expression, his eyes glazed and faraway. But none of that mattered. The longer I looked, the less I saw a man and the more I saw the ethereal light inside him. It flowed beneath his skin in bright rivers, some thick as ropes, others thin as hairs, and coalesced into a ball in his chest. It glowed a bright white that blotted out everything else.

Whatever spell Asagi had cast on him began to wear off. He blinked and shook his head, as if ridding himself of cobwebs. His eyes jerked down to Asagi's hand wrapped around his arm, and he made a startled sound. He tugged against it, growing panic twisting his features. The riot inside me quieted as I took a step forward. He shrank back as I reached out to touch him.

When my fingers made contact with his skin, something happened, a tingle and a snap like a sword settling into its saya. Something flowed between us, insubstantial as breath, carrying with it a tumble of emotions that left me dizzy. Fear, excitement, hunger. No, not hunger— need. His eyes glazed over and his expression calmed. Asagi released him and he didn't run.

"Interesting," Asagi said.

Instinct took over, and I pulled the young man to me. A rope of light cut from just beneath his jawline to below his collar. My mouth watered. I bared my teeth. Asagi caught me by the throat, stopping me short before I could act on that terrible urge. "You leave his life right where it is, understand me?" he snarled. "It doesn't belong to you."

I didn't know what he meant, but I nodded anyway. He released me, and I plunged my newfound fangs into the young man's neck. Light poured out of him and into me, down into my very core, and something dark rose up to meet it. I drank greedily, groaning as my muscles twitched and contracted with something sharper and hotter than arousal. In some dark corner of my mind, I knew it was blood. I knew the metallic taste, the hot, sticky texture, but I didn't care. It filled my veins and blanked my mind. With every pull, it swelled within me, swallowing the light and my riotous emotions with it until I became a monster, feeling only the pleasures it brought.

"Stop, Yoshi!"

Asagi's voice cut through the fog. He grabbed me by the back of my collar, yanked me off the man's neck, and reality snapped back in around me. I tried to hold onto it, that emptiness, terrible as it was. But as the man slipped from my hands, despair crept in. Blood dried on my face, its coppery taste filled my mouth. That man, once so warm and alive, now cooled beneath me.

"What have I done?"

"You've killed him," Asagi growled, swinging his fiery glare back to me.

"But...I..." My head reeled. I reached out a hand to touch the dead man, sure it was all some kind of nightmare and he would disappear into a vapor.

"I thought you were strong. Honorable. A good man." Asagi's voice pinched and his eyes welled. Disgust twisted his mouth into an evil knot. "But you're just a killer."

I protested violently even as my soul shattered, but he turned his back on me. I grabbed at his sleeve and he shoved me hard, knocking me to the ground so that I was face-to-face with the man's corpse, his eyes clouded, his face waxy and pale. I'd taken it, that life that didn't belong to me.

"I am strong," I stammered, pushing myself up off the ground. But Asagi was already gone.

I staggered out into the night, drunk with first blood. Everything was different, brighter, sharper, louder. There were no people, only smears of light in my vision. I bit into one just as I had the first. I took the light into myself and felt cleansed of fear and doubt and the pain of betrayal, only truly realizing what I had done when I saw the corpse I left behind.

I'd taken lives before, but it never felt like this. No matter what noble cause I fought for, death had always felt like a tragedy. This was different. These lives weren't wasted, poured out on some battlefield fighting for men who didn't care about them. These lives were changed, enhanced, elevated, used as fuel for the dark engine that drove me. I killed again and again, plunging myself into the nothing until it felt like home. It was easy. I struck from the shadows. They didn't scream or fight as long as my skin touched theirs. As each body slipped cold from my grip, I remembered the disgust in Asagi's eyes. The next washed it away. I must have killed twenty people in that one night, each one chipping away at my sanity until finally, *finally*, I drowned my human heart in blood and emerged a monster.

After the sun came up, I found Asagi lounging in an izakaya, smoking from a long pipe and whispering in a man's ear. He'd donned all the ornament of our first meeting, his white obi the only indication of his mourning. Cosmetics hid the shadows under his eyes, but they were still red and raw. His smile lit a spark of jealousy, despite how it trembled at the corners. The comfort he'd originally sought in me, he now sought elsewhere.

His expression soured when he saw me lurking in the street outside like a phantom. He flashed a sweet smile at his consort, making some pretty excuse before coming outside to meet me.

I can only imagine how I must have looked, dead-eyed and expressionless, reeking of the blood of my victims. He said nothing at first, just examined me, watching my face for some hint of the emotional mess I was before.

"I am strong," I said, swaying in drunken exhaustion.

His expression hardened into something unreadable. "Is this what you call strength? Look at you. You can barely stand. You've destroyed yourself, turned yourself into a mindless beast. And for what? That's not strength, it's cowardice."

"But...my heart—"

"Is not under control," he spat, "it's controlling you."

"Why did you do this to me?" I asked in a gravelly voice.

Asagi's lips trembled, and his eyes went glassy. "Because...I thought…" He bit the words off, shaking himself and making the pins in his hair swing. When he spoke again, he pushed the words out from between clenched teeth. "It was a mistake. Stay away from me. Tell no one who made you."

And with the pain of those words, I swore never to lose my heart again.

THIRTY

A World Made of Glass

SPRING 2004

I ROCKED BACK ON MY HEELS. I THOUGHT I WAS PAST IT, THAT IT couldn't hurt me anymore, but his words knocked the air out of me. I stumbled backward until I hit the wall, panting, one hand clutching my chest as if he'd punched me. We stood in silence, on opposite sides of a great chasm we could never cross. I'd done as he said. I took the truth of that night and buried it down deep, told no one, not even Hiro. I had no maker.

But as much as I'd tried to smother his presence in my heart, how I'd drowned it in booze and hate, it was still there.

"What's the matter, Yoshi?" he asked, lips curling, though his voice was tired. "Is it hurting you? That heart you pretend you don't have?"

My vision wavered as the door at the end of the hall swung open. Hiro emerged, pale, dark circles etched under his eyes, all traces of the bright, passionate boy I'd taken into my life so many years ago overrun by grief. Asagi was right. I couldn't understand his pain. I lived in the dark. But it was not comfortable and it was not easy, and I would do anything to keep it from devouring Hiro's heart.

"What are you doing here?" His voice was paper thin.

"He's here to save you," Asagi answered with a smug grin.

"I don't need saving."

His words fell hard on my back, making my shoulders hunch. Asagi straightened his collar with a sigh and laid a hand on my arm.

"Maybe this time you should listen."

I brushed him off, my attention focused on Hiro. I wanted to feel all those things he needed me to feel, to give him the things he needed to be whole again. But if I allowed myself to feel his presence in my heart, I would have to feel Asagi's too.

"Fine." I forced the word past the knot in my throat, and it came out mangled. I slipped my hand into my pocket and pulled out Hiro's damaged phone. I bounced it in my palm a couple of times before pulling myself up straight and holding it out.

He blinked, eyes searching as they always did, before reaching out to take it. Our fingers brushed, and in a moment of panic so bright it blinded me, I grabbed him by the wrist.

"I know the monster you're fighting, Hiro," I said in a voice lower than a whisper. "And I know how much easier it is to just feel nothing. But promise me one thing." My grip tightened, and my voice wavered. "Promise me that you won't stop fighting. That you won't give in to the darkness. That you won't be...like me."

His eyes welled and his lips parted. Before he could respond, a commotion just outside the door snapped our attention to it. Two voices —one male, one female. Hiro tensed and sucked in a breath.

"Maia."

My heart rate spiked, and my skin went cold. *Stupid girl!* I jerked Hiro's attention back to me. "You want to hate me? Fine. But that girl needs you," I said from between clenched teeth. "Come back to her."

The door burst open, eliciting a squeal from Asagi, and Maia came tumbling through. Ryo followed closely behind, clutching desperately at her arms. Her efforts redoubled when she spotted Hiro, eyes wide and watery, cheeks flushed. She slipped Ryo's grip and shot down the hall toward us.

I caught her around the waist just before she reached Hiro. She thrashed and clawed at me, calling his name. I wrapped one hand around her arm, the other shoved under the hem of her shirt and pressed flat against the skin of her back.

"Stop, Maia."

My skin warmed where it met hers, tingling with the magic flowing between us. Almost instantly she went still, her face slack, her arms fallen limp at her sides. Her eyes were still wide and staring, and tears marked her cheeks as the door clicked shut behind me.

My fingers interlaced with Maia's, we made a quick exit from the bar. She leaned on me, or I leaned on her, as I led her out of Roppongi. I felt bruised, surely as if I'd been in a fistfight. I saw it in Hiro's eyes, how he clung to the emptiness like a lifeline. He had built a comfortable home for himself there, free from the pain of loss and the slow tortures of eternity. And here I was, ready to burn it all down. And I couldn't even crawl out of my own hole long enough to tell him why.

I wrapped a protective arm around the girl at my side as I led her back to Takanori's apartment. Hiro was as selfish as I was a hypocrite. This girl had just lost her brother and was desperately fighting not to lose another. Did he give any thought to her?

Of course he didn't. No more thought than I gave to him. He may have begged me for power, but I turned him because I wanted him. I took him from his home and the only family he had because I wanted him. Then I reacted with jealousy rather than empathy when he grieved his loss, treating it like a deserved punishment for leaving me. Now he behaved just as coldly. I told him to break off the things that scared him, and instead he broke off the things that hurt him. Just like I did. He'd learned it all from me. Like a child emulating his parent, he'd looked to me for guidance and found an empty shell. So he became one himself.

When we reached the apartment, I asked Maia for her keys, which she obediently handed over. I unlocked the door and pushed it open, wavering a bit in the doorway. The place felt sacred, I like an intruder.

As if sensing my hesitation, Maia squeezed my hand and we walked in together, past the smiling photos, the orderly kitchen, the books in alphabetical order. I saw his fingerprint on everything, this fragile life he'd built for himself—a world made of glass. I wanted to brand him a fool for choosing something so fleeting. But our life, even with its relative permanence, had never felt like this.

By the time we reached the bedroom at the back of the apartment, I was sweating. I pulled back the comforter on the double bed, and Maia slipped under it. I perched on its edge as I tucked it around her. She trembled as her emotions seeped through the remains of my spell, her cheeks flushed and her eyes red-rimmed.

"When is he coming home?" she asked in a weak voice.

"I don't know. Soon." I brushed my fingers through her hair. It was soft like strands of spun silk. "He just needs some space, I think."

She tipped her head up toward me. "You're not as big of a jerk as I thought you were."

"Pretty sure I am."

She sighed and pressed her nose into the pillow. "I miss my brother."

I opened my mouth to respond when it struck me she might have been talking about Hiro.

Exhaustion overtook her, and her shuddering breaths evened out as she eased into sleep. I slid off the edge of the bed and onto the floor, my back against the mattress. Something lying facedown on the carpet near my feet caught my eye—a photograph. I leaned forward and pinched the corner between two fingers, holding my breath as I flipped it over.

It was of Hiro, Maia, and Takanori, bathed in bright sunlight, arms thrown around each other and smiling. Something rose up in my chest and clogged my sinuses. Not jealousy, exactly. Something colder, heavier. Hiro looked at Takanori, expression joyous and open, and there was so much love in his eyes it was almost palpable. He used to look at me that way. He poured his love onto me as if it were endless. I swam in it, bathed in it, soaked it up without giving anything in return. It never occurred to me that it could run out.

Takanori, on the other hand, reflected Hiro's love back like a mirror. His face shone with it. Maia's did too.

Something split open inside me. My chest tightened and my eyes burned. My whole body trembled and ached, and that seductive nothingness called to me. But for the first time, I didn't want to run. I allowed all those hated emotions to wash over me in waves of anger, hurt, grief, and the one I refused to acknowledge. The one that had been there all along.

THIRTY-ONE

Gossip

SUMMER 1994

HIRO HAD BEEN GONE FOR OVER A MONTH. I REPAIRED THE CRACKED frame, closed the door to his room, and carried on as if I'd never opened it, pretending he was just in there sulking and all I had to do was wait him out. He'd come out eventually with his head down and his tail between his legs. Despite his years, he was still just a boy, stubborn and emotional and prone to outbursts. All he needed was time.

The more days passed, the harder it became to convince myself. On more than one drunken night, I'd found myself yelling at his closed door like a deranged person. How dare he leave me like this? How dare he disrespect me, his maker, his partner? I'd made him a king and now he was throwing it away. Didn't he know there was more at stake here than just us?

Eventually, I couldn't stand the sound of my own voice echoing through my empty house, and I took to the streets. With a bottle hanging from my fingers, I wandered like a ghost, my mind on a different timeline. I saw hard-packed earth where now there was asphalt, a wide, blue sky that was now crowded with skyscrapers. I felt the weight of a sword on my hip and Hiro's hand on my arm.

A hush fell over the room when I stumbled through the door of a bar in Takatanobaba. It stood in the same place as the old izakaya. Even many of the patrons were the same, only now the walls were concrete instead of paper, the lights bright neon instead of the soft glow of lanterns. The counter behind which cooks once toiled was now a strip of mahogany in front of a wall of sparkling glass. A modern establishment full of ancient evils.

I pinned each patron with a white-eyed glare, until one by one they returned to their conversations, albeit at a lower volume. Moving as steadily as I could manage, I drifted toward our usual table at the back. It was both conspicuous and private, set up on a raised stage away from the main floor, where we could be seen at all times and only heard if we wanted to be. A place of status. I frowned down at the two chairs pushed close together as if mocking me. I'd never sat here alone before.

I gave one of the chairs a kick, sending it skidding across the floor and crashing into a wall. A waitress shuffled over to me, her tray clutched to her chest like a shield, as I dropped into the remaining chair.

"Sakurai-sama, hisashiburi," she said with a shaky smile.

"My usual, please," I growled without looking at her. She nodded but didn't move, spinning the tray in her fingers. I glanced up to find her eyes on the empty space beside me, brows pulled together and a worried twist to her lips. "What?"

She flinched and pulled back. "Nothing, nothing," she said quickly with another forced smile. "Coming right up."

She scurried away, reappearing moments later with a bottle of nigori sake and a glass. She reeked of questions strong enough to curl my nose. I snatched the bottle out of her hands as she tried to pour it and shooed her away. No matter how hard I tried to ignore them, snatches of conversation slithered into my ears.

So it's true?

I can't believe it. What will happen to us? Are they still protecting us?

He seems angrier than usual. Better stay away—

"Sakurai Hideyoshi."

My blood ran cold at the sound of a dark and familiar voice. I didn't look up at the scrape of the chair I'd kicked being returned and a weight settling into it. I refused. The alcoholic buzz I'd been living in for days burned away in the wake of the raw power that radiated off him. The lights dimmed under the darkness he brought with him. It followed him like a tide, flowing into the cracks and crevices thick as oil.

"What do you want?"

"I ran into Hiro yesterday," Kyo said.

Electricity zinged through my muscles at the mention of his name, followed by an icy panic. I set down my glass so he wouldn't see it shaking.

"He seems to be doing rather well, considering," he said coolly.

I glanced up and caught the corners of his mouth twitching. He was trying to get a rise out of me. I donned my hardest shell, determined to hide the tempest of emotions swirling inside me. My blood ran hot and cold at the same time, the contrast making me nauseous, but my expression never wavered.

"He's met someone, in fact. Seems he's been staying with him since he...well..."

Rage burned in my gut. Met somebody? What somebody? He didn't know anyone but me.

Did he?

I could have sworn I saw Hiro-sama down in Nakano...

My grip went white-knuckle tight around my glass. I thought back to the time just before he left, to his long absences full of excuses—everyday, midday. Almost like an appointment. Or a standing date.

Was he seeing somebody?

Another glass had shown up at some point, and I scowled as Kyo helped himself to my wine. "Why are you telling me this?"

He shrugged. "In case you want to fight for what's yours."

An incredulous laugh boiled up inside me. "And why are you so concerned with what's mine?"

"It's in my best interest, after all."

"Why's that?"

He looked around the room, eyebrows raised as if that was answer enough. I leaned forward over the table and lowered my voice.

"You think I'm not strong enough to control them on my own?"

He glanced at the wine bottle, then back at me. "Do you want to?"

I scowled deeply and something flashed in his eyes.

"Oh, you're strong. I don't doubt that," he said after a deep swallow of wine. "What you lack is power." I frowned, and he released a tired sigh. "Strength is good for vanquishing enemies and conquering kingdoms, but it takes power to hold them. That boy has power. He speaks and they listen. They respect him."

"They don't respect me?"

"They fear you."

Watch what you say. You don't want to end up in one of his cages.

He sat back in his chair and gave a casual shrug. "Don't get me wrong. Fear is useful. But all fear and no love is a recipe for mutiny."

A sick feeling churned in the pit of my stomach. My gaze drifted over the other patrons, only to see half a dozen faces quickly jerk away. The whispered gossip I'd been ignoring now struck like darts in my back. Would they act this way if I were the one who had left and Hiro remained? Would they care?

A slow smile stretched Kyo's face, exposing one bright fang. He finished off his wine, turned the glass upside down on the table, and stood. With a short, insincere bow, he turned and disappeared into the dark.

My drunkenness returned, accompanied by jealousy and a rage so hot it made me sweat. I pushed away from the table hard enough to topple both my chair and the wine bottle, before stomping over to a group two tables down and snatching up one of the men seated there by the collar. He released a shrill cry as I yanked him to his feet.

"Where is he?" I snarled through clenched teeth. The man in my grip just stared wide-eyed, his mouth hanging open. "Hiro. You said you saw him. Where?"

"N-N-N-Nakano," he stammered. "In the Broadway...I think."

I released the man's collar, and he dropped heavily back into his seat. Eyes burned holes in my back as I marched out the door.

What am I doing?

Standing in front of Nakano station, crowds drifting to and fro around me, I felt like a man lost at sea. The farther I got from Kyo, the more obvious his verbal manipulations became. He wanted me angry. He wanted me paranoid. I was a fool, and now I stood exactly where he wanted me to be.

The yawning mouth of Nakano Broadway's street-level entrance flashed from within, the garish lights of shops beckoning like an angler's lure. Day had tipped into evening, and the rush hour surge from the station pushed me toward it. Voices echoed between the glass skylight and the tile floor. Tourists brushed up against me in bursts of indecipherable language. The semisweet smells of a takoyaki vendor itched my nose. It was like being new again, all my senses throbbing from overstimulation.

I found a relatively quiet corner between a hundred-yen shop and a Lawson's and tucked myself into it. The chances of spotting Hiro in this crowd were slim to none, but I searched every face and listened to every heartbeat as they passed. When would he be here? Where would he go? Did he ever hint, ever say? I didn't pay attention. Why hadn't I paid attention?

Evening turned into night, and the shops turned out their lights and shut their doors. The crowds thinned, leaving only a trickle of people from the station cutting through to the surrounding neighborhoods. A headache throbbed between my eyes, and my mouth turned to cotton as my buzz wore off. I shrank against the wall beside me. What a fool I was. I'd worked so hard to convince myself I was okay without Hiro, but one word about him saw me skulking in the shadows like a jilted lover, hungry for a glimpse.

Just as I was about to give up, a familiar voice echoed through the breezeway. My heart flipped and skittered, the flame inside it jumping to life. I could barely see his familiar lean figure framed in the entrance as he approached from the station, a shopping bag in his hands. Another man followed beside him, a small, mousy fellow with a smile that took up his whole face. They walked close together, their silhouettes bumping and merging. He beamed at Hiro and Hiro beamed back, his wellspring of love refilled.

Was this really who he left me for?

No, you idiot. He left because you couldn't say one word.

I cursed and shook my head to rid myself of the intrusive thought. I should have left, satisfied that the rumors were true, but instead I followed. They cut off from the Broadway and down a narrow side street that led to a block of apartment buildings. Once away from the crowds, Hiro slid his hand into his companion's and the man leaned on his shoulder, whispering something in his ear that made him blush. My blood heated with the territorial urge to rip them apart. He was supposed to be miserable. He was supposed to figure out where he really belonged and come home. But he wasn't miserable. He was happy.

They ducked into a stairwell for what I presumed was their building. A bright laugh bounced off the walls, accompanied by Hiro's deeper, more subdued one. I got as close as I dared, close enough to see their shadows merge again. Another sound, this one more intimate, burrowed into my ears, followed by another peal of laughter and a slamming door.

My blood was on fire. Lewd, twisted images of Hiro and that other man burned through me along with Kyo's words. *In case you want to fight for what's yours.* I stomped toward the stairwell, fists clenched and fangs bared, but stopped with my foot on the first step.

No wonder he thought I didn't love him. He was happy, and here I was ready to rip that away for no other reason than my own selfish pride.

I sank down onto the step, my head in my hands. I thought of every time he'd solicited my affection and I'd turned him away. He deserved so much better. He deserved to have that love reflected back on him.

A shadow fell over me, and I knew without looking up who it was.

"Give him time," I said in a tight, gravelly voice.

"How much time?" Kyo asked.

I looked up sharply, a snarl on my lips. "As much as he needs."

I pushed up from the step and glared down my nose at Kyo, as if my physical size were any threat to him. He met my glare blankly and held it for a long time before releasing a tired sigh.

"Fine," he said with a shrug. He gestured up the stairs with his eyes. "Human lives are short after all."

I nodded stiffly, a thread of relief slipping through me, and stomped past him back toward the Broadway.

"I'll need a promise from you though," he called after me. I stopped but didn't turn. "I need you to promise to do your job. To be both Hiro and Hideyoshi to the best of your abilities. And when this ends, as it inevitably will, that you'll make sure he does his job too."

I half-turned to look at him over my shoulder. His expression was blank, his posture relaxed, but the threat hung in the air like a dense fog.

THIRTY-TWO

Explanation

SPRING 2004

MAIA WOKE TO FIND ME SITTING AT THE LITTLE DINING ROOM TABLE, working my way down a bottle of whiskey I'd found in the back of a cabinet. Hiro's taste, something American with a black label. She stood in the doorway of the bedroom, her face scrunched and arms wrapped around her as if she'd just woken from a nightmare.

"You're here," she said. I responded with a slight nod. "What happened? I remember following you to Roppongi, a bar and then...I don't know. It all sort of feels like a dream."

"You got overwhelmed, so I brought you home," I said in a voice thick with whiskey. I couldn't admit to her or myself that standing in front of the two most important people in my life, both of whom rejected me, was more than I could bear. She let out a loud breath, ran a hand over her face, and dropped into a chair across from me. She snatched my half-full glass from my hand, drained it, and held it out for a refill. I bit down on a laugh. I was starting to like this girl.

I filled the glass and she took another drink, hissing as the whiskey burned through her. She was almost pretty once I stopped seeing Takanori in her face, small, delicate like a frost-covered flower, stubbornly refusing to wilt, but ready to shatter at the slightest touch. The whiskey had warmed her cheeks, but the rest of her face was pale, her eyes dark and red-rimmed.

"We found him, didn't we?" she asked.

"Mn." I slipped the glass from her hand, our fingers brushing, and finished it off. I filled it again and pushed it back toward her. My gaze wandered over the soft, Western-style furniture and the little desk in the corner, and despite my best efforts, I found myself trying to piece together a picture of Hiro's life here. "Tell me about him. Your brother."

Her brow creased. "Why?"

I sighed. Truthfully, I didn't know why. Maybe I was just punishing myself. "Because I want to know."

Maia took a sip of the whiskey and let her finger roam over the rim of the glass. "He was...fun. Kind. He had this energy, you know. You could feel it the minute he walked into the room, like all the lights got a little bit brighter. And he would talk and talk..." She released a sad little laugh, her eyes glassy. "About everything. About the latest episode of some variety show or double-entry bookkeeping. There was never silence around him. That's been the hardest part, you know, now that he's gone. The silence."

My throat constricted. "And Hiro? He loved him?"

"Oh yes," she said, eyes brightening again. "You could get cavities just being near those two. And Hiro always seemed so amazed by it all, like he'd never been loved like that before."

I flinched and she cringed.

"Sorry."

I massaged the space between my eyes, and she passed back the empty glass.

"I don't understand," she said, eyes glistening. "This isn't like him to just run away. I understand it's painful and maybe he's...embarrassed about how he behaved toward me. But he loved his life here. Why would he let the landlord just throw it all out like it didn't matter? Why wouldn't he come home?"

I sighed and poured another measure of whiskey into my glass. "It's complicated."

She squinted at me. "Explain it to me."

"I wish I could."

I lifted the glass to take another drink, and she covered it with her hand, a hard, desperate look on her face. I felt for her in that moment, this girl who had been thrust into the middle of something she didn't understand. Her hand was right there. I could explain it all with a touch, but to what end? It would only leave her scared, confused, or worse—with tarnished memories of her brother.

"I'm sorry, Maia." It surprised me how much I meant it.

Her small face twisted, and she ripped the glass from my hand, slamming it down on the table hard enough to splash its contents across the surface. She stood up and pointed to the door.

"Get out."

"Maia—"

"If you're not going to help us, then leave."

"Fine." I stood and backed away from the table, hands up. "Just do me one favor. Stay away from him. Let me handle this."

"Why should I?"

"Because he might be dangerous," I said.

"That's ridiculous."

"That's why he won't come back here. To protect you." I took a deep breath, a knot forming in my stomach. "You should stay away from me too."

She balked, eyes wide and blinking. "Why?"

"When he left me, it had...implications that go beyond just the two of us." The memory of Kyo's threat made the hair on the back of my neck stand up. *Make sure he does his job.*

"What does that even mean?" she asked. She narrowed her eyes and dropped her voice a notch. "Are you yakuza or something? Don't tell me there's a hit on you."

I released a huff of a laugh. "No."

She threw her hands up. "Then what aren't you telling me?"

"Must you always ask so many questions?" I barked, my impatience tipping over into anger. "Just do as I say."

She flinched back, and her eyes welled. My anger fled as quick as it had come, replaced by a cold sense of déjà vu. I'd been here before, using anger to shield secrets I wasn't yet ready to face. Look what it had gotten me. A broken doorframe and an empty house. Perhaps withholding wasn't the best course of action after all.

"It could change everything you think you know about the last ten years," I said, voice hoarse.

She swallowed hard. "As long as it means I can help Hiro."

"It may mean you don't want to."

Her eyes widened, tears spilling down her cheeks. I pointed to her chair at the table.

"Sit."

She hesitated, hands clenched over her chest, before slowly lowering herself back into her seat. I sat across from her, joints stiff, as if all my years had settled into them at once. I took a long, deep breath, poured another measure of whiskey into my mostly empty glass, and drained it in one swallow. Maia's eyes tracked my movements as if I were a snake ready to strike. She flinched when I held my hand out toward her, palm up.

"Give me your hand."

"Why?"

"Do you want to know or not?" I said as evenly as I could manage.

Her throat worked around a swallow, and her jaw clenched, but she eventually laid her hand in mine. I tried not to think about how small it was as my fingers curled around it.

"No matter what you see—"

"See?" she asked, nose scrunched.

"—know that Hiro at no time, ever, had any intention to harm either you or your brother."

"I don't under—" She gasped, and her head lolled forward as if suddenly very drunk. Everywhere our skin touched sizzled and warmed as my magic passed into her. "What...is that?"

"It's me."

She gasped again and tried sluggishly to pull away, but I held her firm.

"Don't resist. It's the easiest way. Close your eyes."

A whimper slipped from her throat, but she complied, her lids falling closed and her expression going slack. My heart trembled as I closed my eyes along with her. Influence usually worked outward, a dulling of the senses sometimes followed by a push. This was different. In order to show her the truth, I would have to let her in. I'd have to peel back all my carefully constructed barriers and expose myself to her, and I wasn't sure how much control I had over what she would see.

"Relax," I said, as much to myself as to her.

I started slow, with feelings more than images. The sounds and smells of another time, the taste of the air, the weight of a sword. Her mind resisted at first, pushing back against the intruder, but I persisted. I eased her into my memories as gently as I could. Little by little, her resistance gave way to curiosity, and I felt her poke at the feelings with nervous fingers, tasting them cautiously as if they may be poisoned. I waited until I no longer felt her pushing back. I opened up further and showed her Hiro the way I saw him when we first met, ethereal as he stood before me in a black kimono, curls escaping from a hastily tied knot at his crown. Physically he hadn't changed, but he looked so much younger then, the wide-eyed and timid romantic. My chest warmed with the sound of his voice. To think, I had nearly forgotten it.

Maia sucked in a breath, and her hand tightened around mine, a reminder that she was in this place with me. I was grateful for that grounding presence. I could lose myself here, bound by the cold thread of regret that accompanied my memories. Looking back, it was so clear. I was a destructive force on his world the moment I stepped into it. What would have become of his life had I not taken it?

My mind took us almost unbidden to the moment I'd turned him, to the coppery taste of blood in my mouth as he went limp in my arms. Maia's hand tightened again, this time as if to dig claws into my skin. Her mind pounded against mine, as if she could break into the memory and save him from me.

"What are you doing to him?" she asked in a high-pitched, breathy voice, words slurred together like a sleep talker.

"Hush, girl."

After that, the memories flowed as memories tend to do, fast and out of order, a rushed and disorganized catalog of the passage of time. My muscles tensed and breathing quickened as I struggled to shape them into something Maia could understand. Instead, they took me to exactly the place I didn't want to be: a brothel surrounded by the pieces of a dismembered boy hunter, a shed with the aftermath of Hiro's bloody revenge, the two of us leaned up against a well as I cleaned blood from his hands and heard him tell me: *I think something's wrong with me.*

Maia made a pained sound and ripped her hand out of mine. I fell back into the present with dizzying abruptness. My body ached as if constricted by thorned vines. Maia's face blurred and stretched as I attempted to focus, but I could just make out the terror and disgust hardening her soft features.

"What…" Her breathing came short and ragged, and she stared at her hands as if they were the ones covered in blood. "What did you… what are you?"

"Hiro will likely never forgive me for what I've shown you." I pulled my own hands back and clutched them in my lap, my knuckles going white.

She stood up from the table and backed away. "You're a monster."

I gritted my teeth until they creaked.

"What did you do to him?"

"I gave him power when he was powerless." The words stuck in my throat even as I uttered them, the same lie I'd been telling myself for centuries, a lie I believed because I didn't want to face the truth, that I was a weak, selfish man and I had taken what I wanted.

"Those people…he…" She looked at her hands again, fingers spread wide, before slapping them over her eyes. "I don't want to see that. I didn't want to see that."

"I know."

"Why did you show me?"

"So you'd know what he's capable of."

"This can't be real."

"It is."

"You're telling me we've been living next to a murderer for a decade? That my brother——" A sob choked her, and she covered her mouth with both hands as if she might be sick. I stood from the table, and she flinched. I didn't blame her for being afraid, but her reaction cut me in a way I wasn't prepared for.

"Don't hate him, Maia," I said gently. "The man you knew, the kind, loving Hiro, may not have been the whole truth, but it wasn't a lie either. He has...something dark inside him, something I put there, and he fights against it every day. Right now..." My voice thickened into a paste, and I choked on every word. "Right now, he might be losing. You caught a glimpse of it today when he grabbed you."

Her face paled even further, and a sound like a cry leaked from her throat.

"He stays away to protect you. If you want to hate someone, hate me."

My heart turned into a lead ball as I turned away from her.

THIRTY-THREE

Time's Up

SPRING 2004

I FELT EYES ON ME THE WHOLE WAY HOME, LITTLE MILLIPEDES OF paranoia that crawled up the back of my neck and down my spine. For some reason, Kyo's request—no, *demand*—from a decade ago echoed in my ears. *Make sure he does his job.* I'd agreed then, but I'd expected Hiro would have a lifetime to grow used to, maybe even a little bored of, a human life. I didn't expect him to find a euphoric love, only to have it ripped from him too soon, leaving a wound more devastating than any Hunter's blade could make, so deep and wide it may never heal.

He wasn't ready. He'd told me as much, and his already fragile mind was buckling under the pressure. But something told me that Kyo wouldn't care. Which was why I wasn't at all surprised to find a silver knife embedded in my front gate with a note.

Time's up.

I clenched my fists so hard my nails dug into my palms. Anger, fear, and regret turned that iron ball in my chest white hot. My gaze darted to shadows around my house, expecting to see flashes of silver. The sway of trees that once felt friendly and safe now looked like the tail of a dragon swinging overhead ready to come down on all of us, spikes and razor-edged scales poised to tear us to shreds.

He knew almost the second Hiro's time with Takanori was over, which meant people were watching. Kyo could have never gotten so close without us noticing. His power shone like a beacon. We thought the Hunters were gone, extinct or at least disinterested. In reality, they were just laying low, biding their time. They could be anyone, the delivery driver, the cashier at the corner convenience store, the old man who rode by on his bicycle nearly every morning. We'd let our guard down and allowed ourselves to be surrounded. Now they were knocking at our door.

Or rather, stabbing it.

I closed my eyes and took a long, deep breath. I had to think clearly, calmly, like the soldier I once was. A mental list of priorities sorted themselves out in my mind. First: protect Hiro. Second: prevent Hunter uprising without provoking a youkai insurrection. Kyo was right about one thing. The youkai were loyal to Hiro, but they feared me. They used to speak of him as if he were some kind of messiah, whispering behind their hands about the day Hiro would return. But the more time passed, the more doubt crept into their voices and the more they kept to his ways out of fear of my judgment rather than any lingering respect for him. It was only a matter of time before they grew tired of my iron-fisted authority and resisted. Youkai were fickle creatures, their thirst for blood and power often outweighing their better judgment. If I pushed too hard, they'd brand me a tyrant worthy of being overthrown. Too much leniency bred lawlessness that was sure to draw the Hunters' eye. Perhaps it already had.

Kyo was right about something else too. As leaders, we worked better together, Hiro and I. He was the heart and I was the sword. But now that heart was drowned in darkness, the hope that once fueled it lost to grief. I didn't know how to give it back to him. I wasn't equipped. I'd fed my heart to the beast the day I was made.

My phone rang in my pocket, and I yanked it out. "What?"

"Don't *what* me," Asagi barked. I drew a breath to bark back, but a tightness in his voice gave me pause. "What have you done?"

An icy lump formed in my belly. "What are you talking about?"

"Why is there a silver knife stuck in my door?"

The cold in my gut spread to my limbs. "It's not meant for you. It's because Hiro is there."

"Not at the bar. At my home. Where Ryo lives." His voice went shrill and trembled as if on the verge of tears. A flash of protective rage burst inside of me—there and gone, but strong enough to leave me feeling confused.

"Are you at home now?"

"Yes."

"Is Ryo with you?"

"No. He's still working."

"Good." My mind spun. Hunters were not only watching me and Hiro, they were watching Asagi too. My mouth went sandpaper dry. "Go back to the bar. Keep him there."

"No," he said sharply. "I have to get him out of Tokyo."

"He's safer with you, with people." I gripped the phone so tight I heard the plastic case creak. "You both are."

"Yoshi—"

"Don't argue with me, Asagi."

"Excuse me? Who do you think you're talking to?" He lowered his voice a notch, and it came through muffled as if he pressed his lips against the receiver. "You may think you control the youkai, but you don't control me. You told me we would be safe. But you can't protect us, can you?"

A hard silence fell between us, filled to the brim with Asagi's disappointment.

"If they want me," Asagi started softly, "the quickest way to get me is through him."

"I know."

"Then they do too." The hard edge was back, but the words still trembled as if Asagi was on the verge of tears. "I can't just sit here and wait for them to take him from me."

I groaned and kicked the gate in front of me, making the silver knife stuck in it shiver. Part of me wanted to bark some childish insult, hang up the phone, and leave him to his own devices, but I had no time for petty grudges. I knew what I had to do, but my pride made it prick like a burr.

"Please," I said between clenched teeth. "Just this once, trust me."

He fell so quiet I thought the line went dead. "What's going on, Yoshi?"

"It's under control."

"That doesn't exactly instill confidence."

"Just do it. I can't worry about you as well."

Another long silence. "You would care if they killed me?"

There was no sarcasm, no malice in the words, and the honesty of Asagi's question made my bones ache. My heart pounded so hard it made me dizzy, and I had to lean on the gate for balance. "Just keep him there."

"Yoshi——"

I hung up before Asagi could argue further. It was a crazy gamble. Asagi was right to be afraid for Ryo's safety. At best, Ryo would be used as a bargaining chip. At worst, a murder weapon pointed right at Asagi's heart. But the Hunters relied on secrecy as much as we did, and I was putting all my money on the theory that they wouldn't snatch a man away in a room full of human—and two youkai—witnesses.

My mind jerked unwillingly back to Maia. If they would use Ryo against Asagi, would they use Maia against Hiro? The love between them was obvious. They had become family in the ten years we'd been apart. If she were hurt because of us, it would break him. Another spike of doubt ran through me as I saw, once again, the terror in her eyes at what I had shown her. In true youkai fashion, I'd taken something from her, something I could never give back. Now she would become a pawn in a game she didn't understand, one that started even before her parents were born. And I wasn't sure if I was enough to protect her.

"Sakurai-sama!"

My head snapped up at the sound of my name whisper-yelled from up the street. A knot of about half a dozen people, all youkai, scurried toward me, heads down and eyes wide. I recognized Hashiguchi's girl, Yui, as well as a few others from the izakaya. All of them had silver daggers in their hands.

"Sakurai-sama." A man with a deep scar on his face and a soldier's bearing skidded to a stop in front of me and bowed. "We're sorry to intrude on you like this—"

"Get on with it," I barked, breathless. What I really wanted to do was duck inside and lock the gate.

"Hunters," he said, his clipped, formal cadence made sharp with anxiety. He held out the knife in his hand, a short, silver tanto with a bone handle. The blade looked old, spotted with tarnish, its grip worn smooth from handling. An heirloom perhaps. "I found this stabbed into my doorframe. I searched the whole area, but found no signs of the intruder besides this. I thought I was the only one, that I had drawn their attention." His eyes dropped, and his head tipped forward. "My discipline has been...lacking as of late."

I crossed my arms and exhaled loudly. He flinched and his gaze flicked up. When no punishment came, he straightened his shoulders and continued.

"Being alone in that house didn't feel safe, so I went to the izakaya. Turns out I wasn't the only one with a knife in their door."

A murmur went through the little crowd as they each held up a silver blade. My blood filled with ice chips, cold and stinging. I thought this was just about me and Hiro, that the blade left for Asagi was to get my attention, but it was bigger than that. They were watching all of us, and they were letting us know that the reign of monsters was about to end.

With a growl I yanked the blade out of my own gate, kicked it open, and gestured the group inside. They hesitated, feet shuffling on the asphalt, and impatience lapped at my insides.

"Did you come all this way to stand in the street?" I snapped, before turning my back and stomping toward the house. Their footsteps tapped up the path behind me like so many beetles, sending a shiver up my spine. This was my home. No one ever came in here, but now it would be infested.

I slid the shoji open, and they filed in one at a time. They each dropped their blades on the chabudai in the center of the room. The blades gleamed evilly in the soft light that filtered in through the walls. I glared down at them, my soldier's mind turning. Six blades. The synchronicity of their discovery suggested they were left simultaneously, which meant at least six men. If they truly had blood on their mind, they'd be working in teams. Two men could subdue a youkai if they were clever. Three or four was better. That was at least eighteen. Eighteen Hunters. Modern men didn't even believe in us anymore. Where did Kyo find and train eighteen men willing to risk their lives to fight monsters?

I ran a hand over my face, a day's growth of beard rasping under my fingers. My mind jumped back to my conversation with Kyo outside of Hiro and Taka's apartment, back when he'd been oh-so-willing to give Hiro the time away he needed. Looking back on it now, I should have known it had been too easy.

He'd used the last decade to build an army.

"What are you thinking?" The scarred man had stepped up beside me, back straight and hands clasped behind him. He watched me out of the corner of his eye while facing the anxious crowd.

"That I have a problem."

"We," he said with a hard tone. "*We* have a problem."

"Mn."

I ran my gaze over the blades again, my mind cataloging all the weaknesses of our position. We were surrounded by tall buildings, allowing for a vantage point to see over the walls around my property. Every bright light painted our shadows against the shoji. Come nightfall, they would shine like a beacon, broadcasting our exact number and position. A well-aimed poison dart could cut right through the paper and into our backs before we even knew the Hunters were out there. Once weakened, they would swarm us like ants, using their superior numbers to overpower and subdue us. Then it would be just a matter of time.

I glanced back at the huddled group. How much torture could they possibly stand? Who would come to save us?

"We could take a fight to them," the soldier said, a gleam in his eye.

I shook my head. "No. These people may be killers, but they're not fighters. Besides, we have no way of knowing who these Hunters are or where they've gone." I thought again of the old man on his bicycle. "They're completely decentralized. They likely didn't even know each other before today."

"How is that possible? With this level of coordination—"

"With today's technology, they could do it with an email."

The soldier's lips pursed, and his weight shifted from one foot to the other. I knew that feeling, the combination of anxiety and excitement, the restless itch that comes from a fight just out of reach. My sword hand twitched. I heard Hiro's voice in my ear.

Not everything can be solved at the end of a sword.

"Get one of the men to help you close the shutters," I said as I turned my back on the group and marched toward the back door.

"Where are you going?"

"I need to think." The shoji snapped closed behind me, and I turned my face up to the sun. I ignored the distinct rumble of the amado being pulled closed and the tense clip of the voices from within. Hiro was right. Not all conflicts could be solved with a sword, but the sword was all I knew. It was my voice when I couldn't speak. As much as I didn't want to admit it, I needed him. When I reached down into my long-forgotten heart and found it cold and barren, I'd leaned on his. And now that he was absent, I feared falling.

After a deep breath, I dug my phone out of my pocket and pressed in a number. I knew he wouldn't answer, but I had to try. After the second ring, the call dumped to voicemail. I expected the generic robot voice. My heart seized when I heard something else, a voice that wasn't Hiro's.

"This is Hiro's phone." A stream of giggles poured through the line, accompanied by the muffled sound of a tussle. "He probably can't figure out how to answer your call because he's a hundred years old."

Hiro's voice in the background: "Taka!"

"You should probably send a telegram instead."

Another stream of giggles followed by a shrill beep.

I opened my mouth to speak, but nothing came. The outgoing message reverberated through me like steel striking steel, a microcosm of their happiness. How could I possibly expect him to settle for what we had?

"They're scared, you know."

I snapped the phone closed at the sound of a soft voice behind me. I turned to find Yui standing in the doorway. She'd always been a quiet girl, soft and devoted to her maker, but since Hashiguchi's death she'd become even quieter, harder. She'd lost a part of herself, and it showed in the hollowness of her eyes.

"They should be scared," I said, turning back to face the yard.

"You should say something," she said. "They look to you."

"Maybe they shouldn't look to me."

"With Hiro gone, you're all they have."

Another dart lanced through my chest. Anger welled up inside me, dark and familiar. I bit down on the urge to lash out at her, to curse Hiro for leaving, but it was all my fault. I ignored Hiro's unhappiness, I drank myself into apathy after he had gone, and when all he needed was someone to lean on, to give his broken heart a rest, I'd demanded he stand on his own and give me the attention I felt I was entitled. Everything leading up to today could be traced back to me.

"Were there signs," I asked haltingly, the words coming out like mud, "with Hashiguchi?"

Yui stepped up next to me, and I felt the weight of her stare on the side of my face. I kept my eyes lowered, turning my phone over and over in my hands.

"Yes," she said with a sigh. "Subtle at first. Bursts of anger followed by long periods of quiet, like he'd drawn into himself. Like he was there but not there. It could last for days or weeks, and just when I'd start to worry, he'd snap out of it and be his usual self again." Her voice trembled, and she took a deep breath before continuing. "Every time, I would just brush it off, but the next time would be worse. Last longer. Until..."

Until.

Until he was a pile of ash on the floor of a basement cage.

I don't want to die alone in a cage.

The air rushed out of me as if I'd been punched. Something swelled inside me that was too big to hide in a box. Hiro was never coming back, not to me. He'd known what was happening to him, knew what his future held, and I'd forced him to watch it over and over all the way to its brutal end. He believed I would do the same thing to him. The worst part was, he was probably right.

"You know where he is, don't you?" she asked softly. I nodded, and her eyes brimmed with tears. "He's not coming back." I shook my head. "What are you going to do?"

I let out a long breath and looked at the sky. "I don't know yet."

She sniffled, and when I looked back down at her, she had her hand pressed to her mouth and her eyes closed. I mumbled a curse, shuffled my feet, clenched and unclenched my hand before reaching out and touching her shoulder. Her eyes popped open, and she jerked a little as if I'd given her a static shock.

"I know I'm not as...good...as Hiro," I said, heat rushing to my cheeks. "But I promise, I won't abandon you."

She sighed and wiped her eyes, the corners of her mouth lifting in a sad smile. "I know."

THIRTY-FOUR

Immortality

SPRING 2004

I DIDN'T SO MUCH AS TWITCH AS A SHARP SQUEAL CUT THE AIR FROM behind me. I sat on the bottom step of Hiro's old apartment, a mostly empty bottle of wine dangling from my fingers. It had been easy to slip away from the house. With the amado drawn closed, the place looked like a coffin. Yui would tell the youkai hiding there that I had gone to seek out information on the Hunters, but really I just felt suffocated, pressed upon on all sides by my failures. I couldn't think, so I'd snuck out of my own home, found the nearest bottle of wine, and attempted to drink until I was numb. Only instead of dulling my emotions, they swirled around inside me like a typhoon.

"I have a broom," Maia said in a shaky voice, shrill with forced bravado. I didn't have to turn to see her clutching it in front of her, its handle thrust out like the head of a spear.

I laughed. "What do you plan to do? Sweep me to death?"

"I'll stab you. Right through the heart."

"That only works in bad American movies," I scoffed, taking another pull off the wine bottle. "Relax, I'm not here to hurt you."

"Why are you here?"

I didn't answer. I honestly didn't know.

"You're drunk."

"Mn." I swung the bottle around in my fingers, and it made a hollow sound as it bumped against the stairs. "Seemed an appropriate reaction."

"To what?"

"Looming genocide."

She gasped, and I turned just enough to catch a glimpse of her over my shoulder.

The broom sagged in her hands, the end of the handle nearly touching the stair in front of her. A laugh bubbled up out of me, dark and slurred.

"Do you want to know the real reason you're scared of me right now?" I started. "The reason you think you can kill me with a broom handle? It's because of us. Me and Hiro. We taught a bunch of undisciplined monsters to exist beyond human eyes. We've become the thing of old books and scary stories and bad movies. And everyone, *everyone*, is safer for it. We were...kings among demons." I sniffed, the typhoon inside me breaking against my sternum. "I had no interest in being a king. But there are people out there depending on us, depending on me, to keep them safe." I gave a dry, snorting laugh. "Hiro was always so good at keeping the peace. Without him, I'm just a brandished sword swinging at anything that gets in my way. He was like the saya. He kept my sharp edge guarded until we needed it, and when we did, he gave me a direction to swing."

"And then he left," she said, her voice soft.

My vision blurred, and I blinked rapidly to clear it. "What good is a sword without a hand to wield it?"

I lifted the bottle again only to have a hand dart over my shoulder and snatch it away. Maia settled on the step just behind me. She'd left her broom on the landing. She wasn't afraid of me anymore.

"You love him," she said.

I clicked my tongue. "Why is it that everyone can see that but him?" I asked, throwing up my hands.

"Have you tried telling him?"

I glanced over my shoulder at her again, and the earnest look in her eyes made my gut clench. "I think it's a bit late for that."

"It's never too late for that," she said. "It may not change anything between you, but it might help him to know."

I frowned and looked away, my vision blurring again.

"So...looming genocide?"

"Believe it or not, there are those who think dangerous creatures such as us shouldn't exist," I said with a wry grin.

"Shocking. And the wine is, what, part of your battle plan?" She hung the bottle over my shoulder by two fingers and dangled it in front of me.

"I think better this way." I reached for the bottle, but she snatched it away. The action brought her so close I could smell her skin—dust and sweat and the sharp scent of cleaning products. The heat of her against my back became too much, and I stood up and took two steps away. I pulled on every piece of armor I had before turning to face her again.

"If things get bad..." My mouth went dry at the possibilities. "They aren't above using the people we care about to get to us. Your connection to Hiro could put you at risk. You should stay here. Lock the door and don't open it. What?"

I stopped as a slow grin stretched her face. "This is why you're here," she said, the bottle still swinging from her fingers. I blinked, baffled. "To warn me."

Heat crawled up the back of my neck.

"I knew you weren't a complete jerk."

I frowned and looked away.

She sighed, stood up, and made a big show of dusting off the seat of her pants before taking a step toward me. "I want to stay with you."

"Stupid girl," I growled. "Just do as I say."

"If you are, as you say, a sword..." She took another step toward me. "...seems like the safest place to be is behind you."

I sucked in a breath as the storm inside me was replaced by a low hum that vibrated my bones. I wanted her with me. I didn't want to let her out of my sight. But Hiro stood behind me, and Asagi, and all those people hiding in my house. There was no room for her.

An errant wind whipped through the space between us, lifting the ends of her hair in a billowing cloud. My fingers were in it before I could stop them, tucking it behind her ear. Her eyes widened a bit, but she didn't step away or stop me.

"The safest place for you is far away from me."

I WAITED UNTIL MAIA WAS SAFE INSIDE, THEN MADE A CIRCUIT OF HER neighborhood with an eye out for immediate threats, though how I would spot them, I wasn't sure. I had been stupid coming here. Hunters were most certainly watching me. If they didn't know about her before, they certainly did now, and I had led them right to her.

Shaking off the impending melancholy, I straightened my back and focused on the crisis in front of me. Kyo had made his presence—and his intentions—known. My instincts were to take the fight to him first, but using violence against someone like him was akin to using a sword to fight back a hurricane. I thought about Hiro, what he would do, what price he would pay for the safety of those under him. There was only one answer.

Everything.

So I took another chance. I gambled on the hope that Kyo, like me, was a man who clung to old habits no matter how the world had changed around him, and I followed my memory to the location of the house where we first met. All the traditional manors were gone, replaced with large, Western-style homes built in a colonial style, remnants of foreign occupation. In the spot where Kyo's home had been stood a wide, two-story building with columns on the front and a wraparound porch. The whole facade was painted white as bleached bone, and even in the day the iron lamps were on, fighting back the lengthening shadows with their unnatural light.

The front door swung open. Silhouetted in the bright light from inside stood a familiar figure. Even from the street, his power made my insides quiver and my muscles tense, braced to fight or run. It radiated off him like a mirage, all the wrath and vengeance of an old god packed into his small frame, with the heat and density of a dying star. Just like the first time we'd met, the awareness of being in the presence of something truly ancient made me feel small, like a bug he would hardly notice crushed under his heel.

He stepped forward out of the glare, closed the door behind him, and leaned against one of the columns. Sweating from every pore, I pulled the silver knife he'd left in my gate from my belt and threw it at the ground beneath his feet.

"I see you got my note," he said, pinching a cigarette out of a pack and popping it between his lips.

"We need to have a conversation."

He flicked open a silver lighter and touched it to the end of his cigarette. "Mn."

"You've been watching us."

"Does that surprise you?" he asked with a smug laugh.

"Why?"

"It's wise to keep an eye on your investments."

I bristled. He was almost aggressively normal. He should be shooting fire from his eyes, not casually smoking a cigarette.

"If you've been watching, then you should know. He's not ready."

His eyebrows bounced up. "He's not?"

"No." I squared my shoulders and held his gaze with a confidence I didn't even remotely feel. "It's not safe, for him or anybody else. He's—"

"Crazy?"

A voice screamed inside me, and I clapped my teeth closed around it. Kyo grinned around his cigarette, popped off the post he'd been leaning on, and took a step toward me. Just one step, but it made me flinch. The shadows pulled tight around him as he moved away from the light, coiling like a great serpent around his feet. He pulled the knife out of the ground and flipped it end over end with one hand while smoking with the other.

"Youkai all over the city have found those in their doors," I said. "We had an agreement."

"We did." He pointed the end of the knife at my nose. "You haven't been keeping up your end."

"I told you, we needed time—"

"And I've given it to you. Now you ask for more?"

I gritted my teeth. My palms itched as I tracked the point of the knife with my eyes.

"Are you still immortal, Sakurai Hideyoshi?" he asked.

My mouth went dry and my chest tightened. I knew what he was asking. Hiro had told me all about their conversation at my house while I'd been imprisoned by Hunters. He wanted to know if we still lived only for each other. I knew my answer. I knew the rhythm of my heart and how even his temporary absence had altered it. And there was a time I thought I knew his. But now it had been wounded, its shape fundamentally changed.

"Yes." The word came out a rasp.

"Are you sure?" He flicked a bit of ash off the end of his cigarette. I expected it to burn a hole in the very earth. "He's had a whole life away from you. Even fell in love."

"That doesn't mean anything. I am still his maker. We are a part of each other."

He nodded—an acknowledgement, not a concession.

"Even if we have...changed..." Just the possibility made my insides ache. "What difference does it make?"

"If you're not immortal, then I might as well kill you." He sounded almost sad. "And this would have been an awful waste of time."

My heart jerked as images of torture flashed behind my eyes, fingers twitching toward the ghost of a sword at my hip. In another time, I would have cut him open for his threats, no matter the consequences. But times were different. I was different. And all the people standing behind me depended on me not losing my head.

"There is...a flaw in your plan." I spoke slowly to keep the tremble out of my voice. Kyo's eyebrows pulled up, and he crossed his arms over his chest, rocking back on his heels. I pointed to the knife in his hand. "You're bluffing."

A smile teased at the corners of his mouth. "Am I?"

"If there is one thing human Hunters can't give up, it's the advantage of surprise. You've given that up with your little display. It's theater, meant to scare us into submission, but now we are alert, prepared. It would take an army to take us down, and you don't have one. But you want us to believe you do."

His smile dropped, and his face turned to stone. My heart skipped. My gamble was paying off.

"No one knows better than we do how hard it is to kill in secret these days," I said, my words steady and confident. "People live in egg crates, stacked one on top of another. We live in a world full of eyes and ears. There are no more dark corners to hide in. Any action against us now would cause a bloodbath you can't contain."

His smile returned, but it was different this time. If I didn't know any better, I'd say it was pride. He took another step toward me. Sweat slid down my back, but I didn't move.

"I was right about you," he said. "You are brave. Brave enough to step into the jaws of the dragon." He tapped the point of the knife against my sternum. I winced with the remembered pain of a silver sword in my chest and Hiro coughing blood for weeks, and suddenly I regretted relinquishing the one weapon that could truly do me harm. "You are right about one thing. Killing youkai is...cumbersome, and my Hunters are no good to me dead, or in prison. So I'll make another deal with you." He flipped the knife around in his hand and held the handle out toward me. "Prove it."

I flinched. "Prove what?"

"That you're still immortal."

My heart dropped to my feet, and my skin went cold. Kyo's smile widened, and he stepped even closer, our chests almost touching.

"Prove it and I'll call them off."

"And if I don't?" The words broke over my barren tongue.

Kyo shrugged. "Then I guess we all have to start over."

Something dropped like a stone in the back of my mind. My knees turned watery, and I struggled to stay steady. When I didn't accept his offered knife, Kyo took a single step back and threw it down. The blade stuck in the earth between my feet, ringing like a bad omen. He took another step backward before pivoting on his heel and sauntering back toward the house, a wavering shadow against a wall of light.

THIRTY-FIVE

Samurai Heart

SPRING 2004

THE SUN HAD SET BEHIND THE SKYLINE BY THE TIME I MADE IT HOME. The amado were still closed, making the house hard and uninviting. I stood staring at it for a long time, my back against the gate. I'd broken my back over the years just to keep this place standing. I'd fought off colonizers and put out fires. I'd repaired or replaced every plank of wood and every screen. I'd even shooed away the vulturous property developers who used to pound on my gate day in and day out before I managed to have the house listed as a historical site. My little plot in Ushigome was much less appealing when they couldn't knock the house down and build a high-rise on top of it.

I lifted my gaze as a familiar shadow passed overhead. Warm nostalgia flooded through me as the hawk dipped low, chirping its signature call. Even as the city grew ever denser around me, the birds still continued to visit, often taking refuge in my trees and under my eaves. Despite their wildness in comparison to their predecessor, my bond with the birds hadn't changed. I admired their nobility and their loyalty. I envied them and their ability to fly above everything, untouchable as the wind. I wondered at the picture they must see and lamented my comparatively small view. How much easier would it be to do the right thing, to know what that right thing even was, if I could see everything at once? How much easier to see the rat in the bush and pluck it out before it chewed holes in everything you valued?

"Keep an eye on things for me, would you?" I asked absently. The hawk called out again as if in answer.

Tension made the air solid as I pushed through the amado and into the house. Half a dozen heads snapped up at my entrance. Drawn faces with wide eyes waited with bated breath for answers I didn't have. The group huddled around the unlit brazier as if the mere idea of a fire gave them comfort. Someone had made tea, and the sharp smell settled in my nose like a memory.

The man with the scarred face rose to his feet and met me in the entrance. "Did you find anything?"

I swallowed hard and shook my head, avoiding his eyes. His shoulders fell a notch, but he kept his face carefully neutral.

"So...what now?"

"Go with the others to Takatanobaba," I said. "It's public, which makes it a less appealing target. Besides, we need to find out if anyone else has been threatened."

His eyes widened. "But—"

"Everything they've done is to incite fear, so don't be afraid." The words came out low and even despite my trembling insides. "Don't forget, they are only human. We are stronger. Stay together. Your best defense is each other. They can't take you down unless you let them."

The soldier's lips tightened, and he gave a tight nod before returning to the group. A ripple of apprehension went through them as he relayed my words. One by one they stood and filtered out the door in single file, bowing as they passed, yet avoiding my eyes. Yui lingered a moment at my side, her eyes wide and wet.

"You're not coming?" she asked. I shook my head, and her brow creased. "They will come for you."

"I know."

She studied my face. I avoided her eyes.

"This won't bring him back to you, you know," she said in a voice almost too soft to hear. My insides felt brittle, as if her words had sapped away what remained of my confidence. One move and I would fall apart altogether.

She released a breath and laid a gentle hand on my arm before joining the others. I didn't breathe again until the gate slammed behind them.

Alone in the dimness, the house felt both vast and suffocating. The wind brushed against the amado, and I heard the rattling bones of every life I'd ever taken. Their whispers followed me as I drifted through the back room and down the hallway toward the back of the house. The door to Hiro's room was cracked open, revealing a line of murky light beyond it. I moved toward it, stopping just outside, and ran my fingers over the damaged doorframe. I thought of all the things I'd taken for granted: Hiro sitting next to me, leaning on my shoulder or dozing quietly with his head in my lap as I absently stroked his hair; the shape of his body in a well-made kimono; the timbre of his voice when he sang for me.

A band tightened around my hardened heart, making it ache with every beat. I longed for all the things I'd once found tedious, for those long, slow days when we only had each other. It had been ages since I'd really felt the heat of his skin under my fingers. I missed him. Even before he left, I'd missed him. I just didn't have the courage to face it. How did we get here?

With a ragged exhale, I turned away from his room and headed to my own. In the far corner sat a heavy wooden chest with a wrought iron lock. I found the key where it was hidden between the yellowed and worm-eaten pages of an old book. It had blackened with age, its surface rough against my skin as I hefted its weight in my palm. I nearly dropped it twice as I shoved it in the lock with stiff fingers. The mechanism resisted, groaned, then finally gave with a grinding thonk.

The chest released a dusty cough as I lifted the lid. Inside were all the things I most treasured—trinkets and baubles and pictures so old they threatened to disintegrate when I touched them. It was easy sometimes to forget how much time had passed, how it moved both fast and slow, a surging tide eroding the rock beneath it and turning it to sand.

My heart ached when I pulled out a long, flat box and opened the lid. The kimono Hiro wore the day we met. It was in remarkable shape considering its age. The hem was falling out and the white undergarments were slightly discolored, but the deep black remained unfaded. I ran the fragile fabric between my fingers and remembered how it looked against his fair skin and made him appear to glow from the inside. The kimono was, of course, property of the house in which he worked so he'd naturally left it behind when we left Kyoto. I'd contacted Hanagawa not long after we arrived in Edo. I was afraid she'd refuse me out of spite for the damage I'd done to her family, but she'd been happy to send it, refusing my offer of payment. "It belongs to him," she'd said. I didn't know why I'd never given it to him.

Regret sitting cold in my gut, I replaced the lid and continued searching for what I was really after. I soon pulled out a pair of black swords. I laid them across my lap, running my fingers along the saya. Each scratch, each mark told a story of battles hard-fought and not always won. They had been my most loyal companions, serving at my side for a lifetime. But the times changed as they always did and they'd been retired, buried like so many other things that had outlived their usefulness. I'd closed them up in a box just like everything else, refused to think about what their loss meant, and it wasn't until I hefted their familiar weight again that I realized just how much losing such a big part of myself had changed me.

I wrapped my hand around the hilt of the katana and pulled. It drew a finger width out of the saya and stopped with a horrible, grinding sound. What a failure of a samurai I was. The katana was supposed to be my soul, and I'd let it rust. The wakizashi was still good though, and I laid it out on the floor in front of me. I found a small bottle of oil and a few sheets of rice paper and set about the task of disassembling and cleaning the blade. Small dots of dirt and rust clung to its edge, and I worked at them slowly, gently, working the steel up to a muted shine. My mind slowed with the practice, my resolve sharpening along with the blade. It awoke something long dormant inside me. My samurai heart—the one willing to sacrifice all for the people standing behind his sword, the very same heart I fed to the beast—beat hot and strong.

My job finished, I snapped the wakizashi back into the saya and went back out into the main room of the house. I walked its perimeter, throwing both the amado and shoji open. Night had fallen, and the darkness poured in like smoke. I turned off all the electric lights and lit oil lamps instead. The wind teased the flames until the whole world flickered.

I could almost believe time had moved backward if it weren't for the ever-present drone and inescapable glow of the city outside. I went down on my knees in the center of the room, back straight, sitting on my heels, and laid the wakizashi out on the floor before me. A sharp, raw feeling started in my stomach, and I pressed my knuckles into the tatami to keep my hands from shaking.

Prove it.

I closed my eyes and took a breath that filled me all the way to my toes. I was gambling again, only this time I'd put my money on Hiro, betting that he could control the monster inside him and that even after all I'd put him through, there was some part of him that still loved me. I found his light in my heart and held it close. I let it warm me in a way I never had before. I clung to it until that belief became a certainty—and when I opened my eyes, I was no longer afraid.

If this all went wrong...well, I'd lived long enough.

I let out my held breath and pulled my phone out of my pocket. I punched in the number, a wry grin tugging at my lips as it rolled to voicemail with the sound of Takanori's bright voice.

I knew he wouldn't answer.

THIRTY-SIX

A Ringing Phone

HIRO

SPRING 2004

I AWOKE TO A BUZZING PHONE. SHARDS OF LIGHT CUT INTO MY EYES AS I forced them open, sending electrical storms through my head. Everything felt strange, almost unreal. My skin tingled with the oversensitivity that comes with being blood-drunk, though the high had long faded. A mattress that was definitely not mine creaked beneath me. The sharp, sweet smell of alcohol permeated everything until even the air felt sticky. Something warm and alive pressed against me, humming with the gentle vibration of blood and breath.

The buzz had stopped by the time I finally managed to open my eyes. I was still in Asagi's back room. I'd dozed off with Rui tucked up against me, wrapped in a blanket with nothing but the top of his head and one bare shoulder visible. His deep, even breaths tickled the skin just over my collar. I ran my finger over the curve of his shoulder, and he moaned and pressed himself tighter against me.

Desire and shame rang through me in sharp, dissonant notes. Rui's blood combined with my compromised mental state painted the events of the day in a strange, sepia sheen. I remembered asking Asagi for help. I remembered him leading me back here and presenting me with a *distraction*. My body heated with the memory of what followed, and I had to resist the urge to slip my hand inside Rui's blanket and over his thigh to touch the mark I'd left there.

Asagi's distraction had worked, at least for a moment. With Rui in my arms and my teeth in his skin, I didn't think about Taka or Hideyoshi or my broken mind. I didn't think about the youkai of Tokyo or how I'd failed them. There was only blood and heat and a reflected desire that didn't quite fill the hole inside me, but at least made it feel less empty.

The phone buzzed again, a short burst indicating a voicemail. I buried my nose in Rui's hair as I fought the dark itch in the back of my mind. Only two people would ever call that phone, and I was in no state to speak to either one of them.

Rui moaned again and stretched his legs, pushing one of them between mine. His eyes fluttered open just a crack, and his face tipped up. Our noses brushed, and his lashes tickled against my skin. "Hiro?"

"How are you feeling?" I asked, brushing a sticky lock of hair out of his eyes. His sculpted locks had begun to disintegrate and now lay in frizzing mats against his face, like a crumpled flower shoved into a pocket and left to wilt. I ran my hands through it as if I could smooth him back out.

"M'okay," he slurred. "Really tired."

"Rest then," I said, looping my arms around his shoulders. "You'll feel better in a day or two."

He hummed and pushed his nose into the crook of my neck. I thought he'd fallen asleep again when he said, "Your phone rang."

"I know."

"You don't want to answer?"

I let out a long sigh before answering. "No."

"What if it's that guy?"

That itch started again. "What guy?"

"Who was here earlier."

"You heard that?"

"Mn." His voice got quiet. He was fading fast. "He sounded...scared."

I scoffed. "Hideyoshi doesn't get scared."

Rui mumbled something against my neck before dropping off to sleep again and leaving me alone with my confused emotions. Scared? What could he possibly be scared of? I couldn't deny a burst of relief when Hideyoshi showed up here with a wild and vulnerable look in his eye. I tried to remember the last time I'd seen him like that, if I'd ever seen him like that, and I'd almost believed he'd finally shown up to fight for me. But then that dark thing inside fed me doubt, reminding me of all the times he'd ignored me, all the times he'd brushed off my cries for help as if I were a gnat buzzing around his face.

My eyes drifted to my phone, hastily thrown on the counter next to the sink, its notification light blinking like a taunt. He wouldn't leave a message. Or if he did, it would only be to tell me how childish I was being and demand I come home. It had to be Maia. I cringed at the memory of her running toward me with tears in her eyes, grief and fear etched across her small face. Hideyoshi had used his touch to calm her, but she must be confused by what she saw. She deserved explanations, but what could I possibly say that wouldn't make the whole thing worse?

She couldn't know. She could never know. It would be better if I just disappeared.

I closed my eyes and buried my face in the musty pillow, trying hard to ignore the growing tension in my gut. I saw that blinking light on the back of my eyelids. My nerves sparked when Rui moved against me again.

"Kuso."

Carefully rolling Rui onto his back, I pushed myself upright and scooted to the edge of the bed. Rui snorted a little but didn't wake, and I tucked the blanket tighter around him before rising to my feet. I stood over the phone, glaring down at it as if I could will that little light to stop blinking.

Without warning, a wave of vertigo struck me, nearly knocking me off my feet. I gasped and grasped at the counter. My knees trembled, and my balance faltered as if the room were spinning on a wobbly axis. My mouth went dry, and my ears filled with a static hiss as a deep pain expanded inside me, then contracted into a white-hot ball in my chest and disappeared, leaving behind a yawning emptiness. I couldn't breathe, as if my lungs had been pulled into that strange vortex and been replaced by a sucking vacuum. Cold sweat broke out on my brow. I doubled over.

And then it was gone.

"What was that?" I'd apparently woken Rui, who now sat straight up in the bed, his blanket sagging down around his chest and pooling at his waist. I wiped the sweat from my face and struggled to stand up straight.

"I don't—"

I was cut off by a loud crash just outside the door. I righted myself quickly and threw the door open. Asagi slouched against the wall surrounded by broken beer bottles, breathing heavily and clutching their chest. Our eyes locked. A realization snapped between us like a whip crack.

Hideyoshi.

I ran. I didn't know how I knew, but I knew I had to get home and fast. Asagi followed hot on my heels, the hard soles of their expensive shoes creating a sharp counterbeat to my pounding heart. I pushed through crowds of pedestrians and ignored street crossings, the edges of my vision black and my chest tight. The emptiness inside me became more and more apparent, and I refused to acknowledge what that could mean.

I smelled the blood before we even reached the gate. Asagi barreled into my back as I whipped it open. We fell through it together. We made it three steps in and froze. The shoji were all thrown open, exposing the entire house to the night. Lamps flickered in the corners, and shadows congealed along the floorboards. It looked empty, and for a moment I was relieved. But as I took a step closer, one particular shadow gained mass and solidified into a lump in almost the exact center of the room.

Asagi made a pained sound and fell to their knees, both hands over their mouth and tears streaming down their cheeks. My insides went cold. I shook my head, refusing to believe what I was seeing. Another step forward and I recognized a shoulder, the curve of a hip, bent legs, surrounded by something darker than the shadows. The smell was so strong, every cell sizzled and popped. I stumbled up the engawa, no longer in control of my own limbs.

"Hi...Hideyoshi?" I fell on my knees just outside the stain on the tatami, hands outstretched but not touching, as if tactile confirmation would suddenly make it real. Hideyoshi lay on his side, legs bent under him as if he'd been kneeling. One hand lay cupped near his face, partially obscuring it from view. The other lay on the hilt of a wakizashi. Though I hadn't seen it in at least a century, I recognized it immediately as the one he'd worn on his hip every day of his life before Meiji took it away, and a sudden surge of misplaced anger flared in my belly.

The blade was covered in blood, and it shone darkly in the lamplight. His clothes, too, were dark with it from chest to knees. It painted a trail down his chin and neck. My throat constricted as I imagined him choking on it.

"Hideyoshi?"

I leaned closer and laid my hand on his shoulder. I tipped him onto his back. His face was devoid of color, lids at half-mast and eyes clouded behind them. I touched his cheek—cold. The buttons on the bottom half of his shirt were undone, exposing his abdomen and a deep, ugly slash across his belly. The ragged edges of his wound showed evidence of multiple cuts, some partially healed. How many times did he have to cut himself before he stopped healing? How long did it take? I thought suddenly of my ringing phone.

I closed my eyes and turned my face away from the mess, tears pressing hard against the back of my eyes. I reached down into my heart, into the space where he should have been, and found it empty. Impossible. He promised me. And yet everything here showed an incredible determination to die.

I took his face in my hands. "Come back," I said in a broken voice, peering into his hooded eyes for any sign he could hear me. But they remained vacant. Desperation and anger mixed into something explosive, and I gave him a violent shake. "That's enough, Hideyoshi. You want to punish me? Fine. Scream at me, beat me, never speak to me again. I deserve it. But this is…"

My words broke off into a stream of sobs. I lowered my head onto his chest, and all I could smell was blood.

"You promised me," I hiccupped. "You promised me you'd never leave me alone. Please. I can't lose both of you."

My despair came to a crest, and the crack in my mind yawned wide. The beast inside me promised escape, and as I listened to my heart and found only silence, I longed for it. Just before it crashed over me, a spark of hope lit up in a back corner of my mind. Blood. He'd bled so much, so much he'd stopped healing. I sat up straight with a gasp.

"He's stuck." I whipped around to face Asagi. They'd made it as far as the engawa and leaned heavily on a post. "He's not gone," I said, voice tight and hysterical.

Asagi let out a shaky sigh. "Hiro…"

"He's not." I turned back to Hideyoshi. My tears dried up, and my skin vibrated with a manic energy. I repositioned myself next to him, pulling his upper body into my lap and cradling his head in the crook of my arm. Blood stuck to my skin and soaked through my pants. The tatami was soggy with it, but I paid no attention. He wasn't gone. Hideyoshi wasn't dead. He wanted to come back, he just needed help.

I didn't even feel the pain as I bit into my own wrist. Blood poured from the tear. I held it over Hideyoshi's lips. It poured dark and thick into his mouth. When the wound healed, I tore it open again, all the while waiting, watching, praying for him to swallow.

But he didn't.

I went cold all over as my blood filled the cavity of his mouth and spilled from the corners. Asagi appeared beside me and placed a gentle hand on my wrist. There was none of their usual animosity, only sorrow, when they looked down into Hideyoshi's face.

"Why would he…" My voice sounded hollow and strange to my ears.

"I don't know."

"Did I do this?" My throat convulsed, and for a moment I thought I would be sick. "Is this my fault?"

Asagi hesitated, just a microsecond, but long enough to eviscerate me. "No."

The darkness beckoned once again. I leaned toward it, all the while with his voice echoing in my ears. *Don't be like me.*

A floorboard creaked from deep inside the house, and Asagi's head snapped up. A man appeared in the hallway. He could have been anybody, plain face, plain suit, a salariman on his way home from work. But he held something in his hand, something that flashed bright in the lamplight—a knife with a silver blade. He stopped well out of reach, impassive eyes tracking Asagi as they slowly stood.

Asagi spun around at the sound of the swinging gate. Another man appeared in the yard, same as the first, his knife held limply by his side. Asagi bared their fangs, manicured nails flashing like talons and muscles tensed as if waiting to pounce.

The two Hunters made eye contact, but neither made a move. They simply watched with narrowed eyes. What were they waiting for? I clutched Hideyoshi tighter. I knew I should stand and face them, but none of the things I'd once cared about mattered anymore. Anger and despair faded to nothing, drifting away like so much smoke, leaving only hunger. Darkness crept in until all I saw was the light from their beating hearts.

Then Hideyoshi moved.

My vision cleared in a snap at the slightest flutter under my fingers where they rested on his jaw. A twitch of his lips, followed by the slow slide of his Adam's apple under his skin. A swallow. My heart that had slowed to a crawl jumped into a quick, fluttering rhythm.

"Hideyoshi?"

Asagi's attention whipped back down to me, eyes wide and disbelieving. I cupped Hideyoshi's face in my hand and stared into his eyes, now squeezed closed, his brow knotted over them. I touched his lips and felt the slightest brush of breath, still cold, but moving.

He exploded to life with a gasp and a scream. His eyes shot open— wide, white, and unseeing. I wrapped my arms around his shoulders as spasms wracked his body. I grabbed his arms as he clutched at the torn flesh of his abdomen.

Asagi joined me in my attempts to restrain him. He snapped like a wild animal. I thrust my wrist between his teeth and he latched on, ripping and pulling and dragging blood out of me in deep swallows. My head spun and my vision blurred as his starving body fought back the death that had claimed it.

"Look at me, Yoshi," Asagi cried, face streaked with tears.

Hideyoshi's eyes rolled, the color slowly coming back. The terrible wound on his belly pulled back together—new, pink skin covering the muscle and viscera. Little by little, the draw on my veins eased and his body relaxed, eyes finally finding their target.

"A..sagi?" he said between gasping breaths, his lips still resting against the skin of my arm.

With a tearful laugh, Asagi collapsed.

"Where's Hiro?"

"Right beside you, bakayarou," Asagi answered.

Hideyoshi looked at the arm in his grip, then up at me with tired, pain-filled eyes. I fell into a fit of relieved sobs. I wrapped my arms tight around him and he let me—his nose pressed against my neck, his now-warm breath against my skin.

"What are you crying for?" Hideyoshi asked.

"I thought you'd left me."

"Stupid boy," he said with a dark laugh. "I made a promise to you, didn't I?"

The all-but-forgotten Hunters took a step forward, and Asagi jumped to their feet again. Blood spotted their designer suit and turned brown against their pale skin. They crouched low, muscles pulled tight and red eyes burning with murderous intent. Power rolled off them in waves strong enough to knock one of the Hunters off their feet. Asagi had always been different from us, but for the first time I saw the predator they could have been if they'd wanted it.

"I haven't killed anyone in a very long time," Asagi snarled, "but I will happily tear the heads off both of you if you take another step."

Hideyoshi laughed. "You would care if they killed me?"

"Shut up," Asagi spat down at him.

"I knew you would come," Hide said in a voice so soft, I knew it was only meant for me.

"I don't understand," I said between sobs. "Why did you do this? Why did you…"

There was a long silence, long enough I thought he'd lost consciousness.

"I had to prove it," he said finally, in a cracked voice.

"Prove what?"

"I'm so sorry, Hiro."

In one swift move, quicker than a man just back from death should be able to do, Hideyoshi scooped up his wakizashi and plunged it into my chest.

THIRTY-SEVEN

Proof

SPRING 2004

HE KNEW EXACTLY HOW TO STRIKE TO MAKE IT QUICK. THE SWORD SLID cleanly between my ribs and straight into my heart. It didn't even hurt. It was as if I'd become untethered from my body, thrust up and out of it by the force of the blow. I saw myself lying there, my arms still draped around Hideyoshi, Asagi with their eyes wide and jaw agape, and Hide with tears on his cheeks as he extracted the bloody blade. Tears. I'd never seen him cry before. He threw the blade away from him as if it alone were to blame, and he cradled my head in his hand as my body collapsed. The last thing I heard was his voice, shaking and broken and desperate.

"Come back."

I was sucked down into the cold black, mind confused and dispersed like a fine mist. The dark, lonely space between life and death surrounded me, enveloped me, pulled me apart. Only one thought managed to form in the void: *Hideyoshi killed me.* In my thinned-out state, I couldn't even find it in me to be angry. It was maybe even a mercy. I thought about Yui and her words when I'd visited her after Hashiguchi's death. Relief. If I stayed here, it would be a relief, wouldn't it? Hideyoshi wouldn't have to watch my slow descent into madness, and I wouldn't die alone in a basement, but here in his arms.

Come back.

His voice vibrated through the dark, the only thing with any form. If I had hands I could touch it, hold the words in my palms and press them into my skin. Another thought formed in the void: I wanted to touch him. I missed him. I didn't want us to end like this.

With a snap, I was ripped from the dark. My disparate mind pulled itself together, and I woke up gasping, choking, pain spreading like a firework in my chest. There was blood in my mouth, and I swallowed greedily.

"Good boy," he said, relief audible in his voice. "You're okay. I've got you."

The pain subsided, and my surroundings came into focus. Hideyoshi held me in a position not unlike the one in which I'd held him, his wrist pressed between my teeth. A pallor still hung on him, but his eyes were sharp as ever, looking down on me with naked desperation. The wound on my chest burned as it pulled itself closed, and I pressed my palm against the new flesh as my laboring heart found its rhythm.

Asagi stood over us, a mix of shock and rage on their face. Even the Hunters stood by, their expressions drawn. Panic sizzled in my veins, coaxing tired muscles to life, and I scooped up Hideyoshi's discarded sword. He barked out a protest as I staggered to my feet and turned to face them. Panting and swaying, I thrust the wakizashi out in front of me. It had been so long since I'd held a sword, it felt foreign, the weight almost more than I could handle. The end trembled as I struggled to catch my breath.

The Hunter in the hallway met my eyes, and the corners of his mouth ticked up. His grip on his knife tightened, and he took a step forward. Asagi faced the other Hunter, their back pressed against mine. I adjusted my stance, and my weakened muscles complained as I lowered my center of gravity.

A mechanical chirp cut through the tension, and the Hunter stopped short. With a huff, he pulled his phone out of his pocket and flipped it open. The light from the small screen lit his face from below, making him appear ghoulish. Another chirp from behind me, and the other Hunter did the same.

Asagi and I exchanged a confused look as the two Hunters scowled at the message on their phones. Almost in unison, they shoved their phones back into their pockets and backed away, their departure marked by the slap of a shoji and a swinging gate.

"What was that?" Asagi asked.

"They got their proof," Hideyoshi answered.

"Proof? Of what?" Asagi asked, turning on him with fangs bared. "Yoshi—"

Asagi's words distorted as if I were listening from underwater. The sword sagged and slipped from my grip. My vision blurred, the floor tilted. The last thing I heard as my knees gave out was Hideyoshi calling my name.

I awoke in Hideyoshi's arms. I knew it was him without even opening my eyes. For a moment I lay very still, my face buried in his broad chest and my hands clutched in his clothes. His heartbeat in my ear was the sweetest music, and I composed operas to its sound. To think I may have never heard it again. The possibility was more than I could bear and one I'd never really considered. Even when I left, part of me took it for granted that he would be here when the time came to return—angry perhaps, but present. I knew there would be consequences to my absence, but I hadn't taken into account the weight of the responsibilities I'd left him with and the danger it put him in. The idea of a world without him made my heart shake, and I wanted to hold onto him and never let go.

But then I remembered. He killed me.

I opened my eyes slowly and lifted my head. Hideyoshi's room took shape around me. Painted scrolls and flowers in vases and books filled with poetry. Soft light filtered in from outside, laying amber shadows across his cheeks and jaw. One of his hands rested on my hip, the other arm under my head and curled around my shoulders. His chest rose and fell with deep, even breathing, his expression slack as if too exhausted to even dream. Darkness still clung to the hollows of his eyes, but his color had otherwise returned. We both wore clean clothes, and our wounds had completely healed. As if it never happened.

Swallowing hard, I carefully extracted myself from his hold and slipped out of the futon. Ignoring the lingering smell of blood, I padded down the hall to the kitchen. I needed to think, to decompress, to figure out what really happened. No matter how much I tried, I couldn't wrap my head around it. Hideyoshi had been dead, truly dead, to the point he'd been carved from my heart. I touched my sternum, remembering the terror and vertigo and *wrongness* of the feeling. It still lingered there in the hollow space where he had been. He was alive now, warm and breathing in the bed next to me, but his heart hadn't returned to mine, and it scared me to think what that could mean.

My cast-iron teapot sat on the counter, dusty with disuse. I washed it out, filled it with clean water, and placed it on the stove to warm. Making tea always calmed me, with its sharp smells and meditative routine. Heat the water, pack the filter, steep the leaves. But for some reason, I couldn't focus. My hands shook, making the glass rattle. I found a tin of loose leaves in the cabinet, but the lid stuck. I dug my fingernails into the seam and forced it with a growl, sending a shower of leaves across the kitchen floor when it finally gave way.

I slammed the tin down on the counter with a curse. Dishes rattled around me, drawing my attention to a blinking light just within reach— my phone. Someone must have picked it up and placed it here. The notification light still blinked from the call I'd missed the night before. I reached for it, guilt already curling in my stomach and solidifying into a hard ball when I flipped it open and read the name. *Hicchan.* It was him, sent seconds before he'd cut himself open. I snapped it shut, closed my eyes, and took a deep breath before opening it again. The voicemail icon flashed, and tears burned behind my eyes as I hovered my finger over the button.

(Silence followed by a cough.) Hiro, this is...you know who this is. Look, I hate talking to these things, so I'm going to just get to the point. I'm about to do something...maybe a little crazy. Really crazy, actually, and you might not understand it, but I think it's something you would do if you were in my position. I am...scared. I'm scared of destroying everything we've spent several lifetimes building. Maybe I

already have. I've failed you in so many ways, I wouldn't blame you if you were really done with me. But in order for this to work, I need to trust you. I do trust you.

I made a promise to myself a very long time ago that if I couldn't come back on my own, I wouldn't. But I also made a promise to you. I know things haven't been right between us for a while now, but I haven't forgotten. So I'll wait as long as I can and trust that I haven't completely lost you. That you'll come for me. But in case it all goes wrong...I hope it's not too late to tell you—

I jerked the phone away from my ear as Hideyoshi's voice was cut off by a shrill beep. I stared at the screen, cheeks wet with tears I hadn't known I was crying. I slapped the phone's side as if I could shake loose those last few words.

"What?" I said from between clenched teeth. "Tell me what?"

"That I love you."

I spun around so fast I nearly fell over, and the phone clattered to the floor. Hide stood in the entrance, his dark, imposing figure softened by the morning light and the tears blurring my vision. My heart jumped so high in my throat, I choked on it. He took a step into the room, and I pressed myself tighter against the counter. He looked different somehow, his usual guarded expression replaced with something warmer.

"That girl, Maia. She really cares about you. She's…" He laughed, ducking his head in a way that was almost bashful. "…annoying. But smart. She sees right through me, I think. She said I should tell you, even if it wouldn't change anything. I thought for sure it was too late—"

"It's…it's not—" I took a deep breath to steady myself, only managing to knock loose a sob. I turned my face away, embarrassed at the scene I was making, but Hide tipped it back with a finger on my chin. His eyes were so open and honest, it broke me.

"Are you okay?" he asked softly.

I shook my head and fell into his chest. I thought he would push me away, tell me to get myself together and grow up, but he just wrapped his arms around my shaking shoulders and held me tight. Relief washed over me, the relief of unwinding an obi tied too tight, of removing pins from your hair that had been poking, of peeling away the costume and letting all the scars underneath show. I was messy and broken, everything throbbed and ached and I was so, so scared. But I also felt safe, because he saw it all and he loved me anyway.

He loved me.

"I thought you were gone," I sobbed into his chest. "I thought you'd left me."

"I know. I'm sorry."

"I still don't understand." I wiped my face on his shirt and raised my head. "Why did you have to go so far?"

Hideyoshi took a breath, held it a moment, then let it out slow before speaking. "We were threatened by Hunters."

I gasped, and my eyes shot open wide. "They're back?"

"I'm not sure they ever really left."

Anger sizzled up my spine. "We had a deal."

"Which we broke."

"You mean I broke," I said, the fire licking through me turning to ice. He ran a hand along my back as the realization sunk in, pressing down on my shoulders and bending my spine. "He came to me once. He warned me but I didn't listen. I just wanted…"

"Takanori."

I nodded and my eyes welled. "I'm sorry. I was selfish and stupid."

Hide's eyes went razor-sharp, and he took my face in his hands. "Would you change anything? Knowing what you know now, would you give up your time with Takanori?"

A flood of memories washed over me, flipbook images of the last ten years, followed by grief so sharp it took my breath away. I could have avoided this pain. I could have walked out of that ramen shop and never returned. But then I wouldn't have had the music of his voice, the warmth of his skin, that sound he made when he kissed me. It may hurt now to look at them, but each of those memories was more precious than the brightest gold or the finest silk. I pulled in a shaky breath and shook my head. Hide wiped away a tear with his thumb.

"Then don't be sorry."

My shoulders sagged, and I pushed my lips against Hideyoshi's palm.

"It doesn't matter anyway. They've been watching us, maybe the whole time, most certainly for the past ten years, waiting for a moment of weakness. I confronted Kyo, and he told me he would call them off if I could prove that we were still…"

"Immortal," I finished on an exhale. "And the only way to do that was for us both to die."

"Mn." Hide nodded sharply, his eyes hard and distant. "This was a test. He doesn't really want to kill us. He needs us for something. Both of us. Together."

"For what?"

He shrugged.

A dark feeling passed over me, and I felt again the cold of that in-between place, the temptation to stay. "It's getting harder. To come back."

Hide's jaw clenched.

"What if I hadn't felt it? When you…" My throat constricted. "What if I was too far gone and hadn't come…"

"I trusted you."

My heart rattled against my ribs, and I let my head fall forward onto his shoulder. We held each other in silence, and I listened again to the sound of his heartbeat, so steady and strong.

"I can't hear you anymore," I said in a voice barely above a whisper.

"I know. Me neither."

"What does that mean?"

"I don't know." His muscles tensed, and he held me a little tighter. "Maybe I got too close or lingered too long. Maybe it's a…punishment."

I didn't have time to think about what that meant before the house vibrated with the distinct sound of high heels hitting hardwood and the scrape of a shoji. Hide released me and moved ahead of me into the main room, his fingers still loosely linked with mine. We found Asagi standing in the doorway, eyes on the dark stain on the tatami.

"Asagi?"

Asagi's head snapped up at the sound of Hide's voice. The color was high on their cheeks, and their eyes glistened. A gust of wind blew in behind them, making the gauzy skirt of their white dress billow around them like smoke. They pulled in a shaky breath over parted lips before pulling their gaze away and busying themselves with removing their shoes.

"Is everything all right?" I asked. Asagi didn't answer, a deep crease forming across the bridge of their nose. High-heeled sandals dangled by straps from their fingers as they crossed onto the tatami on bare feet. Asagi kept their eyes lowered and their face hard as they moved toward us, stopped in front of Hideyoshi, and slapped him hard enough to knock him off-balance.

"How dare you?" Asagi growled.

Hide released a shocked laugh, a hand on his bruised cheek. "How dare I?"

"Yes, how dare you." Asagi's red eyes practically glowed with anger. "How dare you throw your life away. I gave you this life, and you treat it like it's expendable. Like it's something that can be bargained with. And what about him?" Asagi jabbed a finger in my direction. "He's half-mad already. What do you think would happen to him if he lost you? Don't you care about anything but yourself?"

"Of course I—"

"Shut up," Asagi snapped. "You are forbidden to die before me unless I allow it, which I DO NOT. Understand me?"

A smile teased at the corners of Hide's mouth. "Mn."

"Good," Asagi huffed, out of breath. They smoothed their hands down their dress as they took a moment to compose themselves. "Fix your floor. It stinks like death in here."

Asagi turned and stomped out the door without even bothering to put on their shoes. Hideyoshi watched them go in shocked silence, eyes wide and blinking. A laugh bubbled up inside me, and I pressed the back of my hand to my mouth to suppress it.

"I'm glad this amuses you," Hide said.

"Well, you did deserve it." I took a deep breath to calm my hysterics. "They care about you, you know."

"He hates me."

I shrugged. "Both things can be true."

Hide sighed. "You don't seem surprised."

"That Asagi's your maker?"

He nodded again.

"It makes a lot of things make sense. You two have been pecking at each other like hens for as long as I've known you." Hide made a sour face at my remark but didn't argue. I moved closer to him and rested my nose on his shoulder. "Why didn't you tell me?"

"Maybe I was embarrassed," he answered after a thoughtful moment.

"Of Asagi?"

"No. Of me."

Hide's eyes went hazy, and I saw the past there, full of hardships and regrets. His armor came back on, articulating piece by piece in the tightening of his muscles, the stubborn line of his back, and the hardening of his jaw. I slipped my hand into his, and it tightened around mine almost desperately. After two hundred years, I thought I'd known every facet of him. It was a relief to know I was wrong.

"Hide," I whined against his shoulder. "I'm hungry."

He grunted in agreement.

I swung our clasped hands between us. "Come out with me?"

"Stupid boy," he said with a click of his tongue. "It's broad daylight. Just wait—"

"But I'm still healing," I said with a pout, touching my fingers to my chest. A lie, of course, and he knew it, but I batted my eyes at him anyway. "It's all your fault and you won't even come with me? You're a horrible man."

He rolled his eyes as I wrapped myself around his arm. "Enough," he huffed, shaking me off. He stomped out the door without looking back, and my heart fluttered as I skipped off after him.

THIRTY-EIGHT

Obsession

SUMMER 2004

I WAS SITTING OUTSIDE, ONE LEG SWINGING OFF THE ENGAWA, THE OTHER crooked up beneath me and cradling a shamisen, when Maia slipped through the front gate. A soft breeze curled around me, and I plucked a lazy tune to accompany it. I'd been home a few days when I got the urge to play again. I found the practice comforting in a way I hadn't expected. Though the darkness had receded, it wasn't gone, my emotions still volatile, and when I found myself sad or anxious or even angry for no real reason, I poured those feelings out into music. It made them more tangible somehow, easier to deal with, and as the notes drifted and dissipated, those emotions did too, leaving behind a deep calm.

"That's beautiful," Maia said with a warm smile that trembled around the edges. She clasped her hands together at her waist, and her fingers wound over each other in nervous knots that broke my heart. I hadn't seen her since she'd appeared behind Hideyoshi in Asagi's bar. I should have reached out to her after the dust settled, but I was too cowardly to even pick up the phone.

"I'm rusty," I said with a self-conscious laugh, as I lay my palm across the body of the instrument to mute the strings. "I haven't played in a long time."

"How long...exactly?"

Her weight shifted from one foot to the other as she searched my face for answers. I released a long, tired sigh. Hide had told me, of course, about their conversations and what he'd shown her, and I saw it twist the lines of her face as she tried to reconcile that man with the one she knew. I had no answers for her. Even to me, they felt like two different people. One I'd found in my time with her and Taka, the other a monster I hardly knew. I hated that she'd seen that man, hated the doubt and fear it put in her eyes, and it lit a spark of resentment deep inside me.

"Don't be angry at him, Hiro," she said as if she could see the train of my thoughts.

"He shouldn't have scared you like that. It was cruel."

"It wasn't," she said quickly. "He was trying to protect me, I think. I would have gone running after you no matter what. He just wanted me to know that you were—"

"Dangerous?"

She let out a breath, and some of her tension left with it. She stepped forward and dropped down beside me on the engawa. Her eyes were soft and watery, and it was all I could do not to pull her into my arms. "You're not dangerous, Hiro."

I gave a dry laugh. "I am, actually."

"Well, I'm not scared of you."

She met my eyes with startling conviction, and I found myself flinching away. I swallowed hard and plucked at my shamisen.

"Did he know?" she asked gently.

I shook my head. "I must have tried to tell him a hundred times. Then he got sick and...I don't know. I think the last thing he needed was to believe everything I'd told him was a lie."

"Was it?"

"Not the important things."

Silence fell over us again, broken only by the strings vibrating under my fingers. I glanced at Maia out of the corner of my eye and caught her looking over her shoulder into the house.

"He's here, you know."

She jerked her head back forward, cheeks pink as if she'd been caught doing something scandalous. "What? Who?"

"Hideyoshi, of course," I laughed, flicking her between her eyebrows. "He's the real reason you're here, isn't he?"

She blushed so hard even the tips of her ears were red. "What? No! I mean…"

"It's okay," I said, giving her cheek a playful pinch. "I think he likes you too. He's doing this thing where he's…communicating." I shivered with a melodramatic roll of my eyes that made her laugh. "He must bring up your name half a dozen times a day."

Maia's eyes widened. "What does he say?"

I scratched my chin and hummed in thought. "That you're irritating and ask too many questions."

She groaned and slapped her hands over her face. She reminded me so much of Taka in that moment, it hurt.

"Don't worry," I said. "Coming from him, that's a compliment."

"How is that a compliment?" she asked from behind her hands.

I shrugged. "He cares enough to notice."

Her fingers parted over one eye, and she peeked out at me. I gave her a smile of encouragement, and she dropped her hands with a sigh.

"Are you sure?" she asked. "I mean, aren't you two…"

I sucked in a breath. Hideyoshi and I *had* done a great deal of talking in the past few days, about who we were as individuals as well as a couple. It was amazing how much we'd left unsaid in our time together. I couldn't deny a small twinge of jealousy when he spoke of her and that genuine spark of interest danced in his eyes. But I knew it had no bearing on his love for me, just as my relationship with Taka didn't change my love for him. And she would be good for him. She was strong enough to stand up to him and self-confident enough to withstand when he pulled away. If anyone could force him out of his shell, it would be her.

"We have a literal eternity together," I answered. "I think a little break every once in a while might do us some good."

She studied me a long moment, disbelief etched in her face.

"Just do me one favor, okay? Be careful."

Her brows pulled together. "I'm not afraid—"

"I'm not worried about you," I said. "I'm worried about him." Her brows shot up into her hairline, and I laughed. "He puts on a strong face, but he's more vulnerable than you think. And it's...scary being in a relationship with someone who's not like us, because he knows—not fears, *knows*—that one day, no matter what happens between you or how your relationship plays out, he will lose you." A glimmer of pain passed through me, and I swallowed the lump in my throat. "It's the price we pay. So be gentle with him when you feel him holding back or pulling away."

She pulled in a long, slow breath, her eyes going far away as the truth settled over her. Her hands wound themselves into a knot again, and she pulled her lip between her teeth.

"Go on," I said, breaking the tension by sweeping the plectrum over the strings of my shamisen. "He's probably out back trying to woo those dumb birds. You'll be doing him a favor."

She offered me a kind smile before blowing out a breath and pushing herself to her feet. She took a couple of steps toward the house before stopping and turning back.

"Oh, I almost forgot," she said. "There's some guy hanging around outside your gate."

A needle of anxiety pierced my gut. "A guy? What guy?"

"I don't know. Young-ish, nervous, kind of looks like Harajuku threw up on him."

Rui.

I laughed and waved her off, but my heart was in my throat. The second she disappeared inside, I jumped up off the engawa, hesitating only slightly before swinging the gate open and pushing my head outside. A strange contradiction of feelings swirled inside me as I spotted him pacing a row on the sidewalk across the street, spiky hair hanging in his eyes and chains dangling from his hips. I'd thought of him often in the past few days. Not just of the taste of his blood, though it had found its way into my fantasies more than once, but also of the depths of his eyes, the shape of his body under a blanket, the soft way his tongue lingered on my name like a benediction.

But it was obsession that brought him here. His blood in me called to him like a siren song, a fact I had to keep in the front of my mind. My fascination with him, however, came from a different place. It took me by surprise. His presence was like a balm on my wounded heart. He was beautiful and broken in a way that felt both familiar and completely alien. I had the violent urge to protect him and devour him all at once. It was probably best to stay away. I didn't know if I could.

Rui's pacing stopped abruptly as I emerged from behind the gate. Those deep, molten eyes widened, and his lips parted on a gasp.

"Hey," I said. I couldn't get the single word out without my voice cracking, and it sent heat crawling up the back of my neck.

"Hey." His deep, gravelly voice tickled over my skin. He licked his lips and shoved his hands in his pockets, weight shifting forward as if he would cross the street but didn't dare. "I don't...really know why I'm here."

"It's obsession," I said, swallowing around the tightness in my throat. "It happens sometimes when we...it'll pass after some time away. Probably."

He nodded, a crease forming between his manicured brows. I didn't know why I told him that. I wasn't even sure it was true.

"What if I don't want it to pass?"

I gasped. Objections piled up and dissolved on my tongue.

"I know what I'm feeling isn't real," he said, and my veins buzzed as he finally took a step closer. "Asagi told me how all this works before..."

"Then you should know what we did was dangerous."

He nodded, his heavy earrings clacking around his ears. "I do. But it also felt..."

"Good?" I answered breathlessly. His cheeks darkened, and he nodded. A craving burned through me, and I shoved my hands in my pockets to keep them from shaking. "Aren't you scared?"

He shrugged. "Maybe. But I was so numb before." He took another step closer, and my resolve melted in that small distance. "I like the way this feels. Like flying and falling all at once. Like listening to loud music that makes your heart race so hard it hurts. I know it's not real, but it's better than feeling nothing."

"Rui—"

"Just have a drink with me." He jumped forward again, now within reaching distance, and I balled my hands into my jeans to keep them from moving. He laughed, a dark, brittle thing. "Like a real one. With booze."

Say no. Say no. Say no.

"Okay."

His face brightened, and as if on some mutual agreement, we both turned and walked in the vague direction of Shinjuku. He drifted closer to me with every step, and I let myself relax as our shoulders bumped together. I knew deep down I was likely setting myself up for yet another heartache. I had just warned Maia about the dangers of human relationships, and here I was ready to jump into another one. But then again, like Maia and Hideyoshi, maybe he would be good for me. A distraction might be just what I needed.

つづく

Epilogue

NAKAMURA MEI

IT'S FUNNY HOW THE SMALLEST THINGS CAN CHANGE THE COURSE OF your whole life. For me, it was ten yen. Ten fucking yen. Worse than that. Ten yen short of a fucking coffee. Standing in front of a vending machine, a cigarette dangling from my lips and a hangover pounding in my ears, I stared mournfully at a handful of coins, so sure that little can would be the answer to all my problems. The rising sun turned the sky gray between buildings that felt too close, their tops bowing toward me in mocking attention.

I should have gone back to bed.

"Two hundred fifty. Two hundred fifty," I repeated to myself, counting the two hundred and forty yen in my hand for the hundredth time, as if it might have changed in the last five seconds. I leaned my forehead on the machine and groaned. It was the fourth shot that did me in, something pink and sickly sweet shoved into my hand by a girl whose face was a blurry smear on my memory. My usually carefully manicured honey-blond hair stuck to the back of my neck. Or was it the pitcher of beer bought by one of my subordinates and unceremoniously sloshed all over the table in his attempt to pour? My hands were still tacky with it, the smell soaked into my clothes.

"You are so fired," I growled into the crook of my elbow.

A shadow fell over me, followed by the sound of metal on metal and a mechanical beep. I looked up just in time to see a tanned and tattooed hand withdraw from the coin slot and shove itself back into the pocket of a pair of navy blue dickies.

"Thank you, GOD!" I cried, shoving my handful of coins into the slot and jabbing the button. I heard a little snort of laughter as I tore into the little can, almost choking on the contents as it went hot down my throat. It was half gone before I remembered myself, wiping my mouth with an embarrassed grin. "Thank you, sir. I owe you my—"

Youkai.

"Your life?" he finished. Golden cheeks lifted, and his whole face crinkled when he smiled. "Is your life so cheap it can be bought with ten yen?"

It was so obvious, sometimes I wondered how everyone on the street didn't notice. His voice was too crisp, his skin too bright, his posture too relaxed to be real. But people didn't believe in monsters even when they were right in front of them, even when they were chewing on their necks.

"My sanity, maybe," I said with a nervous laugh, lifting the little can to him as I took another drink.

"Well, maybe you can pay it back someday," he said, turning and tossing a little wave over his shoulder as he continued down the street.

Naturally, I followed him. Because I'm a fucking idiot.

Mattaku, these Tokyo youkai were boring. Tame as fucking house cats, and he was no different. I followed him for hours, watched him shop, eat, even pick up dry cleaning. Everything so dreadfully ordinary, I began to question myself. Had I just been hunting so long, I saw youkai everywhere? But there was the way he moved, smooth and calm and perfectly measured. Humans all carry with them a sort of tension, an ingrained fear of the unknown and the knowledge that, at any moment, we could die. He moved with the nonchalance of someone untouchable, with the ease of someone who hadn't feared death in a very long time.

Eventually, we ended up at a cheap and rather dirty-looking hotel tucked into a forgotten corner of Akihabara. A weathered sign by the door boasted hourly rates in sloppy, hand-painted characters and murky neon light filtered through dusty windows. I hung back along the street as the monster tapped a keycard against a pad by the door, worn in the center from the thousand cards before it, and slipped inside.

"Is this where you're living, you bastard?" I muttered to myself, lighting another cigarette and sweeping my eyes over the property for a good stakeout position. I wanted in. I wanted to stand where he was standing, lie in the bed he slept in. I wanted to know everything about him—what he ate, what he drank, who he fucked, what trophies and trinkets he kept. I wanted to crawl inside his head and know his every thought, wish, and nightmare.

I wanted to know what he lived for. I wanted to kill him.

I plopped myself down on a horribly uncomfortable bus stop bench with a view of the door and waited. A light flicked on two stories up, and his shadow moved behind the curtains. I leaned forward and listened hard, as if I might catch the sound of his music on the wind.

What I caught was worse. Or better, I guess, depending on perspective. The sound of hard-soled shoes on concrete. I cursed and dove to the ground behind the bench, making the old lady next to me squeal. A long, lean frame moved sleek and catlike through the crowded streets toward me. Sugiyama Minato. That smug son of a bitch. The man I hated but secretly wanted to be. I imagined our leader, if we actually had one, would be like him, a chess player always fifteen moves ahead. I, on the other hand, could barely plan ahead as far as lunchtime.

We'd worked a hunt together a few years ago, one of my first. He'd shown up in front of the boutique where I worked with a note written by brush on fancy paper. On it was nothing but an address and a name. He was good, great, with needle-sharp instincts and a cold brutality that chilled me to my bones. He knew exactly where to strike, what button to push. I was timid then, struggling to see the monsters behind the human faces, but he taught me to see them as they truly were—beasts in human skin, skin he peeled away piece by piece until they revealed themselves.

After that first kill, he made me stand and watch for hours as the monster's body disintegrated into dust. I vomited in a trash can. His face never changed. And I never saw youkai as human again.

I must have stumbled upon his hunt. It would be my ass if he knew I was here, threatening to blow it for him.

I held my breath as he crossed the street. As annoyed as I was to see him, part of me thrilled at the thought of watching him work. I inched closer as he approached the door, my skin tingling. And then he did the strangest thing.

He pulled out a key and went inside.

"Son of a bitch," I muttered to myself. Keeping low, I dashed across the street and caught the heavy, metal door just before it clicked closed. I held my breath, listening to the echo of his footsteps as they ricocheted off the walls. I peered through the crack just as he stepped into an elevator.

Once the elevator doors closed, I shot through the doorway and into the stairwell at the end of the hall. Taking the steps two at a time, I reached the second floor landing in less than a second and pressed myself against the door, ignoring the sticky film beneath my cheek. A tinny *ding* announced the elevator's arrival, and I counted to five before easing the door open. A hallway lined with rooms opened up perpendicular to the elevators, and I followed on tiptoes as he took a hard turn to the right, stopped three doors down, and knocked.

"FUCKING son of a bitch!" I snarled under my breath as Minato bowed and the youkai welcomed him in. That traitorous motherfucker. This wasn't a hunt. It was a meet-up.

Once Minato was safely tucked inside, I crept closer, cringing at the Velcro sound my every step made against the grimy linoleum. I pressed myself to the wall and leaned my ear against the door. Muffled voices and shuffling footsteps. Nothing distinct enough to tell what they were talking about, but Minato's voice had the sharp, crisp feel particular to polite Japanese. He was lowering himself, talking to that thing as if he were his superior.

My blood boiled, and despite my distaste for the man, my heart broke a little. I'd heard of others becoming entranced, even obsessed with their youkai prey after getting too close, but it was always some lesser Hunter. A cautionary tale about another's failure. If it could happen to Minato, the strongest among us...

I jumped and darted around the corner as the voices stopped and the footsteps drew closer to the door. The two of them exited shortly after, still conversing in hushed tones. I held my breath at the scraping sound of a sudden stop and pivot.

"Is there a problem, sir?" Minato asked.

Sir.

"Nope," the youkai said casually as his shoes squeaked against the tile again, followed by the ding and whoosh of the departing elevator.

I didn't release my breath until the hall was silent. I peeked slowly around the corner with one eye, making double-sure the coast was clear before approaching the door again. My original goal hadn't changed. I still wanted in. The purpose, however, was entirely different.

To find out if Minato had really betrayed us and why.

As any experienced thief knows, hotel room locks, especially cheap ones, are a joke. A credit card slipped inside the jam and a sharp strike to the frame were enough to dislodge the locking mechanism, and it swung open easily. I slipped inside and found exactly what one would expect: stained carpets, gaudy wallpaper, and a sagging bed. Other than the general grimness of the place, the room was pristine, the bed perfectly made, toiletries still in their hermetically sealed wrappings, not even a stray coffee cup on the bedside table. I curled my nose and tried my damndest to touch things as little as possible as I opened drawer after empty drawer.

He didn't live here, probably hadn't been here more than a few hours. He must have picked it special for his meeting with Minato. I cursed and was about to slam the last drawer shut when I noticed something wedged in the corner. A little Polaroid, facedown and slightly stuck in the grimy surface. I grimaced and peeled it up with a fingernail. My heart stopped when I saw what it was.

It was me.

He hit me so fast, it knocked the wind out of me. He pinned me against the wall, his teeth in my neck before I could even wonder why I didn't hear the door open. Pain whipped through me, fiery and all-consuming, as if every vein were a lit fuse burning its way to my heart. He pulled the blood from me so fast, I couldn't even scream, and within seconds my vision blurred. Then, as quickly as I had been taken, he released me and I fell heavily to the floor, unconscious before I hit the ground.

I thought it would be dark, but instead I dropped into a space so bright, it was featureless. White light pierced through my very skin, brighter than the floodlights on Tokyo Tower, colder than the moon. My limbs felt blurry and indistinct, like an out-of-focus photo. Even my mind seemed soft somehow. I knew what had just happened to me, the danger and the shame, but it all seemed far away and unimportant. I thought maybe I was dead, but then I heard a voice, a whisper in my ear, but not in my ear.

I like the way you taste.

I shivered as the voice consumed me, filling me up like something viscous and liquid until I became just a vessel. I couldn't see anything, not even myself, but I felt hands on me, rough and strong, tracing every line of me, defining my fuzzy parts. I felt recreated, like an idea without form until he drew me and made me real.

Who are you?

A rush of images flashed against my eyelids like photos in a flipbook. Different eras, different settings, but all the same man. The man with a bulldog face and tattooed fingers who walked like a god. And a name. Kyo.

Why didn't you kill me?

Because I want you for mine.

My newly defined body filled with warmth. My heart raced as it condensed and intensified, twisting into a deep carnal pleasure that left me gasping. If I could move, I'd be squirming. If I had a voice, I'd be moaning. Every part of me sizzled and popped until I became nothing but that volatile ball of heat in my pelvis.

I snapped awake, panting and sweating. My neck throbbed, and when I touched it, my fingers came away sticky. My stomach dropped through the floor and landed somewhere on the street outside. I'd been bitten. My judgment regarding youkai would never be trusted again. My life as a Hunter was over. I would rather he'd killed me.

I cracked my eyes open, and the room bent and distorted as if looking through a funhouse mirror. Minato stood over me, the hard lines of his usually impassive face twisted in disgust. When he saw I was coming to, he went down on his knee and gave me a slap.

"Naptime's over," he said coldly, grabbing me by the arm in an attempt to pull me to my feet. "Let's go."

"Get the fuck off me!" I cried, jerking away. My voice came out broken and slurred, my motions so sluggish that every attempt to escape only entangled me further in his grip. Tears burned in my eyes, but I refused to let them fall. "Fucking traitor! You let him do this to me!"

"I don't let him do anything," he said with the same cool patience one would give a child or an invalid.

"You're working for him."

"So are you."

I froze, staring at him dumbfounded.

"You take your orders from me, I take my orders from him, our secret immortal head. He's old and powerful beyond measure, his plans too far-reaching for our mortal minds to comprehend. It's useless to fight it, so just GET UP!"

He yanked me roughly to my feet and pushed me into the bathroom, grabbing a towel and throwing it at me before slamming the door. I slouched against the countertop and tried to stop the room from spinning. I splashed water on my gaunt and pale face and dabbed at the wound on my neck, trying like hell to ignore my painful erection as I struggled to come to grips with this new reality. Kyo, the voice in my head, the heat lingering under my skin. Our leader and a youkai. It didn't make sense.

After reciting times tables and the entire Dragons outfield and picturing my grandmother naked, I felt a little more normal and exited the bathroom on wobbly legs. The room was empty, but the door was open, and the occasional plume of smoke told me Minato was waiting just outside. He hardly looked at me as I rejoined him. He stomped his cigarette out on the tile, kicked it into a corner with half a dozen others, and loped back toward the elevators. It went without saying that I was to follow.

It was as if someone turned the dial up on the sun, and I cringed against it as we emerged back out onto the street. My hangover returned tenfold, making my stomach lurch. We walked for what seemed like forever. Still weak from my ordeal, I struggled to keep up, barely staying on my feet by the time we arrived at our destination, a mansion, big as I've ever seen, gaudy in the Western style with wide windows and pillars all around. I leaned against one, breathless and shaking, begging Minato to just give me a moment, but he refused, grabbing my arm and pulling me inside.

White. Everything was white and ultra-modern and lit up so bright it hurt my eyes. It felt surreal, and for a moment I wondered if I was still dreaming. Minato jerked me through the house and down a long hallway that twisted under my feet like something from a Stephen King movie. We stopped in front of a door at the end, big and heavy and so white as to become featureless, and Minato released me long enough to straighten his collar before knocking.

A grunt sounded from inside, and Minato swung the door open. On the other side was the youkai, Kyo, a spot of inky dark on this white world. Like everything else, the room was too bright and empty, save for a double bed clothed in white linens and a wing-backed armchair shoved in the corner. He stood near a window, leaning against the sill, and the shifting light from outside played across his face like monsters, shadows of little devils sliding down his nose. He turned, and his lips twisted when he saw me.

Minato tossed me in and slammed the door behind me before I could even try to escape, leaving me standing there, back pressed against the wall, facing the monster that had attacked me. My body was a confused swarm of instinct and emotion, fear telling me to run away from him, something else telling me to run toward him. My muscles didn't know what to do, so they locked down, freezing me to the spot, the only sound my ragged, unsteady breathing.

"You know, they say," he said finally, his voice brushing over my skin like fingertips, "that a human, once bitten, forms a sort of attachment to their attacker."

He took a slow step toward me and my breath caught. Another and I was trembling. The heat I'd felt in my dream—if it even was a dream —returned strong enough to make me sweat. I pressed my back into the door. It felt like being torn in two. He was one of them, a monster, a youkai, yet my body pulled to his like gravity.

"They even become...obsessed." He took my hand in his and raised it to his lips. I flinched. When did he get so close? He grinned, exposing a single, bright white fang, and allowed it to graze the inside of my wrist. "Is that what you're feeling now? Obsession?"

"Ah, fuck," I whimpered, my skin tingling under the heat of his breath. I couldn't make myself pull away. Heart pounding, head swimming, my knees finally buckled underneath me and sent me crashing forward into his arms. He caught me easily, tossing me face-first into the bed behind him.

I landed with a groan. My hard-on from earlier was back and throbbing painfully beneath me. I reached for it and he caught me by the wrist, pulling both my arms over my head and restraining me with one hand. His grip was firm and unyielding, but gentle too. The power in it, the ability to effortlessly crush my bones to powder, both terrified and thrilled me, and I found myself flushing despite my recent blood loss.

"Please," I breathed into the mattress, "please, just kill me or let me go." He gave a sharp, wheezing laugh as he pulled up the hem of my shirt, exposing my bare back. He traced a burning hot line down my spine with his fingernail, made hotter as he traced the cut with his tongue.

"But I just love the way you taste."

I moaned as the crackling feeling from the dream returned. His hand on my wrists tightened just enough to ache, and then he was gone, dropping me into a weightless, dizzying void.

"You know my secret," he said from somewhere behind me, "so your life now belongs to me. Understand?"

What little blood was left in me rushed in my ears. Even though he'd released me, I hadn't moved from the position he put me in, and I curled my fingers into the bedding.

"I've prepared a room for you. You will live here. As long as you behave yourself, you'll never want for anything."

"Why?" I croaked, my voice muffled by the mattress.

"So I can protect you," he said, like it was the most obvious thing in the world.

"What do you want from me?"

"I want you to feed me."

I lifted my head just enough to find him leaning against the wall, arms crossed over his chest. "That's all?"

An amused smile pulled at his lips. "You sound disappointed."

I sank back down into the mattress, ice water filling the space around my heart. God, what was wrong with me?

"Sleep," he said, popping off the wall and moving toward the door. "I'll have a job for you tomorrow."

I blacked out. Then he was there in my dreams, whispering, teasing, until I felt myself crack in two—the part that hated him, hated the pain and deception, and the part that wanted him to the point of obsession, wanted the ache of his bite and the touch of his mind. I didn't know if I wanted to sleep forever or never sleep again.

The next day I got a tattoo. A twisted black heart in the place he first bit me. And from that day on, I was his, completely and irrevocably. For better or worse.

All because I was ten yen short of a coffee.

つづく

Thank you for reading! Did you enjoy?

Please add your review! Then, sign up for the City Owl Press newsletter to receive notice of all book releases!

And don't miss more dark paranormal fantasy like CHASING DESTINY by City Owl Authors, Sydney Ashcroft & Dani Nichols. Turn the page for a sneak peek!

Sneak Peek of Chasing Destiny

BY SYDNEY ASHCROFT & DANI NICHOLS

Berlin, Germany 1941

Sometimes, the call of angels demanded sacrifice, and this was the second time Akantha was deep within the heart of Germany during a world war. Akantha, now known as Alexis Rowland, had many jobs in the past twenty-four hundred years, but this was by far the worst and her least favorite. Two years as a spy in Nazi Germany wasn't glamorous, but it was necessary if the Allies had a chance of winning the war.

Voices drifted in from the open windows near the ceiling, and Akantha paused in photographing documents containing sensitive information. Other people in the offices at this time of the night was not an uncommon thing, but she recognized both voices and continued to listen. Himmler spoke freely when he thought no one else was around. Not everything was on the classified papers she looked at daily, and every bit of information helped.

"We have a spy problem," Karl Wolff, adjutant to Himmler, said. Thoughts of watching the life pour out of both men always brought a small smile to her face. "Our couriers carrying orders for the commanders for Operation Barbarossa were ambushed. We assume the information is now in the hands of the enemy. "

"Enemy spies are a hazard of war," Himmler responded. What would he think if he knew one sat in the next room listening? She allowed herself the briefest of smiles.

"Yes, but this one is quite concerning. The mission was top secret and very few individuals were aware of the couriers' missions. The whole eastern operation could be in jeopardy."

Akantha's heart raced in her chest and blood thundered in her ears, drowning out the soft whoosh of the fan overhead. As Himmler's secretary, she was allowed access to the most sensitive information, and she passed it along to the resistance and Allied forces. Did they suspect her? The fear of being discovered sat in her stomach like a rock—cold, hard, and immovable.

"This is serious," Himmler agreed. "We need to find this person immediately. This is something that will reach the Führer, and I must answer to him. Who had access to this information?"

"You, me, your secretary, and three others."

Panic welled up, creating a lump in her throat, but she forced herself to remain calm. Panicking never solved anything and usually produced disastrous results. She'd stay calm and find a way to cast suspicion off her. It wouldn't take them long to find out she passed the information on to the Special Operations Executive if she didn't keep it together.

"I want you to ferret out this spy and bring him to me. I will deal with him personally."

"Of course, sir. Will this impact our plans for Russia?"

"I do not believe so."

Akantha looked at the papers and folders on the desk in front of her. She brought the camera up but stopped when she heard them continue.

"Our troops continue to move through Italy," Wolff reported. "A spear is rumored to be in the Vatican. Mussolini is cooperating with our search, though he is not aware of what we are searching for."

"Good. Acquiring the spear is our number one priority at the moment," Himmler replied. "Legends say it holds unimaginable power and can shape the fate of the world. I am confident the *Ahnenerbe* will find it. It's imperative we have it, even if we have to bring every spear we find back to Germany."

She sat down in the wooden chair and gripped the armrests, her knuckles turning white. The last thing the world needed was the Nazis getting their hands on the Spear of Destiny. They couldn't be talking about anything else. Himmler was obsessed with the occult and had sent teams all over the world searching for legendary, even mythical, objects. Others would have to pass information on to the SOE. Akantha had a new mission.

"Understood, sir," Wolff replied. "What about the one from Vienna?"

"I don't believe it's the true spear. Something so powerful, so important, would not be kept in such an obvious place."

"The Führer thinks it is the true spear."

Silence roared and each tick of the clock on the wall lasted an eternity.

"It is not." A chill froze her spine and her stomach twisted into a Gordian knot. Did he know more than he let on?

"Herr Holtz believes it is elsewhere."

Her heart pounded as she waited for Himmler to respond. "Herr Holtz will take as many troops as he needs. I want any rumored to be the true spear brought to Wewelsburg. With the Spear of Destiny in our hands, we will be unstoppable."

"It shall be done."

"How goes the search for the other items?" Himmler asked.

Other items? Fear wrapped icy hands around her heart. A myriad of weapons rumored to have power existed, and the Nazis getting their hands on any of them was unimaginable. It was bad enough bullets, bombs and tanks caused death on a scale unprecedented in history, but now the Nazis were looking for items that could alter the world in unfathomable ways. Millions would die. Tens of millions. Her own immortal existence was threatened as well, along with the existence of people she had known for centuries.

"The search continues, but so far we haven't been able to find any of the other items."

"I had hoped the news would be better. The summer solstice approaches and I would like to have all the items in our possession by then."

"We will have them."

"Good."

Silence settled over the two rooms and she wondered if they had left. The door to the office opened and Himmler's form filled the doorway. His head tilted to the side when he spotted her sitting at his desk. "Alexis? It's late. What are you doing in here?"

She slid her hands into the pockets of her jacket as casually as she could, slipping the small Minox Riga in. "It's only nine. I was going over your schedule for tomorrow and organizing all the paperwork for you to review." Despite the pounding in her chest and thundering in her ears, she kept a calm outward appearance. She placed her hands on the desk, hoping he didn't take notice of how they shook. This wasn't the first time he had walked in on her going through papers, looking for information. The prepared response slipped past her lips as natural as breathing.

Akantha took the position of Himmler's secretary when Hedwig Potthast left. A few months passed before she could get into his bed, but the invaluable information she collected made her personal sacrifices worth something. She played the good little Nazi and was paid in valuable information she then passed along to SOE contacts. Even in the heart of Berlin, people resisted Nazi rule.

"You work too much, my dear." He moved around the desk to stand next to her. Her eyes rose to meet his smiling face.

"Your schedule is complex and takes time to organize. Working odd hours isn't unheard of for either of us."

He nodded. "Yes, we do tend to work around the clock."

"You're too important to the cause for me to allow you to fail." The bitter words came out seamlessly across her tongue. Boosting his ego always worked to take his mind off what she was doing. The last thing she needed was him questioning why she was going through papers containing sensitive information.

"Everyone must contribute to the cause as they can," he said. "I do what I can." Himmler smiled benevolently.

"I left a copy of tomorrow's schedule on your desk."

"Did you put in a few hours in the afternoon tomorrow for me to visit my family?"

"Of course," she answered. His plans presented her with the opportunity to sneak out of Berlin and start looking for the spear. Akantha usually used the time when he went to visit his wife, or his other mistress, to meet her contact in Berlin and pass information along to the Allies. It was dangerous, but she enjoyed the thrill.

He held out a hand to her.

Breathing deeply, she gathered her courage. Tyranny, like hell, was not easily conquered. She remembered reading Thomas Paine's words back in 1776 during the dawn of the American Revolution. A long time had passed, but the words still rang true. Hitler, with the backing of the juggernaut of the German army, was a tyrant and needed to be stopped. Placing her hand in his, she rose from the chair. She forced a smile as he stepped closer. His head lowered and his mouth covered hers.

Her stomach churned from the false intimacy and she fought to keep from pulling away. Revulsion welled up every time he touched her. Screwing her courage to the sticking place, she returned the kiss.

A slight sigh slipped past her lips when the kiss ended. Every moment around him was a test of self-control and every time he touched her she wanted to take a long bath and scrub her skin raw. "It's time we should be out of here and in bed," he whispered. Sex was a useful tool to get information and one she didn't mind using even if it meant cozying up with the enemy. She may regret sleeping with him for a century or two, but if it helped stop the Nazis it would be worth the burden of regret.

"Yes, it is," she agreed while thinking of interesting ways to kill him. One day he would die a slow and painful death by her hand and she would enjoy every second of it.

"Then come," he said as he brought her hand up and placed a kiss on her knuckles.

The door squeaked behind them and hope welled up. With luck he would be pulled away for the evening and she would be able to slip away earlier than planned.

He turned on his heel and faced the source. Akantha looked around Himmler, spotting a low-ranking officer. "I apologize for the interruption. Herr Holtz is downstairs."

"Very well," Himmler said. "I will go down and see him now."

The officer saluted and disappeared from the doorway. Himmler turned back to face her. "It seems our immediate plans are to be postponed."

She feigned disappointment. "Duties always come first."

"Yes, but I would rather keep our plans."

A genuine smile appeared on her face. Let him think it was for their 'plans', but it was more relief. She wouldn't have to tolerate his vile touch tonight. "As would I."

"I must see to Herr Holtz." He turned toward the door, took one step, and stopped. He turned back to her. "Come with me," he said and held out his hand.

"Is there something you require?" She straightened her uniform, looking every inch the loyal Nazi she was supposed to be.

"No, but I would like you by my side."

She regarded him for a long moment and nodded. Did he suspect something? He never had qualms about leaving her alone in his office. Nervously she wiped the palms of her hands on her skirt. She followed him out of the office.

The spacious building in the heart of Berlin functioned as the headquarters of the SS and it housed some of the top officers. Although Himmler had a private house in the suburbs for his family, he rarely stayed there. Instead, he stayed as close to Hitler and the center of power as he could. Despite the late hour, bright lights reflected off the polished marble of the floor. Plush carpet ran down the middle of the hall and stolen works of art adorned the walls. The looted paintings spoke to the art lover in her, and her fingers itched to tear them off the walls and return them to their rightful owners. The thought of the Nazis looting museums and stealing from people was another thing to hold against them. She clenched her hands into fists as she imagined reaching out and strangling the man walking in front of her.

She followed him through the building and ignored the few people they passed. They all gave Himmler a wide berth and looked past her. She preferred it that way. It allowed her to move more freely and gather much-needed information. She followed him and froze in the doorway when she saw the individual standing in the center of the room.

Six hundred years ago, when she had a different life and name, she first saw his face, but it cut through the present and let the past rush back in a torrent. "Matheus," she whispered as her heart skipped a beat.

Don't stop now. Keep reading with your copy of CHASING DESTINY by City Owl Authors, Sydney Ashcroft & Dani Nichols

And find more from Courtney Maguire at www. courtneymaguirewrites.com

Glossary of Japanese Terms

Aho – (Kansai dialect) idiot

Amado – exterior shutters made of solid wood to protect the home from elements or for security when the house is empty

Bakayaro – vulgar; stupid bastard

Bokken – wooden practice sword

Chabudai – small, short-legged table

-chan – familiar honorific often used for women, children, and people with a close relationship

Chikushou – curse similar to "son of a bitch" or "dammit"

Daimyo – feudal lord

Damare – vulgar; shut up

Domo arigatou gozaimashita – formal; thank you

-dono – honorific roughly translating to "lord" or "master"

Eboshi – tall formal cap made from silk or paper coated in black lacquer

Edo – Former name of Tokyo; castle town centered around Edo castle and the home of the shogun

Engawa – strip of wood flooring that runs around the outside of the house, similar to a porch; can be closed in using wooden shutters during bad weather or when the house is empty for security

Futon – traditional bedding that is laid out on the floor for sleeping and then rolled up and stored in a closet during the day

Fuzakeruna – vulgar; lit. "stop messing around." In this construction, the meaning is harsher, closer to "Fuck off!"

Geisha – lit. entertainer or artist

Genkan – entryway, traditionally where shoes are left upon entering the house

Geta – flat wooden sandal elevated off the ground by wooden prongs

-gumi – group

Hakama – a type of split skirt worn over the kimono and tied at the waist

Hajimemashite – nice to meet you

-han – (Kansai dialect) honorific; same as -san

Haori – hip- or thigh-length jacket worn over the kimono

Haori-himo – cord that holds the haori closed

Hikyaku – feudal Japanese version of the pony express; system of messengers that carried packages and correspondence on foot.

Hinoki – type of cypress; hinoki oil is often used in soaps and bath oils and has a calming effect

Hisashiburi – "long time no see"

Irrashai – a call of welcome said by shop workers to patrons as they enter their shop

Isseki nichou – idiom; one stone, two birds

Itai – ouch!

Izakaya – informal bar that serves drinks and snacks

Jinbei – matching top and trousers made of light material and worn as nightwear or house clothes

Kamidana – small Shinto altar

Kamishimo – sleeveless jacket with exaggerated shoulders worn by samurai and court officials as part of their formal costume

Kanzashi – elaborate hairpins

Katana – traditional sword of the samurai

Keigo – formal Japanese

Kikentai no ichi – idiom; sword, body, and soul are one

Kisouma – small, hardy horse traditionally used by samurai

Koi – decorative carp

-kun – honorific less polite than -san, used generally among men when addressing someone younger or of lower social status

Kuso – vulgar; shit

Kusogaki – vulgar; lit. "shit brat"

Mattaku – as an exclamation, "My goodness!"

Nagajuban – simple robe worn under a kimono

Naito-Shinjuku – post town located just outside Edo, now the modern day ward of Shinjuku, Tokyo

Natto – fermented soy beans

Ne – particle asking for agreement, similar to "right?" or "isn't it?"

Nihonshu – rice wine

O- – honorific attached to the front of a name or title for increased formality

Obi – wide belt worn around the waist over a kimono

Ofuro – bath

Oiran – high-ranking courtesan

Ojamashimasu – lit. "I will disturb you." Polite greeting used when entering a house

Okaasan/Okan – mother (Kansai dialect)

Okiya – combination house and drinking establishment that houses geisha

Okyakusama – formal; customer/guest

Omedetou – congratulations

O-nee/Oneesan – sister

Otsukaresama deshita – lit. "you are tired;" used to acknowledge someone's hard work

Ponto-cho – located in Hanamachi district in Kyoto, traditional home of geiko and maiko

Ranma – carved wood details found above doors and below ceilings

Ryo – denomination of money in the form of rectangular gold plates; value based roughly on a year's supply of rice

Sakura – cherry blossom

Samurai – military nobles and retainers of daimyo

Saya – sword sheath

Seiza – lit. "proper sitting;" posture while sitting on the knees with back straight

Shakuhachi – traditional Japanese flute

Shamisen – traditional three-stringed instrument

Shimabara – Kyoto geisha district

Shinai – bamboo practice sword

Shitsurei shimasu – lit. "excuse my interrupting;" can be used when entering or leaving a room or conversation

Shogun – hereditary military leaders

Shoji – Door or window made from a lattice frame covered with paper. Used as both walls and room dividers that can be opened or removed

Suzuri – flat grinding stone used to make ink

Taikomochi – lit. "drum carriers;" filled a similar role to court jesters and acted as both entertainers and military advisers

Takagari – hawking

Takatanobaba – archaic pronunciation of Takadanobaba; neighborhood in Shinjuku

Tatami – mats made from rice straw and rush used as flooring

Tekiya – predecessors to modern Yakuza

Tokonoma – alcove used to display art or flower arrangements

Tonsu – storage cabinet

Usotsuki – liar

Wakizashi – short sword

Yoroshiku – lit. "please treat me favorably"

Yotsuya Oukido – boundary gate used as a sort of check point for inspection of goods and horses

Youkai – "mysterious calamity;" used to refer to supernatural beings in Japanese folklore

Yukata – lit. "bathing clothes;" lightweight version of a kimono

Zaisu – basically a chair with no legs used on tatami floors

Want even more dark paranormal fantasy? Try CHASING DESTINY by City Owl Authors, Sydney Ashcroft & Dani Nichols, and find more from Courtney Maguire at www.courtneymaguirewrites.com

If there was anything Akantha hated more than the Nazis, it was Damianos.

For twenty-four hundred years, Akantha has dedicated her life to defending mortals from destruction, yet the Nazis are determined not just to rule the world but destroy it. Working as a spy for one of Hitler's highest ranking officers, she learns that the Nazis are set to get their hands on the ultimate weapon, the Spear of Destiny. She will need the help of the one man she hoped she'd never see again to stop them. Loving Damianos was never a problem. Trusting him is another story. Forgiving him is impossible.

Akantha is the Nazis' most wanted as she races them through Europe to locate the spear. The road is lined with bullets, betrayal, soldiers, and heartbreak. She must navigate it all, along with her past with Damianos, if she is to find the spear. Her life and the fate of the world hang on her success…or failure.

Fans of Indiana Jones and Wonder Woman are sure to love this fast-paced adventure about a new form of immortal hero. Not quite a goddess, not a mere mortal. A woman with a curse and a destiny she isn't sure she is ready to face.

Please sign up for the City Owl Press newsletter for chances to win special subscriber-only contests and giveaways as well as receiving information on upcoming releases and special excerpts.

All reviews are **welcome** and **appreciated**. Please consider leaving one on your favorite social media and book buying sites.

For books in the world of romance and speculative fiction that embody Innovation, Creativity, and Affordability, check out City Owl Press at www.cityowlpress.com.

Acknowledgments

Blood Bound is above all a book about grief, grief over the loss of a relationship, a loved one, a family member, or even loss of self and all the forms it can take. As I write this, I am suffering my own form of grief--grief for the loss of an idol.

The passing of Anne Rice has brought up many complicated feelings for her fans and fans of the vampire paranormal genre in general. She has an admittedly complicated and often messy legacy, but it would be disingenuous not to acknowledge how formative her work has been both for me as a writer and for the genre in general. As a teenager, I devoured The Vampire Chronicles books (I've read The Vampire Lestat and The Vampire Armand more times than is healthy). They were the first explicitly queer books I'd ever read and tackled dark and often taboo subjects with an honest openness I'd never experienced before. She portrayed her monsters as human first without denying the horrifying reality underneath. They experience love and loss, appreciate the beauty in all things, and have hearts that can be broken--but they will also burn you alive in a house fire if you cross them. I was both drawn to them and repelled by them, a juxtaposition I find intensely appealing and strive for in my own monsters.

Without her, I wouldn't be the writer--or the person--I am now. Without her vampires, there are no youkai. So thank you, Anne Rice.

I would also like to thank once again my editor, Heather McCorkle, boss lady extraordinaire, Tina Moss, and the whole team at City Owl Press for continuing to champion my weird ideas. Thank you to Jennifer Worrell who has suffered through many an early draft and to my friend Avion Blackstone who I kind of tricked into beta reading for me. You are a great friend and I hope you know how much I appreciate you even though I'm bad at saying it.

Last but certainly not least, I'd like to thank you, the readers. I've been getting so many lovely messages from you guys about my books and you have no idea how much that makes my day. Thank you for taking this journey with me. I love you all.

About the Author

COURTNEY MAGUIRE is a University of Texas graduate from Corpus Christi, Texas. Drawn to Austin by a voracious appetite for music, she spent most of her young adult life in dark, divey venues nursing a love for the sublimely weird. A self-proclaimed fangirl with a press pass, she combined her love of music and writing as the primary contributor for  Japanese music and culture blog, Project: Lixx, interviewing Japanese rock and roll icons and providing live event coverage for appearances across the country.

www.courtneymaguirewrites.com

 twitter.com/PretentiousAho

 instagram.com/courtneymaguirewrites

 facebook.com/CourtneyMaguireWrites

About the Publisher

City Owl Press is a cutting edge indie publishing company, bringing the world of romance and speculative fiction to discerning readers.

Escape Your World. Get Lost in Ours!

www.cityowlpress.com

 facebook.com/YourCityOwlPress

 twitter.com/cityowlpress

 instagram.com/cityowlbooks

 pinterest.com/cityowlpress

www.ingramcontent.com/pod-product-compliance
Lightning Source LLC
Chambersburg PA
CBHW031212260626
47169CB00007B/2036